NOT YOUR AVERAGE HOT GUY

ALSO BY GWENDA BOND

Stranger Things: Suspicious Minds

YOUNG ADULT

Dead Air
Strange Alchemy
Lois Lane: Triple Threat
Girl Over Paris
Girl in the Shadows
Lois Lane: Double Down
Lois Lane: Fallout
Girl on a Wire
Blackwood
The Woken Gods

MIDDLE GRADE

The Sphinx's Secret
The Lost Legacy

NOT YOUR AVERAGE HOT GUY

A ROMANTIC COMEDY
AT THE (POSSIBLE) END OF THE WORLD

GWENDA BOND

ST. MARTIN'S GRIFFIN
NEW YORK

First published in the United States by St. Martin's Griffin, an imprint of St. Martin's Publishing Group

www.stmartins.com

Designed by Devan Norman

Library of Congress Cataloging-in-Publication Data

Names: Bond, Gwenda, author.
Title: Not your average hot guy : a romantic comedy at the (possible) end of the world / Gwenda Bond.
Description: First Edition. | New York : St. Martin's Griffin, 2021.
Identifiers: LCCN 2021016068 | ISBN 9781250771742 (trade paperback) | ISBN 9781250771759 (ebook)
Subjects: GSAFD: Horror fiction. | Science fiction.
Classification: LCC PS3602.O65648 N68 2021 | DDC 813/.6—dc23
LC record available at https://lccn.loc.gov/2021016068

Our books may be purchased in bulk for promotional, educational, or business use. Please contact your local bookseller or the Macmillan Corporate and Premium Sales Department at 1-800-221-7945, extension 5442, or by email at MacmillanSpecialMarkets@macmillan.com.

First Edition: 2021

10 9 8 7 6 5 4 3 2 1

For every woman who could save the world,
because she learned how from books

48 HOURS

(AND UNTOLD MILLENNIA) ON THE CLOCK

PART ONE

IN THE BEGINNING

"Why is a raven like a writing-desk?"

. . . .

"Have you guessed the riddle yet?" the Hatter said, turning to Alice again.

"No, I give it up," Alice replied: "What's the answer?"

"I haven't the slightest idea," said the Hatter.

ALICE'S ADVENTURES IN WONDERLAND,

LEWIS CARROLL

Is this not the true romantic feeling; not to desire to escape life, but to prevent life from escaping you.

THOMAS WOLFE

CHAPTER ONE

CALLIE

LEXINGTON, KENTUCKY

Hmm." My mother puts her hands on her hips and inspects the waiting area with a slight frown. She's wearing a T-shirt with her favorite Time Lord on the front.

I try to imagine what she's seeing. Because everything is just as it should be: the giant metal lock with the name of our family business—THE GREAT ESCAPE—hangs straight and shiny on the wall; the counter and hardwood floor are pristine; T-shirts and key chains and water bottles saying WE GREAT ESCAPED wait in stock bins; iPads for customers to bring into their chosen rooms sit in a fully charged line; and, of course, the all-important release forms are plentiful.

"I feel like I'm forgetting something, Callie-expialidocious," Mom says, walking around to give everything a higher level of scrutiny.

"That seems unlikely," I say.

Because Mom doesn't forget things. Her mind is the proverbial steel trap. If you want to know how Bletchley Park broke
the Enigma code during World War II to help defeat the Ger-
mans *or* the names of the key people who worked on the team
(it wasn't just Alan Turing), she can recite the answers without
pause. Same if you can't remember which episode of *Star Trek*
is the one where Kirk kisses Uhura.

(It's "Plato's Stepchildren"—I'm not even that into classic
TV, but I inherited her legendary affinity for collecting random
pieces of knowledge. Though I do my best to make mine even
more obscure. I'm particularly drawn to occult factoids. Historical ghost stories? Every single era of witch burning? Famous grimoires for a thousand, Alex? I'm your girl.)

No, she's not *forgetting* anything. I know exactly why Mom
is postponing her departure. She's freaking herself out about
leaving. I understand. I'd be doing the same thing. I also inherited her predisposition to hermit in my favorite places and
trust new people slowly, when I end up trusting them at all. A
big event filled with strangers? Speechifying in front of them?
Nightmare territory.

"It'll be fine," I tell her. "Go. You don't want to be late. This
is a big deal."

Mom's frown melts away, replaced by a cocky grin. "It is,
isn't it?"

"Huge." I sweep out my arms. "Planet-sized."

The Association of Escape Room and Countdown Games
named her Owner of the Year and she's off to their conference
in Nashville for the weekend to accept the award. Meanwhile,
I volunteered to hold down the fort with the (in my opinion,
unnecessary) help of my older brother, Jared.

We're the best escape room business in the country. I help

Mom write and run the games and find all our props in my copious spare time. Yes, it's decently copious. I graduated from college in the spring with a history degree, only to discover that there are no jobs for someone with my specialty. We've all decided being doomed to repeat history is fine, I guess. I'll admit I'm flailing a bit—school wasn't much of a challenge for me, well, ever. The read-all-the-books thing. I can even adequately math.

Adulthood seems to require different skills, ones I didn't realize I needed. I'm also single. Apparently relationships require different skills too.

"Still," Mom says, and her frown returns. "I was hoping Jared would show up before I left."

"I'm sure he's on his way," I say.

Jared is a freak of nature, by which I mean smart *and* good at extroverting and social situations. He's in his second year of law school, which he took to the way perfect human specimens take to becoming lawyers. I'm sure he has not just straight As, but a million friends and a canon of party anecdotes.

Meanwhile, I'm considering going to graduate school to become more (or less?) employable, fantasizing about the giant libraries it will afford me access to hide away in. *Ah, crusty old book spines and teeny tiny type, how I dream of thee.* Mostly, my mom is okay with my struggle to figure out what to do with my life. But she knows we're anxiety twins.

She focuses on me. Her hands rise to my shoulders. "Callie, you're going to do great this weekend," she says, sensing my secret nerves that I'll manage to mess this up. "Everyone on the books is routine. The odds a tricky situation will come up are low. Jared will be here. But I don't have to go . . ."

"It really will be fine." When that doesn't seem to convince her and I can practically hear *her* anxious nature telling her to stay home and skip the awards, I fall on the sword of my pride. "And you're right. Jared will be here anytime."

"Okay." She squeezes my shoulders, then lifts her hands away as the tone of the door opening sounds. "Call me if *anything* happens."

I turn expecting to see my brother, but brighten at the sight of my best friend for life and the ever after, Mag. A freshly applied glittering fuchsia lip stain pops against their brown skin and baggy gray silky T-shirt. David Bowie is their forever patron saint, a fixed star in their ever-evolving constellation of style. Mag landed a job as a graphic designer for a local ad agency immediately after graduation.

"We are not going to need to bother you in any way," Mag says. "Go, be fancy."

Mag and I met after church during toddlerdom and our friendship was sealed when we renamed all our dolls after superheroes and had them attack the other kids' Barbies (liberating them from the control of Planet Blonde; we could be judgy). I trust Mag always, and they trust me.

"I know what it is!" Mom thrusts her hand up and snaps her fingers. "The extra clues. You know people always crumple at least one. They're in the—"

"Extra clue cabinet, neatly labeled," I return, giving her a helpful-daughter stare. "And yes, there are plenty, we made new ones last weekend. You are not forgetting anything. Go."

"Okay, fine." At long last Mom retrieves her purse from behind the counter. "But no new bookings. Just what we already have. And you'll call me if *anything* happens?"

"Scout's honor," I say.

"You were never a scout."

"I was," Mag chimes in. "Eagle and everything."

"Close enough, then," Mom says.

"Plus, you know I'm not going to get into trouble."

"You're having a tough time lately. You could use some trouble." She pauses. "Not this weekend, though, please. Text me when your brother gets here, and I'll see you Sunday night."

"Jared's coming here?" Mag asks. "Tonight?"

"Yes, to supervise," I say and roll my eyes where only Mag can see. "Love you, Mom. Now get going."

"Okay." She presses a quick kiss to my cheek and then she's finally out the door.

We watch her all the way to the car and wave again after she's behind the wheel of the minivan. She waves back, and then she's gone for real, pulling out of the parking lot.

Mag looks at me and then raises both hands in the air. "Keg arrives in ten, party starts in six!"

We both burst out laughing. "I think you mean the party of six arrives in ten," I say. "I better head upstairs."

"Aye, aye, Captain Callie." Mag salutes me.

I'm a little giddy with the freedom of a weekend . . . running my mom's business like someone who has their act together. And hanging out with my bestie, since we don't get to do that enough these days.

I take up my perch between the control room monitors that show every inch of the escape rooms so we can provide clues or see attempted cheating or theft. I'll be running this side of the evening's adventures, and that starts with sizing up the customers as they enter. Mag's talking to tonight's first group in the lobby now while I listen in.

I instantly categorize the six-pack of guys as "Frat Boys Out for the Evening." They're in khakis and GO CATS T-shirts. Going by Mag's slight nose wrinkle, I'm guessing that inhaling their general aroma is like being inside an Axe Body Spray factory. We get a fair number of these guys, and I prefer the sorority version. Besides better taste in scents, *they* don't tend to break at least one piece of furniture per visit. Speaking of which . . .

"You don't need to move any heavy pieces of furniture," Mag says slowly, making sure the group is listening. "Nothing comes off the wall. Anything lightweight can be moved or removed, but you won't need to bust into anything. Got it?"

"Sure," the leader says. He's got a fresh-from-spring-break tan. "Hey, what's the fastest time anyone's ever made it out in?"

"Eighty percent don't. But forty-one minutes," Mag says.

"We're going for thirty," he declares. His bros cheer and exchange high-fives.

I roll my eyes and eat popcorn, literally, by the handful, as Mag leads them up the hall and completes giving them the drill. Mag unlocks the outer chamber of Tesla's Laboratory, the room they chose of the three we currently offer. The group is admitted into an alcove designed to look like a ye olde street, complete with faux gaslight lamps. Mag tells them how many hints they can have (five), that they all have to raise their hands in agreement to get one, that the prompts will show on the corner monitors along with the countdown timer, and so on. Then they're finally locked in and my control-freaky fun begins.

I start the clock. The first second ticks off: 59:59.

The guys attack their first challenge—figuring out how to get into the lab from the doorstep they've been left on. They remove the envelope from the postbox beside it with their first clue. One of them reads it and I tune him out, since I wrote it and I know it by heart: *Dear colleague, I'm afraid that Edison's men have been spotted in the area again . . . Three of them . . .*

The theme of this room is Mom's brainchild, based on the infamous rivalry between inventors Nicola Tesla and Thomas Edison. Sure, everyone knows Edison's name, but Tesla is responsible for the alternating current system of electricity that powers most of our houses and other buildings. (Tesla would rank high on a list of history's strangest geniuses. He once fell in love with a pigeon that had gray-tipped wings and flew around outside his window. We put a painting meant to be of her inside the room.)

The boys proceed to run their hands over every part of the walls and above the doors. And one of them is either sniffing or licking the fake cobblestones. It's hard to tell from this angle.

"Read the clue again," I mutter.

A furry white dog paw lands on my thigh. Then, before I can even react, a second paw joins the first and a long snoot noses up into my face.

"Down, Bosch," I say, and put her legs gently back on the floor. I scratch her on the head. Our freckle-nosed dog is a little spoiled. She's a rescue and had a rough life before winning the "pets who are spoiled but not in ways that make them uncomfortable like outfits and constant baby talk" lottery, so I don't feel too bad about it. Or at all bad, really.

Bosch waits, brown woe-eyes of doom on me.

"Fine." I offer her a small handful of popcorn.

She nibbles it straight from my palm, then circles three times and settles back down in her bed two feet away.

The guys have their hands up when I glance back to the

monitor. First hint already? Most people get through this part without using one.

We rank clues from easy to hard. I click my way down the menu and select a heavy-handed one. You don't want to give a difficult clue in a situation like this.

They squint at the monitor, which now reads: *Knock on the door.*

One of them does, then another waves the letter. "Oh, wait, it says there were three men. Try three times!"

One knocks three times with a fist.

"You can do this," I say, rooting for them. Sure, we design the games and the stories and clues to be difficult, but we also play fair. Everything needed to get out is provided, and we give players three to six clues on top of that. Creating a game no one ever wins is no fun. Also, no one would ever come back.

"What if we use this?" one guys asks. They've spent six precious minutes on this.

"Hallelujah," I say, when he points to the knocker mounted on the wall beside the door. He takes it in his hand and does the deed while the others wait. They cheer when a brass key falls from the ceiling on the third knock. It hits the cobblestones with a satisfying clatter.

"We did it!" They retrieve the key and let themselves into the lab room where the rest of the puzzles await.

I toss Bosch another piece of popcorn, which she tries and fails to catch in midair. Goofy dog. My phone buzzes.

Mag: They in yet?

Me: Just.

Mag: You have snacks?

Me: Come on up. Rosé in the fridge.

A few minutes later, Mag slips into the chair beside mine and sets two coffee mugs half-full of rosé on the desk. I pass over the bag of white cheddar popcorn. "How are the guys doing?" they ask around a mouthful.

"Better than you'd think, and not as bad I expected either. Maybe we misjudged them."

The guys navigate the inside of the room, designed to be a combination lab/office space. Locked trunks and sinister-looking beakers abound. They already managed to figure out the combo to the first lock, on the desk's middle drawer, and are now working on the second one.

I drum my fingers on the desk and watch the monitor. "You staying over tonight?"

Mag's apartment is way across town, and they volunteered to help out all weekend. But they've also been dating someone new. And cagey about the details, claiming it's too early to talk about.

"If you don't mind."

"Mind? Bosch is going to do a dance."

Bosch trots over at her name and Mag humors the dog by taking her paws and leading her in a dance as graceful as a human-pooch waltz can be.

"Jared is too, but he probably won't bother us much," I say.

Mag doesn't respond, so I assume they're about as confident of that as I am.

We watch on the monitors, groaning when the group misses

big pieces of the puzzle. When they're almost out of time, Mag gets up and salutes. "I'll go get ready to take the 'we didn't escape' photos with these guys and open back up for our next victims."

"Customers," I correct.

As predicted, our first group doesn't make it out before the hour elapses. But they also made it slightly farther than I had assumed *and* they didn't break any furniture. I head downstairs after they leave to reset the room. A bridal shower booked it for tomorrow morning and if I do it now, we can get out of here after the next group. Mom kept things light, and I do my best not to be insulted by that. I could've handled a heavier load. Though Jared is still nowhere to be seen. My phone buzzes at that moment and I check it. It's him: Had to help a friend with test prep. Leaving now. See you at home later? You're okay to close up solo, right?

I text back yes and then message Mom he's here so she won't worry. He's on his way, so it's a white lie. After, I replace the letter in the envelope, reset the locks. The guys didn't even muss the clues.

"They might grow up to be responsible, contributing members of society." *Unlike me.*

I turn out the lights, let the door lock behind me, and go back to the control room. As soon as I sit down, I see our next group has arrived.

"Holy wow," I say, leaning forward. "Now this is interesting."

And not what I'd call routine.

The group is mixed gender and cosplaying something I'm not familiar with (my geek fu must be slipping). They wear black capes that look high quality and those eerie plague doctor masks with the long, creepy, curving beaks. The masks are costumes now, but they were real enough when they were adopted in Paris in the 1600s to deal with bubonic plague sufferers. The beaks were stuffed with sweet (or at least better)–smelling substances and straw, meant to protect the wearer from breathing both the stench and the tainted air around their patients.

"Really getting into character for the room." Because they booked my baby, the first of our countdown games fully designed by me: the Chamber of Black Magic. It's super hard, super detailed, and supremely spooky. I poured every occult, demonic thing that gives me the worst heebie-jeebies into it.

On-screen, Mag holds up a finger at the group and then goes back behind the counter and bends down. My phone buzzes a moment later:

Mag: They don't want to sign the waivers.

Me: They have to. But you can let one sign for the whole group.

Mag: kk.

Mag informs them of this, and a tall thin man steps forward and scribbles on the sheet. I have the weirdest feeling when his mask angles directly up at the concealed camera in the corner.

I feel like he sees me.

I send Mag another message: Ask who they are.

Mag humors me, and I strain to hear the man's response. "The name is on the form."

Mag tosses a frustrated squint at the camera, then glances down at the paperwork. "Okay, Mr. Solomon Elerion."

The man looks up into the corner again. And then . . .

The others follow his lead. They all look right through the lens, at me. Like they *know* I'm here. It must be a trick of the masks, right?

Except no.

"*Of course* they know I'm here. Duh." I laugh at myself. I doubt it's the first escape room rodeo for people who come in dressed as plague doctors of the night. "A few capes and masks and a refusal to chitchat and I start to lose my chill, Bosch. Don't tell anyone."

But I don't look away until the group finally stops staring up at me.

CHAPTER TWO

LUKE

'm presently sitting at a desk not unlike any other. It's oblong and wood, the usual desk kind of thing. The only distinguishing characteristic it possesses is its location.

I'm in Hell. Not the figurative kind, the literal kind.

I'm sure you're curious. What's it like, then? Your feet toasty warm? Pitchfork poking your butt cheeks? That's what you're thinking.

I can't say I blame you. I'm told my butt cheeks are quite something. The early twenties are the peak butt years, or so the demonic laundress and tailor horde would have me believe.

At the moment, my long-suffering tutor, Porsoth, head and wings of an owl, body of a pig and the size of an overlarge child, walking upright and wearing a long black robe, is droning on about the history of demonic pacts with humans. "While the rules do apply, they apply more to human beings than our breed, who are in possession of an ability to create excess loopholes," he continues, stopping to fuss with his wide scholar's collar.

I won't bore you with what he says next. So . . . what lies beyond this drafty stone room in the managerial branch?

Outside, the vast plains of Hell are bordered by mountains with a million pointed peaks of jagged glass. The infamous rivers section off various parts of the kingdom. My favorite, the Phlegethon, a river of flames, circles and slashes through the territory, burning all who dare touch the fiery flow and offering no oblivion to those who dive deep seeking escape. Gates of rickety bone and charred metal keep forfeited souls in or out of various torments and delights, as the demons overseeing their punishment intend. In the center of it all is my father's castle. The Gray Keep rises with spindly turrets and branching walls, forming the shape of a giant, gray-black tree reaching ever upward toward the overcast sky.

If *you* were here, however, you wouldn't necessarily see—or feel—the same things I do. Hell is accommodating in a very specific, peculiar way for humans. It and its demons know you better than you know yourself.

If you were here, maybe you'd look out on a great sea of jowly men in business suits telling you what to do, or maybe really sad dogs that you couldn't help make unsad in any way, or perhaps clowns would set fire to your clothes and then cream-pie your face over and over again (there's a rumor this one happened). It would all depend on which circle you've found your way to. The bottom line is: you know your despair kinks better than I could ever guess and so does Hell . . .

I will tell you that Hell is rarely other people. More often it's the lack of other people.

This isn't *my* Hell, though it might as well be—and maybe I'm wrong about that. Father, aka Lucifer Morningstar himself, rules this kingdom, and one day he intends for me to do the same. The screams of the damned are but a distant echo from here in the Keep, where I'm enduring another lesson from my tutor while waiting for the demon in charge of my internship to show up and be disappointed. Again.

"It's always good to start with the corruption of your peers," my know-it-all, unholier-than-thou supervisor Lucifuge Rofocale, He Who Flees the Light, likes to say. "That's how your father got where he is today."

The implied critique being that I'm not going to get much of anywhere if I don't improve. Thus, Porsoth's focus on interactions between demons and humans, at Rofocale's order.

I've been reporting to Rofocale for months now. The first few weeks involved shadowing him. Then I graduated to popping on and off Earth to find groups of people at bars and score some immortal souls. Every time I return, Rofocale asks for a number. At first, he was hopeful. No longer.

It's always zero. I haven't managed to seal the soul deal even once.

In fact, I haven't come across anyone who motivates me to reach for more than the shallowest depths of depravity. The other people my age I meet—both the rare demonic ones I'm kept separate from and the ones on Earth—seem like aliens. Once you win a soul it's yours to look after, by which I mean harvest and torment, and who wants that kind of responsibility? I'm supposed to, but I don't. A hazard of my childhood, maybe, of having a father with an actual god complex. Anyway, it's past time for me to just get over it, locate some humans to get to know and trust me, and then *enjoy* manipulating them into eternal damnation so I can come back and spit out a re-spectable number to Rofocale.

Anything would be better than sitting here behind this lit-erally god-damned desk contemplating the future all mapped out for me in nine hellacious circles.

But I can't quite muster the energy. I'm not good at doing what I'm supposed to. It's a thing. My father has noticed it, which no good can come of.

Amazingly, when Rofocale's steps sound in the hall, mov-ing fast, my motivation also materializes.

"He's coming," I say, sitting up straighter.

Porsoth blinks those big owl eyes at me and fidgets. "Prince, you might want to—er, possibly it would be best if you were not . . ." He raises the slender hand at the end of his wing.

For once, I have the same thought as my tutor. There's noth-ing grand or particularly dashing about the way I leap to my feet and look around in search of a way to seem like I wasn't occupying *his* desk as Rofocale marches into the room rocking some scaled-out gray skin and a crimson suit that fits him like it was made by the underworld's second best tailor—which it was. He's like some kind of flashier demonic Darth Vader.

(Vader *is* based on one of Hell's own, someone who made the infernal deal with a devil or lesser demon. When deals with the devil go out of fashion in Hollywood, Hell will have truly achieved blizzard conditions.)

"Porsoth," he says with a nod.

"Sire." My tutor looks at the floor, even though they're not of dissimilar ranks.

"You may leave us," Rofocale says. Without protest, Porsoth leaves, hooves clicking as he goes.

"Prince of Hell." Rofocale pauses to moue his lips with dis-taste as he considers me.

Yes, I'm aware of how you loathe me; it's mutual.

"Report, please," he says. "How many souls have you gained since we last spoke?"

"None . . . yet." I play it casual. "But I'm just about to head out for some *extremely* effective tempting and corrupting."

Rofocale narrows his eyes. Black, obviously. With pinpoint red pupils, because he's never heard of overkill. He looks skeptical, which hurts . . .

Not at all. Rofocale couldn't hurt me if he wanted to.

Except, perhaps, in the literal sense or by tattling to my father about my extremely ineffectual efforts.

Either would be bad. I suspect that my father's management team, especially Rofocale and Sathariel, and their attendant demon hordes, think me a poor prospect from a noble bloodline. They're probably already planning to overthrow me when the time comes. Whatever the case, I don't want those two looking at me with their creepy eyes and horned visages and plotting, whispering together.

My father is difficult enough to deal with as it is.

"Luke, I understand you've been encouraged in this lack of focus. Your tutor is too soft on you. But it's well past time to get serious. You have a responsibility—"

"'As the heir,'" I chime in before he can finish.

His forehead becomes an actual thundercloud. How does he do that? Before I can ask, he says, "I've had enough of this. Your behavior is unacceptable. You interrupt me. You . . . you . . . sit behind my desk when I'm not here."

"Oh, is this yours?" I put in, giving the wood a tap with

my fist. I know I'm going too far but that's my specialty. Other than getting souls.

I should know to worry when there is a pause lengthy enough for the thundercloud forehead trick to fade. Rofocale tilts his head, black-and-red eyes narrowing again. Not skeptical this time. Speculative.

I move from behind the desk, gesturing that it's all his. "I apologize, sir," I say to lay the contrition on thick. "My father . . ."

"Your father," he says, letting the words linger as he passes me and slides into the chair. He repeats the words, probably knowing how unwelcome they are. "Your father has asked for a progress report on you in two moonrises, with the aim of promoting you. You have two days. Or he will see you for the failure you are. You may think yourself unique and thus protected, but you aren't. He's already troubled by your continued lack of wings."

That hurts, as I'm also troubled by it. Most demons grow their wings as children. I'm into adulthood and nothing so far.

Rofocale's eyes go unfocused for a beat, although I thought he was getting into a good lather. Me? *My* heart beats slower, my blood grows cold. Two days until he makes a report to my father. I'm well aware that I don't know what the old sire is capable of. Or, I reconsider, I'm well aware that his limits are boundless. Loyalty? Not a strong suit. Bloodlines? Blood is cheap.

And then there's the part of me I pretend doesn't exist. The part that wants to make him proud. To surprise him in a good way for once. To be worthy.

In this home for the unworthy.

Rofocale continues his tirade. "I encourage you to finally get serious this evening—"

He breaks off again, distracted.

I've seen Rofocale's unfocused look on Dad's face before. Rofocale is tuning in to another frequency, another realm or plane of existence. Something is happening that caught his attention, even here, even while angry with me.

"What is it, sir?" I ask, figuring respect is a good bet here. I stand straight, hands clasped before me, and with my feet at a position on the stone floor that might be military or diplomatic—I remember the stance from some lesson or other of Porsoth's.

"You can tell something is wrong?" he asks, surprised, paying attention to me again.

"That your awareness changed."

"There might be hope for you yet." Rofocale sighs. "I don't care if you succeed or fail, but I do care if you fail on my watch. So . . ." He stops again, grimaces.

I say, "If you need to be somewhere else, I understand."

He peers at me to see if I'm being a smart-ass. I'm not.

"It's a cult," he says. "They sometimes invoke my name in addition to your father's. They're about to get their hands on a grimoire."

I whistle. "A real one."

"Yes, which means I'm about to be summoned."

"This cult," I ask, my mind racing. "Admirers of our kingdom?"

He nods. "You could say that."

One thing I do remember from my assigned reading—I don't always tune out Porsoth—is that cultists and witches and warlocks and proactive Satanists and the like often get harvested en masse. It's easier to get them to make the bargain when they have a big ask—they also tend to believe their devotion will result in less torment. Believers in the devil are always trying to outsmart the devil.

I've never been summoned, obviously, as a lowly intern, even if I am the prince of Hell. But an ideal solution to my immediate problem puts itself together in my mind.

"You want me to harvest souls ASAP, correct?" I ask.

Rofocale says, "As we've established."

Perfect. "Let me answer the summoning instead."

"What?" He blinks, taken aback. "Why?"

"They'd only be summoning you if they wanted to ask for something. Right? Something they'd offer up their souls for?"

"I don't know about this," he says, taking my meaning. "These situations can get tricky."

Details, details. "But how many people in the cult?"

"Thirteen total," he says. "And, yes, they will offer up their souls for the boon they require."

"If I brought them all in, that would be a decent number."

"It would also make up for not being pure souls of innocents," Rofocale says, mulling it over. Finally, he shrugs. "I hate summonings, and you need numbers. Just be careful. Don't screw this up. Remember, you have two moonrises. Then I report. Don't keep me waiting." He pauses. "In his dark glory."

"Let us reside," I respond. Then I wait. He pulls out a thick hide-bound ledger and runs his fingers down the columns. Names and numbers and notations are side by side in neat rows. He adds a few words to one. Astonished, I realize he's *working*.

I set a hand on the desk in front of me. "Um, what now?"

He doesn't so much as glance up. "Now we wait for the summoning and then I send you in my stead. It shouldn't be long."

For once, I'm eager to get moving.

CHAPTER THREE

CALLIE

These guys are weird. Even beyond the staring and the masks.

I can tell by how quickly Mag rushes through the rules that they must be even more disconcerting up close. Soon enough, they're shut into the alcove outside the Chamber of Black Magic. I designed this outer area to appear as a ye olde English graveyard. The players' goal is to find the hidden entrance to a crypt used by a coven for dark magic rituals. Once inside, they must locate the clues to stop a dangerous spell in order to escape through a hidden exit.

Like I said, I went all out on this one. Mom and I hit every estate sale within a hundred miles for months to deck it out with properly aged items that hit the right forbidding occult note.

I start the clock: 59:59 . . . 59:58 . . .

My phone buzzes as Mag texts:

Mag: Yikes.

Mag: Should I come up?

This group makes me uneasy. I want my attention solely on them.

Me: Right? Better stay put.

Mag: kk.

I focus on the monitors, where some kind of unusual collusion is going on. Instead of scrambling around and studying each of the five fake headstones for clues or feeling up the front of the crypt on the back wall, they gather in a knot and remove something from a leather bag. One of them unwraps whatever it is from cloth, and then another whips out a lighter. A distinctive, unmistakable flare of flame follows.

No *fire* isn't in our rules, strictly speaking. But it probably should be. And it would have been if we'd anticipated anyone might think it *is* allowed. I wonder if I should interrupt them . . . On the other hand, they're adults, not frat boys, and so maybe I should see *what* the lighter is for first.

Okay, right call. I think.

The lighter is for a weird lumpy candle with five wicks, lit one by one. The glow from all of them together makes the security camera focus a little less great. It also makes the guy who's holding the candle—the thin, tall Solomon Elerion— even spookier, with flickering shadows along his mask, a black hollow beneath the curving beak. Inhuman-looking.

"Shivers, Bosch, shivers," I say. Bosch grunts in response and settles down for a nap.

The group takes up a chant then, in what sounds like Latin. They make their way to the faux crypt wall at the back of the alcove. Papier-mâché gargoyles gape along the edges like they're screaming secrets. A date and a forbidding skull symbol appear above the door.

They have to press the right spots on the door to open it.

But they don't do that. Instead Solomon with the short, lumpy candelabra thing steps out of the group and raises his free hand. The door begins to slide open, and another of the cosplayers dives forward to help it along.

"That shouldn't have happened."

I sit in my chair desperately trying to figure out how in the world they got the door to open. They don't seem surprised though. Without pause, they enter the room.

Maybe they talked to someone who's done it before? Or maybe I missed one of them pressing on the spots while I was focusing on the lighting of the candelabra?

That has to be it.

The fake torch lights in the crypt are brighter. I won't miss anything else.

I admire my work, as I do every time I see it. (And Mom's, of course.) There's the cauldron with dry-ice smoke triggered by the opening door. There's the tomb sitting above the floor with a cypher-style lock on it against the far wall. There are spell books and jars with slimy eye of newt–looking things and human eyeball–looking things and as many potential clues as possible to disguise the real ones.

The Chamber of Black Magic is intentionally the hardest

puzzle we offer. To get out, the players have to put together the contents of a powerful magic spell that will then reveal the location and combination of the secret exit.

Only *one* person has figured it out so far: Mom.

They quickly move toward the tomb, which also has my pièce de résistance of set dressing on it. Open and displaying moldy brown pages is a legitimate super-early printing of the *Grand Grimoire*, a legendary French text that outlines a ritual to summon a high-level demon. Mom even suggested we eBay or Sotheby's it, because it's probably worth thousands.

"No," I'd said, clutching the giant brick of a book to my chest. "It has that old-book smell. This is the perfect touch. It's worth thousands to us already."

"Fine," she'd said. "You and old books. Get a room."

"Ha," I'd replied.

Not that she's wrong. Every time someone lays a finger on it, I want to stop them. But I would never *admit* that. The grimoire is necessary to the story in the room. So what if I feel a bizarre sense of ownership over it?

The plague doctors touch it reverently at least, all of them seemingly, while spooky candelabra guy stays off to one side. Until, at last, Solomon approaches for his turn. He sets the candle down on the table beside the book, then closes the cover. He picks the grimoire up, hefting its weight on his hand. Then he lifts the candle with his other hand and says something I can't make out.

I check and discover they've spent ten minutes to get this far.

"Better get cracking," I say, before I realize one of them is pushing the faux tomb around on its tracks. I sit up straighter. "What? There's no way—"

But I watch it happen. I watch as the tomb slides around, and they push it up flush against the wall, where it clicks into place. The empty space left below is the hidden exit. A few steps down, then along a dark hallway and back up again, and boom, they'll be in the upstairs hall. Out. Escaped. In ten minutes.

"No. Way." My face pinches with disbelief. "No. You didn't solve it."

They didn't even solve *one* of the mini-puzzles to get to the big one at the end.

This does not stop the billowing cape-wearers from descending through the exit. I could swear Solomon Elerion looks at the camera again, almost in challenge, before he steps down holding *my book.*

"Nope," I say. "Too bad for you we don't allow cheaters, buddy."

Before I can think better of it, I'm out of my chair and running down the stairs from the control room. When I get to the hallway that leads to each room's entrance and exit, I spot a confused Mag at the far end. I hesitate, knowing I should open the Chamber of Black Magic's exit and confront them—but truth is, I've never been down there. I designed it because that was the scariest thing I could think of, subterranean and dark. My two secret phobias when put together.

Mag doesn't know what happened, that they cheated. But it won't matter, there's no time to explain. Mag *will* know there's no possible way they made it out in such a short amount of time.

In seconds, the party is flowing out the door.

"Hold it right there," I say. "We have cameras in the rooms. I know what you did."

They form a river of awful cape-wearing cheaters between Mag and me.

"You don't know anything," Solomon says. He has my book

in one hand and the candle in his other, flames licking the air. "Step aside."

"Callie, what should I do?" Mag asks.

The other cape-and-mask wearers press against the wall to let Solomon approach me. Trembling, I look past him to Mag. "Lock the front door."

I sound braver than I feel. I *feel* like I'm out of the control room and thus out of control. What a night for Mom to be gone. She'd probably tell me to let him go.

But I can't bear to. "You are *not* leaving with that book. I'll call the cops. Mag, lock the door."

Mag goes to do it. I get even less brave when I finally understand what kind of lumpy candle Solomon Elerion is holding.

Lumpy because it's a blob of flesh that used to be someone's hand. Desiccated, old, maybe as old as the grimoire he holds in his other one. If such things were real, it would even explain how they got in and out of the room. My skin goes clammy, because my reading on occult topics is plenty extensive enough to recognize . . .

"A Hand of Glory? Am I supposed to believe that's *real*?" I ask.

"Yes, it's a real one," Solomon says. "Not only that. It's the first. Why do you care if we take the grimoire?" He pauses. "Are you a guardian?"

I blink. I'm sweating. The hallway seems to close in around us.

He's telling me that the gross relic in his hand is a *real* Hand of Glory, the hand of a murderer who died on the gallows. The hand that "did the deed." And, oh yes, I search my random-fact-retaining brain, the hand is combined with the fat from the dead person to make the candle one that will burn. Its power? Supposedly to open any door.

Like they did. You saw it. There's no other way they got through so quickly.

His lips curl into a smile. "I'll ask again . . . Are you a guardian?"

"I—I can't let you take the book." My words are an iceberg lumbering from my throat.

"I don't see how you can prevent it."

Maybe Mag's busy calling the cops and I can distract him until they come. "What would you do if you could go back in time?" I babble, trying not to look at the burning hand or inhale too deeply. "Because I'd have rubbed this house with unguent from the gall of a black cat, the fat of a white hen, or, um, the blood of a screech-owl. Compounded during the dog-days, obviously."

Only *I* would immediately go to facts from another old book, another grimoire, the *Petit Albert* from 1722. It details how to make a Hand of Glory *and* how to protect yourself from one.

Solomon's head tilts, the beak-like nose of the mask slicing the air. "You *are* a guardian. How else would you know these things?" He shakes his head. "Whoever did the reconnaissance on this place is fired. Bring them. They're guardians. This one at least."

"Wait a sec," I say. "What do you mean, 'bring them'?"

But I understand soon enough when two of the masked people advance and stop on either side of me. Solomon leads the way to the front door and out, and I struggle as they grab my arms and drag me along behind him. Mag, brown eyes drowning in fear, waits at the threshold when we reach it, flanked by two more of the group.

"This is a mistake," I explain. "Really. No guardians here. You can take the book. I should've let you from the beginning."

Mag asks, "What is going on?"

"You called the cops?" I ask, hopefully.

Mag shakes their head. "Should I have?"

I consider how to answer. "We're being kidnapped by some kind of cult."

"Oh," Mag says faintly. "Right. So that guy *is* holding a gross old hand?"

"Stop talking," the woman holding my right arm says. "Give us your phones."

Mag and I exchange a look, then fish them from our pockets and hand them over. The woman sets them on the countertop. Then we're grabbed again and pushed through the door.

"Wait!" I plant my feet on the parking lot pavement, with enough force to make the guy holding my other arm stumble. We have to leave some sort of something that might be a clue to our whereabouts. "Let me at least lock it and put up a sign. We have more customers coming."

Before they can say no, I wriggle my arms free and run back inside. I could lock the door and leave them out there. But . . . I'm no hero and I can't let them take Mag alone, can I? No way. I can't even get one of our phones into my pocket.

I *can* scribble a note while the two masked people stand watching and then tape it to the glass door and flip the lock. It contains a lie, meant to be a hint for Jared.

CLOSED FOR FAMILY EMERGENCY
WE REGRET ANY INCONVENIENCE

Although when Jared does show up, he'll call Mom. Is that so bad?

Yes, it is. I didn't even make it through the first night successfully. She'll never leave again.

Though that's probably not as bad as wherever the black murder van they push Mag and me into is taking us.

"Maybe you shouldn't have said the blindfold thing," Mag whispers.

"You think?" I whisper back.

I hear the strain in their voice. I can't see them though, because I nervously babbled some more that it wasn't smart of our captors to let us watch where we're going. Which led to rummaging around and some kind of cloth wrapped around our heads. They haven't bound our wrists, but we were assured they will if we try to remove said blindfolds.

A huge understatement to say this is not shaping up like the weekend I planned. I pray that Jared or someone will find the note and get us out of this insanity . . . somehow . . . and back to safety, where we can pretend none of this ever happened.

"Sorry," Mag says. "That was snarky."

"Snark is allowed."

"Quiet!" a woman barks.

"You guys are really unpleasant," I inform them. I can't imagine the situation getting worse at this point. The moment I say that I do though. Unpleasant isn't the half of what's possible. These are evil people. Evil people have taken us.

I picture us never getting away. Mom showing up after Jared calls her to find the business abandoned, my cryptic sign on the door. Will it take him two hours to notice we never showed up at home and go investigate? Will that be too long?

No. There's no point to that kind of thinking. Yet. *Pay*

attention, I tell myself. It's the best clue I give anyone at the Great Escape.

So I focus. I listen. I track the changes in our speed the best I can. I count the number of turns we take and how far apart they are. My best guess is that we got on New Circle and drove a fair way, then got off and drove until we entered a rural area. We could be anywhere in our county or the next one over. Or the next. Why do TV and movies always make figuring this stuff out so much easier?

Right, because it's not usually a book nerd and her fashion-forward best friend.

The van stops, finally. The door slides open, and I reach beside me to find Mag's hand. I give it a squeeze. "We'll get out of this," I say, though I have zero reason to believe it's true. "I promise."

Now I'm lying to my BFF. Banner day in the Johnson household.

Mag whispers back, "You can't promise that."

They're not wrong, but . . . "I did though."

"Quiet," Solomon Elerion says. I recognize his voice. "And stay that way when you get out."

If he wants us to be quiet that must mean there are people around to hear. My shoulder is grabbed and I'm hefted up out of my seat. Then my feet are on solid ground.

"Mag," I say, and wait for them to respond, so I know they're out and on the ground too.

"Callie?"

"Run!" I rip off my blindfold, and have a moment to blink and get oriented before I stumble forward. Mag does the same, but of course the plague doctors are on top of us again.

It doesn't even matter.

I look around.

The only thing out here is woods and more woods. And, as they turn us, a house.

Big and gothic. Two stories of decaying mansion that must have been gleaming white and pretty once. Night sounds rise around us, loud, underscoring how in the middle of nowhere we are.

But something about the house strikes me as familiar.

"I was just testing you," Solomon says. "Rookies."

"Guardians," I say on a gamble, because I don't like the tone of "rookies." Rookies might be expendable; guardians sound important.

He shrugs and after a vague nod we're being carted toward the house. Someone flips on the porch light and unlocks the door, and they bring us inside.

As we come in, there's a wide living room off to one side and a parlor on the other. And a set of stairs, which is where they take us.

Not before we get a look at the parlor though. It's been emptied of furniture and a large pentagram has been traced out in what looks like reddish dirt on the floor. Candles, fat and black, line the windows and edges of the walls, unlit as yet. Occult symbols are traced within the star in black and white.

"Wait." I snort. "You're Satanists or witches or something? You know that stuff is a hoax?"

"Sure." Solomon Elerion sneers beneath the beak of his mask, then removes it. His face is long and pale. He stares at us with bottomless eyes. "Like the Hand of Glory was a hoax."

I am forced to concede the point with my silence. He still has my book in his hands.

We're taken up the stairs and pushed into an empty bedroom.

Empty except for one thing, anyway. There's a painting left on one of the walls, a very Hieronymus Bosch knockoff filled with cavorting and dark revelry—and given that I named my dog after the painter who specialized in scenes of torment—I remember it. Now I know why the house is familiar.

The "chosen" ones shut and lock the door and Mag and I face each other, then take in the bleak landscape. There's what looks like a closet door and one window. Besides the painting, that's it.

"This is where we got the grimoire," I say. "We came to the estate sale. I remember that painting."

"Nobody bought it?" Mag says with a squint. "It's pretty good."

"That's the weird thing about this situation?"

We smile weakly at each other, but it's covering up a world of emotions and too many questions without answers and a kind of fear that's like numbness.

"So I didn't see this coming," Mag says.

"I did in my crystal ball of strange Satanic cults," I quip. "How do we get out of here?"

"You don't think they'd, you know, sacrifice us, do you?"

Thanks for that idea, Mag. I hadn't gotten there yet.

"I'm sure I'm chewy. All that sitting," I say. "Not good for the ritual cannibalism."

"At least you're still funny."

We nod at each other.

"If only this had rules and we could solve it." I hesitate. "It probably does though. We just need to figure them out."

"Right," Mag says. "It's a start. And Jared will figure out we're gone."

"He will eventually. Time to do the 'top to bottom' on this

room," I say, referencing stage one in approaching every escape room.

We're both quiet as we circle the space. Mag opens a closet, filled with a few leftover pillows and knickknacks but not much else. I check the windows and find them not only nailed shut, but painted shut too, with black paint. "Subtle."

I try the door, rattling the knob. No one tells me to knock it off, so I guess there's no watchdog outside.

"We could break the window." I consider the height. The ground is at least thirty feet down. "And leap to our death."

"Next option."

"Okay, so they came to our place for the book. It was obviously what they wanted."

"Good point." Mag sits down on the floor, leaning against the wall. "What is that book?"

"It's a grimoire. It, uh, supposedly summons the devil. Or the devil's right-hand man . . . Or is it left-hand man? Anyway."

Mag's eyes are wide. "But you said that stuff is fake. A hoax. Downstairs."

"I thought it was." I pause. "I think it is."

"I don't want to know what a Hand of Glory is, do I?"

I consider it seriously. "No, you really don't."

Then I bend down to examine the lock on the door more thoroughly. "I might be able to pick this."

"Really?"

"Really." I went to a lock convention with Mom that had demos and games where people competed to get through them fastest. I sat through boring seminars where we learned about various locks, and practiced a few times at home. This one's old.

"If I had something to pick it with."

Old lock, old door, old house. If one of us had muscles, we'd probably be able to bust through it. There's a slim chance we could do it together. Before I can suggest it, the door flies open.

"You're needed downstairs," Solomon Elerion says, two of his minions beside him. "As guardians, we'll want to present you as gifts."

Downstairs is closer to the front door. And I'm out of ideas. "Yes, of course," I say.

I take Mag's hand and squeeze. They squeeze back. Neither of us is alone, whatever happens.

Solomon makes a mocking "after you" gesture and we walk out and down the stairs side by side. The air in the old house is stale and cool. Like we're in the waiting room of a hospital or a cemetery. All is darkness on the stairs, the lights off now, the flicker of the candlelight ahead the only thing we have to see by.

"You're really into creating an atmosphere, aren't you?" I ask, but I feel a grudging admiration. I find myself pretending this is an escape room. Some secret gag. A whole new kind of game.

I wish.

When we reach the parlor, everyone else has their masks and capes on, still. There are more of them. I count thirteen. Solomon Elerion gestures for us to stand near an old fireplace. Far from the door.

The thick grimoire is open in his hands and, as he intones the words, some of the others do things with incense burners and candles and what appear to be drops of blood around the edges of the circle.

Mag and I stand, our grip on each other's hands tightening as horror sinks in. Deep.

At last, Solomon claps the book closed with a sharp crack. It's echoed by lightning and loud thunder outside. The bones of the house creak and shake around us, and there's a growing darkness and smoke in the center of the pentagram.

Someone is here who wasn't before.

They did it.

They summoned the devil's left-hand man.

CHAPTER FOUR

LUKE

Rofocale sets down his bone pen and goes still for a moment. "It's time. But again, these situations can be . . . fluid. Are you positive you're up to this? You'll be careful?"

Careful. I don't laugh. Somehow. "Careful is my middle name."

We both know it's actually Astaroth, because he's the former good angel, now bad angel, who introduced my father to my mother.

"I'm being serious, Luke." His gray visage is as judgmental as it gets. The effect is compounded by the imposing stone behind him, and the giant desk in front. "You have to be serious for once too."

I nod, deciding that's better than anything I might say. And I am *very* serious about not landing myself in boiling hot water with Father. Failure isn't something he tolerates with grace, infernal or otherwise.

"Fine." He sighs and waves for me to lean over the desk. "This may sting a bit."

"You'll enjoy that."

"Greatly." He touches my shoulder.

Like that, the knowledge of the summoning burns through me like fire through a dry forest. I know precisely where I'm headed and who will be there chanting at me when I arrive. It tugs at me, the calling steady and going nowhere until it's answered.

"Smell you later," I say.

As he shakes his head with disappointment, I leap into the air and traverse the universe in the blink of an eye.

Arriving in the cult's lair, I find myself in the middle of a pentagram. It's slightly disconcerting. Not that I don't enjoy a pentagram as much as the next resident of the Gray Keep, but it *is* a confining nexus of energy.

In other words, I feel as if I can't just leave again if I want to. Because I can't.

Oh, so this is why Rofocale let me be summoned instead. Crap duty. Got it.

There's a lot I don't know. A lot of Rofocale's and Porsoth's lessons I've neglected to pay attention to. Usually I'd say that's a good thing, but there are some situations where you want to be able to channel the disenchanted, hardened point of view of a cynical demonic lord who's seen it all.

I didn't really think about that when I volunteered. But then I remember Rofocale's appointment with Father, the reason I *did* volunteer. Luke Astaroth Morningstar, prince of Hell, reporting for soul collection duty. Get the deal made, add thirteen souls to my tally, get out.

"Great," a female voice says, and I recognize the sarcasm like I would my own, "you summoned a male model. What's he going to do without a catwalk?"

I sniff and straighten to my full height. She's not wrong about my looks. My appearance is human, and it's not bragging to say the most attractive type. My brilliant blue eyes can mesmerize. I'm in jeans, black boots, and a leather jacket so cool it should be a sin and probably is. Yet what she said didn't feel like a compliment. Turning, I find the girl who spoke, and I . . . feel something odd when I look at her.

She has shoulder-length brown hair that is frankly the color of tree bark and green eyes that are grassy but intelligent and she's scared to be here for some reason but, boy, is it impressive how little she shows it. None of those things are the most noteworthy detail about her.

She's *good*. She radiates it like sunshine. She has faith in the world.

This is not love at first sight, it's way better: it's *interest* at first sight. I haven't felt that in . . . ever. I've never looked at someone and felt anything remotely like this. A pull toward her.

This is turning into a very strange evening.

I like that.

As long as I don't get trapped here. Because *why* is someone good in this place with these cultists? Rofocale might have finally been right about something. This might be tricky after all. I decide not to ask about any of that, about her. It would give away too much.

But I can't let her remark pass without counter.

"I have a brain too, you know. You could at least assume I'm here because of that," I say, as if I'm wounded by the girl's dismissal. Which I would never admit I almost am.

Her mouth makes an O of surprise, and then, I swear to you, she rolls her eyes at me right in the middle of this parlor surrounded by cultists and candles.

My heart beats in my chest. I'm sure it does that all the time, that it's been there all along, but I hardly ever *remember* it's there. I hardly ever *feel* it.

She shakes her head. "Having the best cheekbones in Hell isn't enough?"

"The Best Cheekbones in Hell is the name of my next band," I say.

Beside her is a person whose gender is on a spectrum that touches the masculine and the feminine. "Don't taunt the demon," I hear this person whisper. Their name is Mag.

And the name of the girl with the sharp tongue is Callisto, but she goes by Callie. Being able to know a few basic things about pretty much everyone on Earth with a tiny amount of focus and without earning it is one of my favorites of my gifts. I should probably feel bad about the intrusion. But unlike Callie and Mag, I'm not good. I'm the opposite.

"Demons like being taunted," I say.

Mag swallows.

A man, name of Solomon Elerion, so my gift tells me, clears his throat. Solomon Elerion? How cute, he's taken a Biblical king and prophet and matched it with a demon's name to form his own. Unlike the others, he wears no beaked mask, only the same black cape. He's the spokesperson for this little forced gathering, the leader.

"Greetings, Lucifuge Rofocale, esteemed minister of Hell," he says with a frown at Callie and Mag.

Callie scowls at him.

I decide to go along with the assumption I'm Rofocale. Best

not let them know they've caught a more important title than his.

"See," I say to her, "I'm a minister of governance. Show some respect."

She doesn't react either way. I notice how hard she grips Mag's hand, and how hard Mag grips hers back. *Why are they here?*

"We brought them as a gift to you," Solomon Elerion says, and I face him. Deeply evil vibe, not a shred of decency in this one. His soul is mine for the taking. He hardly seems to want it. "As I'm sure you know, they are guardians," he adds.

I don't let myself look over at them. Those two are many unusual things, but guardians? Pesky humans chosen by Heaven to train as holy warriors and to combat the work of my father's helpers on Earth? There aren't that many guardians left these days, and they tend to stick together in roving, righteous packs. Hmm . . .

I know without even checking that these two aren't for me. Their souls have been claimed by the Above and to get them back on the market would take more work than I would be willing to do. Not when there's far easier prey in hand.

And a deadline to meet.

"Well met, Solomon Elerion." I've heard Rofocale say such things. "And, ah, thanks."

Callie, eyes of grass green, hair of bark, soul of good, snorts. I turn to see her head shake in disgust. She and Rofocale would probably get along like gangbusters. I continue to be so interested in my reaction to her that it pains me to look away.

But I do. I wave my hand to suggest the leader get on with it. "What can I do for you, Solomon Elerion? I assume you've summoned me for a reason."

Please don't let it be capture. The pentagram pulses beneath my feet and the air feels closer, more confining, at the thought.

"We are willing to trade our immortal souls in exchange for a certain boon we believe you can grant us."

See how easy this is? I grin. "Go on."

He continues. "Our number is an unholy thirteen, and our devotion to the Dark Prince is the strongest you will find."

"King," I correct automatically, without thinking.

His eyebrows lift. "The Dark King," he says, clearly with pleasure at learning a secret of Hell.

I suddenly *wish* Careful were my middle name. "And?" I prompt.

He takes a step closer to the pentagram, but he doesn't breach it. "We have dedicated our lives to bringing about his kingdom on Earth. We offer you not only our souls, but the boon we seek will be used to accomplish this. We hope we will be favored by him in return."

They don't understand—they never do, the evil ones—that's not how it works. Father encourages bad, but he wishes for good. The worse the stains on a soul, the worse the punishment. He sees us as a force of balance. He wants to be proven right, that mankind was a corruption of the highest order to the purity being an angel above promised. But he's still disappointed by every soul that does prove him right. And disappointment makes him do very bad things.

He's a mass of contradictions, Father.

I hedge. "I am certain you will receive particular treatment in the kingdom beyond."

Solomon Elerion bares his teeth, and then I understand it's a smile. Save me from cultists. No, save cultists from me—or don't. *Remember why you're here.*

"What is the boon you desire? If it is in my power, I shall grant it."

He takes a moment to gather himself, eager to spill but not wanting to seem so. I cast my senses around the room, seeking more information about the situation . . . and discover Callie and her friend Mag are here because they were kidnapped. These cloak-wearing cultists stole the book from Callie and her family and brought the two of them here to hand them over to me. I frown.

Then, I focus harder.

The cult calls itself the Order of Elerion, and Solomon here is only the latest to hold that name, it turns out. They have a longing for great power and have spent centuries working toward tonight. They've obtained a lot of divine and infernal secrets and items to get here.

I don't like them. Not because of their mission, which is frankly in line with my own here this evening and my father's larger goals. But because of the kidnapping of Callisto and her friend. This . . . caring . . . is a new sensation.

Novelty is important. I'm not bored in the least. I decide to *lean in,* as they say, and torment him a bit. "What is this boon you seek? It better be good for me too, because your souls aren't really A-plus material. None of you even play instruments, so you're useless to my new band."

"Oh?" Solomon gives me a look, then sweeps his eyes down to the pentagram. He knows I'm trapped. "And why would you not want our souls?"

I curl my lip. "Why on Earth *would* I want your souls?"

Except, of course, I desperately need them. *Why in the devil's name did I say that?*

Solomon's eyes widen and he takes a step forward—still not

quite far enough to break the pentagram and let me escape it. He's got too much presence of mind for that.

I have to get those souls. I force my face into an expression that seems more appropriate for negotiation. "As I asked before, what is the boon you require in exchange?"

"We would like the Spear of Destiny," Solomon says. "The Holy Lance."

Not a small ask.

But I reach out with my senses, prepared to say yes. The spear is the one that was used by the Roman soldier Longinus to pierce Jesus's side as he hung on the cross, sacrificing himself to give humanity a path to redemption (one path of many, to be sure—most religions have some truth about them). It's endowed with the power to bestow God's full might to whoever has it. Many evil men have tried to take possession of it over the thousands of years since, and a small group of do-gooders managed to hide it away to prevent that. No one who wants to use it to help Father has gotten this far.

They're ambitious, I'll give them that. There's just one problem.

"I can't give it to you."

Solomon opens his mouth.

I speak before he can. "It's in a sacred place. Where I can't go. So *I* can't give it to you."

"No spear, no deal," he says and any deference vanishes. I feel the lines of the pentagram that surround me like the cage walls they are.

"*But,*" I say, "because of that little favor I did where your souls are still intact for now, I can tell you where it is. Then you can retrieve it."

He hesitates. "All right. I suppose we have a deal."

I nod, pretending I'm not flooded with relief. And already second-guessing my actions.

"Where is it?" he asks.

"It is in the gardens of Quinta da Regaleira in Portugal. You will find it beneath the chapel."

"Thank you." Solomon Elerion inclines his head. He still doesn't smudge the edge of the pentagram to free me, however.

"Our business is thus concluded." Another phrase I've heard Rofocale use. It's a little stuffy for my taste, but I'm in a pinch.

Solomon smiles at me, that baring of teeth. "Not until we have the spear."

"That, person who is not my friend, is not the deal," I say. "You forget your place. You seek to trap me and you haven't even made good on your promised gifts."

"What gifts?" he asks, perplexed. He's forgotten Callie and Mag.

I smile. My best smile. The smile the wolf who wore sheep's clothing wishes it could smile. But sexier. I have officially lost my mind.

"Her," I say and fix my attention on Callie.

"No way!" she says, hand on her hip. Her eyes are narrowed and rage-filled. Maybe I misjudged the green. Maybe it's the green of a stormy ocean, not grass. "They can't do that! I'm not *theirs* to give!"

"Done," says Solomon, flatly, like he doesn't get why anyone would want her but won't judge. Also, like he worries about my sanity.

"No way!" she says. "Did you hear a word I said? I am my own person. You cannot trade me for . . . for . . ."

"And her friend goes free too," I add.

Callie stops midprotest. She looks at Mag. She swallows.

"No," Mag says. "No freaking way."

"Fine," Callie says.

It's not fine. I can feel the hatred boil off of her. I bet she's already planning to find "instructions on how to kill a minister of Hell" in some dusty tome like the one these guys stole.

"You can have them both, as promised," Solomon says.

But here I am, still bound in this pentagram.

At that precise moment, as I'm about to despair of getting out of this entire situation and to my eternal surprise, Callie leaps forward. She grabs one of the tall burning candles and brandishes it at the bad Solomon. He recoils with as much surprise as me, and bless her, he does as she intends before he realizes she intends it. She drives him forward, and he breaks the pentagram.

I immediately fly above it, not a showy distance, just a foot or so. I breathe easier the second my feet leave that bound patch of Earth.

Callie shoots me a look like she'd love to see if I'm flammable, but drops the candlestick. Several cape-wearers dart forward to pick it up and an awkward scene ensues while they try to put out the flame.

"Our business is thus concluded for now," I say. "My . . . guardians . . . and I will be going."

"You leave now, our souls remain ours," Solomon Elerion says.

He's right, of course. I never specifically stated my terms for the deal meant they'd give their souls. In my rush to torment him, I questioned their value and then only made a deal to tell them the location and help them get the spear.

I've screwed myself to the max and let him come up with a loophole.

Currently, I have zero leverage. I hate him with all the fires of the Phlegethon.

"We'll see about that," I say.

Callie and Mag are already hand in hand again and headed for the door. I stick with them as we leave, exiting into the cool night and its freedom.

"Where are we going?" I ask.

"We're going home," Callie says. "You can go back to Hell."

Is she truly so ungrateful? Am I that bad? No, I'm not. At least, not right this second. What I am is in big, deep trouble. I still have zero souls. Why am I always my own worst enemy?

Because it's more fun this way.

"Not without you," I say.

It's the obvious solution. The only solution. I'll need an intermediary or two to get back in a position to force the issue of the cult's souls. Which means having *good* company who can retrieve the spear they desire first. Even if I could get into the spot where it is, I can't directly prevent them from getting it now. I should've paid more attention to Porsoth and his talk of deals.

I need Callie's help to get the cult's souls by my deadline. Well, I need *someone's*. But it's hers that I want.

Mag looks over at me. "I don't suppose you have a phone we can use."

"I'm from Hell, not Luddite-ville," I say and hand mine over. My thumbprint smokes a little as I unlock it and I expect them to be impressed.

Callie reaches out and takes it, holding it in a way to make as little contact as possible. "He still uses the worst rideshare," she says, in an "of course, ugh" tone. She and Rofocale really *will* hit it off. "Crap. Not a car within fifty miles of this place," she says after a few swipes.

"But in sixty?" Mag asks, hopefully.

"Nope. We start walking," Callie says. "Until we can, I don't know, hitchhike or get a car or be murdered on the side of the road. We're definitely not sticking around here."

"What about me?" I try again. "I might be able to help. You *are* mine now."

Callie turns and smiles sweetly under the moonlight. Maybe she's seen reason. I am a handy ally to have. And a devastatingly handsome one.

I want to tempt her. Badly.

"I told you, go back to Hell. We're not actually 'guardians,' whatever that is. So I'm not interested in anything you have to say."

She seems to mean it, and she's leaving again. Mag chases after her. But I'm the devil's son, and I already told you about my eyes. They're nothing next to my cleverness.

"Not interested? Really?" I say and stop. I know she'll stop walking too, momentarily. "I find that hard to believe. You *are* a guardian. It's your job to foil evil plots like the one back there. I can't believe you're not going to do it. That you're just going to walk away."

Her feet plant on the ground in a way I can't help but find oh so satisfying.

"What?" she demands.

And I know she's mine for the rest of the evening, in every way that matters.

CHAPTER FIVE

CALLIE

The devil's minister stands there, smirking at me.

Lucifuge Rofocale. The devil's minister . . . who looks like he's my age and really should be modeling or in a band. What's that about? Is it one of his powers that I simply want to stare at him, because he's the most beautiful person I've ever seen? Right now, I *need* an explanation for all of this. I don't care for the one he just rolled out.

"I asked you a question," I say. "What do you mean? We're not guardians."

The smirk transforms into a smile. I pretend not to notice that it is blindingly hot. He probably can't help his effect on people—a side effect of being from Hell or something. He's a living bad idea, a smoldering honey trap.

He leans forward. Into my space. I have the ridiculous urge to move closer. Instead I step back.

"It's true that both of you aren't. But *you* are." He frowns, and the tiniest line appears between his perfect eyebrows. "Although it is mysterious how you could have gotten this far without knowing."

At my side, Mag coughs. I'm relieved they haven't lost the power of speech as I have. "What even are guardians?" they ask.

"From your perspective, they're the good guys," he says.

"And from yours?" I volley back.

"Inconvenient, but sometimes interesting." He winks at me.

Every hormone in my body responds with a command to fall to his gorgeous feet already. Why fight it?

I throw my head back, stifling a scream of frustration. *Down, body. Let brain do its thing.*

The moon above us is bright and fat, nearly full. Scientific name, waxing gibbous. I scan and confirm the woods that surround us are horror movie central casting woods, sans scientific name. They remind me of half the sinister woodcuts in the books I presumed were faux occult texts before tonight. I expect two girls to come racing out of them in white sheet togas with a chainsaw-toting masked madman behind them at any second. Or a coven. Or a devil.

I do not like these thoughts any more than my reaction to that wink.

I do not like any part of this situation. I want to be safe at the office back behind the monitors. Or at home watching the kind of movie with cults or black rites that—and this is key—*stay on-screen.*

But if I were in either one of those places, someone else would be there too, I realize. Someone else who must be freaking out.

Bosch. Bosch the very goofy, very neurotic rescue dog. Who we left alone at the Great Escape. *Oh no.* What if Jared showed up already and called Mom because we didn't get home yet? But I can't even worry about that because . . .

Because poor Bosch.

"The guardian stuff can wait," I say to Mag. "Dog."

"Oh no." They search the horizon as if a car will magically appear.

"You need a favor?" the handsome demon asks, and gives me a smile obviously meant to be charming. I feel as if I'm about to be swallowed whole by a snake. And enjoy it.

"You can't read minds, can you?" I ask, suspicious.

He huffs a sigh. "Not really. Which is good, because I bet that would get awfully dull."

I seethe, about to protest that while I may seem outwardly boring my thoughts definitely aren't.

"But, no, I'm not reading yours right now, if that's what you're asking," he says. "I do feel like you need something, though. From me."

What is happening? Wild night, kidnapped by a cult, Bosch and mom's business abandoned on my watch and now a hotter-than-Hell demon insists I'm a guardian, that's what. I hate asking, but what choice do I have? He's right. I do need something. "Can you help us get back to town? I mean, before you leave."

"Before I go back to Hell?" He's outright grinning now. He looks at Mag. "She *is* asking me for a favor, isn't she?" Now he looks back at me. "I'm growing on you."

I cross my arms. He appeared out of nowhere, so I'm assuming he can do it again. "Do you have magical zappity travel powers that can get us where we need to be or not?"

Mag casts a worried glance back at the big, dark, creepy house where I had the misfortune to find and purchase the grimoire I now blame for this mess. "What she means is, can you please get us out of here? We would like that," Mag says. "Stat."

"Don't worry about the cult," he says. "They're busy for now."

But I can see that Mag is worried. That's enough for me to fully cave.

"Okay, yes, I need a favor, Lucifuge Rofocale. Can you take us to my family's business or not?"

Be nicer to the minister of Hell, Callie. I'm afraid to. I want to be home. I want Mag not to be scared and worried anymore. I want to not deal with the guardian questions, and what they might mean for me. I want to pretend he's a boring, hideous troll. I want to go back to being in the control room, safe.

"It's just Luke," he says.

"Luke." I pause. "Why are you so sure they won't come after us?"

"Because they're busy using more of their liberated magical items to prepare for their journey to Portugal tonight. Obviously."

"Oh. That doesn't sound good." But it's none of my business.

"I can get you to where you want to go," he says, "in one piece even." He leans in toward us and this time I don't step back. "Well, two. I'm assuming you prefer to remain distinct entities."

"Uh, you assume correctly," Mag says.

"Distinct entities," I mutter. Who talks like that? "We're going to the Great Escape," and I rattle off the address just in case.

"Got it," he says, before extending his hand to me. "You have to hold my hand."

Why was I bothering to worry about ax murderers? The man

in front of me seems infinitely more dangerous, the most dangerous thing I've ever seen. The moonlight makes his face a shadow and his hair the pale gold of a halo.

Despite every ounce of good judgment I possess, I take his hand. He folds his fingers around mine, and I'm securely in his grasp. It's like having the nerves of my entire body in my palm. He could talk me into anything right now. My skin sings for more of his touch. I've never experienced anything like this.

No way am I letting him know any of that.

"You can hold onto my jacket," he says to Mag. His face is angled in their direction, but I can feel the heat of his gaze on me.

"I think someone likes you," Mag says to me. They take a light hold of Luke's jacket sleeve with a glance to Luke's and my linked hands.

I can feel my ears turning red, something that always happens when I'm upset or embarrassed. "Great," I say, playing it off and ignoring the throbbing heat in my palm . . . and elsewhere. "'Dear Prudence, I need some advice—what do you do when you find out the minister of Hell is into you and you were hoping to do something with your life that doesn't involve Satan's best pals? P.S. What should I do with my life? Because I have no idea . . .'"

Something zaps me with the force of a lightning strike.

Sure, this is how I die, being a pretend-brave smart-ass to one of the devil's minions. Sorry, Mag.

I should've winked back is to be my dying thought.

Or so I'm convinced for a long moment. There is a rumble and rattle like we're too close to train tracks and black shadows swoop around us and my ears detect what my gut says are screams but my brain doesn't want to work too hard to identify.

Then, those things stop. All of them. At once.

My feet are on solid ground. My eyes open to the familiar, comforting sight of the lobby of the Great Escape. My hand is still in Luke's.

"You okay?" he asks, tightening his grip a fraction.

"Better now," I say, steadied. I force myself not to cling, and take my hand back.

Mag's and my phones are still on the counter. I pick mine up and see—with crushing relief—no missed calls or texts from Mom. That settled, I shout: "Bosch!"

I take off when I remember Bosch is likely closed in the office upstairs. Mag and Luke follow.

"Bosch?" Luke asks, behind me.

I ignore him. I take the steps two at a time and fling the door open. Bosch comes barreling at me with a skidding of paws on hardwood floor and frantic yelps. I bend to catch her and ease her back into the control room.

"It's okay. Good girl, good girl."

"She named her dog Bosch?" Luke asks.

Mag shrugs. "After some scary art."

"Hieronymus Bosch's art isn't scary, it was visionary," I say, not for the first time. Though I know it's a ridiculous thing to be saying at this exact moment and it's also not easy getting the words out around Bosch's full tackle-and-lick mode.

"I agree," Luke says. "One of my favorite painters."

"Callie and you agree on something. How about that?" Mag says.

I stare down into Bosch's calming brown eyes. Isn't it time for Luke to get going?

"Don't you have a crossroads to be at?" I ask, invoking one of the most well-known myths about the devil—what I assumed were myths before tonight anyway. I instantly worry about being so in-his-face. What if he tries to possess my soul? Why do I keep challenging him? It's not like me. Usually I save my color commentary for rooms where the people it's directed at are not. It's reserved for conversations between me and Mag, sometimes Jared or Mom.

"You keep trying to get rid of me, it might work," Luke says.

His bottom lip juts out a little.

He's pouting.

In a ranking of cutest, most devastating expressions, his would be up there. I don't *want* to get rid of him at all.

This night keeps getting stranger. But that ends now.

I turn my head to Mag. "I guess this is all over, then. I still can't believe we had cheating cultists here."

"Cheating cultists who kidnapped us," Mag says.

"Who were into Latin and brought a dead murderer's hand with them, all of which is on video." I gesture to the monitors around us.

"Who put us near a pentagram," Mag says.

We're both getting into this now. "And summoned the minister of Hell," I say. "The minister with the best cheekbones in Hell."

Luke sniffs, but the pout disappears.

"Who were willing to trade us to him," Mag says, and whatever fun we were having dies with the words. That was a close call. Far too close for any sort of comfort.

"In a bargain for the Spear of Longinus." The words are heavy as lead in my mouth.

I stand and point an accusatory finger at Luke. "You told them where it is. You're going to let them have it."

Luke frowns, his blond eyebrows drawing together. "Kind of my job. They summoned me."

Bosch is checking Luke out, sniffing his boots. I wonder if they smell of sulfur. Not that I detected anything when I was holding his hand, except the burning desire to climb him. Maybe I'm wrong, but I have a terrible feeling that even though we're free this is all extremely bad. Everything that's gone down tonight.

"Luke?" I say.

"Yes." His brow unfurrows. He's immediately at attention. It makes me incredibly self-conscious.

"Please tell me that the spear is a myth, that it's got no power. That whatever those guys think they're up to, it's all just a big dud."

Luke studies our surroundings. He's taking in the monitors, our chairs, the clue cabinet that is actually a retired library card catalogue, Bosch's dog bed. I may not be that much of a student of human nature outside our escape rooms, but I am fairly certain he's stalling.

"Right?" I ask. "It's all imaginary?"

Luke pivots and fixes me with a stare. I focus on his forehead so I won't notice what color his eyes are.

Too late. An almost clear blue.

"Not exactly," he says.

"Does your asking this have anything to do with the guardian business?" Mag says to me. "You're going to figure things out, Callie."

"It doesn't," I say, quickly. For whatever reason, I'd rather

Luke not hear about my personal flailing. "I'm just curious. How 'not exactly'?"

Bosch collapses onto her belly with a sigh. A tense silence ensues.

"Not at all exactly," Luke says finally. "The Holy Lance has long been hidden for a reason. Many have tried to find it, but none have gotten so close in"—he pauses, and it's like he's accessing the cloud or something—"at least a century."

"What is this thing they want anyway?" Mag asks.

"It's a spear used by a Roman soldier when Jesus was hanging on the cross. One that came into contact with his blood when it was used to stab him," I say.

Mag and I both grew up going to church more or less every Sunday. Our recreational reading may not be the same, so Mag may not know about these kinds of mystical legends, but they know enough to blink with an understanding of how sacred such an object would be.

"It is a weapon that can be used for many things," Luke says.

I have a sneaking suspicion he's trying to downplay this. Why? Because he wants them to succeed?

"And those assmasks are going to get it and bring about Hell on Earth?" I ask. "And you're not going to do anything about it?"

He scrubs a hand over the back of his neck and studies the ceiling—I have the weirdest thought that he looks like he's saying a silent prayer. Yeah, right. Then he shrugs a shoulder languorously. It's not an adjective I use often, but it fits. A state of pleasant inertia. I can guess at the answer before he speaks.

"I can't, really," he says. "Even if I wanted to. It's the sort of thing Fa—the boss likes. But it's not going to be a good thing. For anyone."

I stand my ground, which is an unfamiliar sensation. "Why can't you?"

"I'd have to have someone else who could interfere directly with their task. I made a deal with them." He starts for the door. "I suppose I should get going. It was truly lovely to make your acquaintances." He gives me a look, then Mag, then Bosch. Then me again.

My mind works the situation like a puzzle. He's going to leave. Of course he is. He'll probably go back wherever he came from. Hell. Like I told him to. The devil's left-hand man isn't going to stop what those guys are doing. They're going *to Portugal* next to get the Lance of Longinus. The Spear of Destiny. The Holy Lance.

The smart thing would be to wave good-bye to this blond angel-faced demon lord and act like none of this ever happened. Within a week it'll feel like some distant memory, a movie I watched. It's too weird to have happened to me. I read books. I have a useless degree and a brain stuffed with facts. I help my mom out. I hang out with my best friend when they have time. I dream of libraries with impossibly tall ceilings.

That's pretty much it.

Or it has been until now.

See, I've read plenty about this particular relic. Hitler wanted to get his hands on it, which says it all. I thought it was in a private collection on display in Vienna . . . and that its powers were probably fictional. But . . .

If Hands of Glory and the other things we've seen tonight are real, if the *Grand Grimoire* summoned Lucifuge Rofocale here, and he says this is real too, I have no evidence to suggest it isn't. We're the only people who know this is happening. That leaves one solution to this puzzle, and only one. A spike of fear shoots through me, even as I feel the grim satisfaction of knowing I'm correct.

"Wait." I step forward and grab Luke's shoulder before he's quite out the door. "Were you serious before? About me being some kind of guardian?"

He doesn't turn around. I drop my hand.

"Yes," he says. "A guardian who, apparently, somehow managed not to get instructed in the art of your sacred duty to fight evil."

That's what I'm afraid of. But it makes sense of everything that's gone down tonight. I can't ignore things that make sense. Something drew me to that book.

And, if I'm being honest, I want a purpose. A calling. This may be way over my pay grade (which is slightly above minimum wage), but it's also looking a lot like the answer to my major life problems. This *matters*.

"We have to stop them from getting it," I say.

"*What?*" Mag asks with a double take.

"We can't let them get the spear," I say.

Luke is silent and still and I hold my breath. He's not going to help us. His job is letting the bad guys win. He said so. He's a *demon*.

Maybe his leaving is for the best anyway. I don't trust myself around him.

But he turns to face me.

"I knew the minute I saw you," he says, "that you wouldn't be boring."

He grins his ridiculously hot grin. What in the world have I gotten myself into?

CHAPTER SIX

LUKE

That was close. I'd almost been forced to come to terms with the fact Callie might not take the bait.

Oh me of little faith.

This is how I wanted the evening to go, more or less—considering my royal screw-up and my impending deadline. I even get to be someone else for a change. Rofocale doesn't know how good he has it. He could be having unexpected adventures with fascinating people all the time, constrained only by his less personal fear of my father, and instead busies himself keeping his ledger up to date behind that behemoth he calls a desk and hanging out with the most torturous and tortured people the infernal kingdom has to offer.

"I regret this already," Callie says, and I can tell she means it. I can also tell she responds to my attention and touch—the slight change in her breathing, her eyes lingering on my face and form—even though she won't admit it. Yet.

Though, for the record, I can't read minds. Father sometimes seems to be able to, but true omniscience is for the shiny heavenly type of ruler, not the fallen likes of us. I meant what I said before though: Can you imagine how dull it would be the majority of the time? *Feed the dog, pet the cat, I'm sleepy, I'm hungry.* I'm so bored just thinking about human thoughts I can hardly stand it.

Maybe it wouldn't be so boring right this second, however, as I watch Callie close her eyes and presumably come to terms with the choice she's made. *Right now* I'd give up 10 percent of my good looks for a peek in that brain.

Don't worry. I'd still be the most handsome devil you've ever met.

"Are you all right?" Mag asks her. "We really don't have to do this, you know." They lower their voice. "There's no reason to trust him."

"There's every reason not to," Callie says, opening her eyes. "I don't. But we need information."

Mag purses their lips. "If you say so. But . . ."

Callie ignores the beginning of her friend's objection. "Why are you willing to help us?" she asks me.

I shrug. "I don't have anything better to do."

She frowns.

She let me convince her so easily that she's a guardian, steering her smack into the decision I hoped she would make. I picked up on a bit of . . . frustration with her current circumstances there for the exploiting.

But I realize almost too late that I can't gloat too much *or* be too blasé. Persuasion is one of my gifts. The hard sell isn't. I'll have to give her a better reason. "Like I said, it won't be good for anyone—including me. I like things the way they are. I've got a pretty sweet setup. Hell on Earth would mess that up."

"Excuse me if I'm the only one not getting the whole

picture here. But what are we actually talking about doing?" Mag asks. "Going back to that house with that cult? Because: No. Way."

Callie raises her eyebrows. She doesn't know precisely what's next.

I do. And I can't have her overthinking her decision. I had to let her come to it on her own, but she can talk herself back out of it too. That would be the safe choice, and I suspect after just this small amount of time with her that she is excellent at those.

"Is there someone who can watch your . . . Bosch?" I ask.

I've seen enough to know that the pooch is not getting left behind alone and I don't think we need to bring a dog along with us. We have hounds in the office, but they aren't nearly this charming. More what I'd call slavering beasts.

"She can stay at home with Jared, depending how long we'll be," Callie says. "We have to be here to open tomorrow." Her forehead wrinkles.

"You want to prevent a cult from gaining the Spear of Destiny and also open on time tomorrow?" I ask.

She nods. "Yes."

There's a challenge in it.

"We can try to do both." I should be up-front about something, because it's to my advantage. "I can't actually prevent them from getting the spear. They summoned me appropriately and a bargain was struck before you broke the summoning pentagram."

"That worked?" Callie flushes with pleasure. "I wasn't sure, but I've read things that made me think it might. Mostly I just wanted to distract them."

Flattery is my friend, and, in this case, also true. "You have killer instincts. And yes. Otherwise he could've kept me there indefinitely."

"We can't just let them get it. Unless we're already too late?" Callie asks. Almost hopeful.

"We can try to beat them to it," I say. "You could get it first."

"I really would rather never see those guys again." Mag has gathered their arms around themself and shivers despite a lack of cold. Can't say I blame them. Solomon Elerion is not my favorite sort of human either.

"You don't have to go," Callie says in a way that tells me she is praying Mag won't take her up on it. "I can do it solo."

Mag blows out a breath. "Nice try, Cal. I'm not leaving you alone with . . . Luke."

I grin at them. "Cheer up. I'm not so scary. We'll have fun."

"We're saving the world or something like that," Callie says. "It is not for fun."

I'm playing it Antarctica cool, giving her the impression there's no other option. Which isn't a lie. I couldn't do anything to stop the cult's plan without her. And there *is* a part of me that wants to.

Another interesting discovery.

Not as interesting as finally divesting the cult members of their souls and satisfying Father will be, but . . .

"Suit yourself." I shrug. "I plan to have fun."

I get the narrowed eyes of disapproval once more.

"Luke, you should know . . ." Mag says. "Callie loathes bad boys."

"Who said I was bad?"

They look at each other. "Aren't most people who live in Hell?" Callie asks, all skepticism.

"Judgmental," I return.

Now I get a shrug back.

"Most of them are," I say.

"Not all?" She stops, curious. Then retrieves a leash from the desktop, and clips it to Bosch's collar.

Technically, every denizen of Hell belongs there. "Would I be helping you save the world if I were all bad?"

"Probably." Callie brushes past me, and I resist the impulse to reach out and pull her close. That would be the best way to make her run. I almost do it anyway.

I'm saved from the impulse when she heads for the door, dog in tow. "We're walking home, by the way. I don't want Bosch getting zappity time-space traveled like we did."

"Probably best," I say, "since we're then going to Portugal. Look, I swear I'll let you know the moment you can't trust me anymore. Deal?"

I still want to touch her. So I hold out my hand.

Callie turns, hesitates. "Is this going to give you power over me or my immortal soul or anything like that?"

If only it were that easy, good Callie. I'd have to stop lying to you for that.

"No."

I fold her fingers in mine again. I like the feel of her skin too much. I lightly stroke her wrist with a finger. Her breath hitches.

We lock eyes. The intensity surprises me. Neither of us looks away.

I want her to tell me every thought in her head and then kiss her until neither of us is thinking anymore. This feels dangerous, which is as new as anything. But then what about this situation isn't? I am, frankly, fascinated. Maybe for the first time.

Mag waves a hand between me and Callie, breaking the

moment of connection. "Did you say something about going to Portugal?" Mag asks, with something like dread.

"To the city of Sintra," I confirm as Callie removes her fingers from mine. I pretend to be unaffected, as if I don't have the immediate desire to reach for her again. "That's where the Quinta de Regaleira estate is. Hopefully we'll have time to poke around a bit. I think you'll like it."

"Portugal," Mag says.

"You always wanted to go abroad," Callie says, apparently recovered from our moment and bright-siding.

"Not like this," Mag says. "Will we get passport stamps? No, we don't even have passports."

"I could probably fake something up," I put in. Forgery is another innate gift of mine. "But technically no passports are needed for zappitying."

"Is that what you're calling it now too?" Callie shakes her head.

The term is ridiculous, but I used it so I can't admit it now. "I guess so."

Callie brings Bosch to the door, and we follow her down the stairs.

I hesitate. I'm compelled to issue a warning. "This is probably going to be both difficult and treacherous. You understand? I don't see the cultists giving up on getting the spear without a fight."

"We *know* it's dangerous," Callie says, a tone even I recognize as *c'mon, duh* in her voice. "*Hello.* But why plan on fighting? I help build escape rooms. And you say I'm a guardian. We'll trick them. Or we'll trap them. Or both."

Mag says nothing.

But the confident gleam in Callie's eye makes me feel a

new burst of happiness that the evening has proceeded as it has. Which, in turn, makes me slightly uncomfortable. Other people's emotions don't typically factor into my decision-making.

I'm not bothered enough to put an end to this evening of exciting cult-thwarting festivities though. "I can't wait to see your work," I say.

The truth feels strange on my tongue.

Bosch trots along happily, while Callie, Mag, and I descend into an uneasy silence as we traverse the narrow shoulder of the pavement.

Callie's house turns out to be less than a mile's walk from the shopping center that houses the business. The road is fairly well trafficked, and so I wave my fingers and let some shadows conceal us without bragging about it. Something tells me Callie would protest about me hiding us with no real cause. She likes protesting.

I want to talk to them—to *her*—but I also don't want to seem like an overeager pain in the buttocks (no matter how nice mine are and, again, I've been assured they're exquisite). Truth is, my sojourns on Earth have been as lonely—maybe more—than my time at lessons or as Rofocale's intern. The conversations I've had with these two are among the best in my memory. It's against my nature to be cautious, but I tread carefully here.

We're going to have an adventure. And inside forty-eight hours I have to show back up at home with souls or this is likely to be my one and only adventure.

"Why are you so quiet all of a sudden?" Callie asks. She squints over at me. Suspicious.

"No reason." I consider whistling, but decide it would come across too creepy.

"I don't believe you," she says with an adorable uptilt of her nose. "So, what can you tell us about these cultists that we don't already know? What kind of assumptions will they make?"

I blink and reaccess everything I know about Solomon Elerion and his merry band of lunatics.

"The Order of Elerion is approximately four hundred years old, but it's remained a fringe group in terms of size. Thirteen members, always. Believes artifacts that contain magic were left behind on Earth expressly for the battle between good and evil. Various churches and many individuals went out of their way to hide a lot of these objects, so they aren't easy to lay hands on. The Holy Lance, which would allow them to make what they think is the infernal plan for Earth a reality, has been the cult's ultimate goal all along. Unlike most cults, they are filled with true believers to the core. No one has ever left."

"Wow," she says.

"What?"

She shakes her head, almost in awe. "The way you rattled that off. It was . . ."

I could swear the word she's about to use is *sexy*. But then she shakes her head again in a way that is obviously meant to clear it. "What do you mean 'what they think is the infernal plan for Earth'?"

I'd rather go back to the first thought, but her question is perceptive. "Lucifer views his role very specifically. He will punish those who lose their souls, but he wants people to surprise him. He views the infernal and the divine's eternal conflict as a stabilizing force of sorts."

"Huh." Callie absorbs that. "Okay, back to the cult. It has men and women, though? And different ages? Like we saw tonight. So progressive as far as small, non-dude-wants-a-bunch-of-wives-slash-sex-slaves cults go?"

She's right. They're not one of *those* cults. "Yes, but women as full members in the last twenty years only."

"Got it. And what kind of training do they have? Weaknesses? Anything like that?"

Callie is taking all this in as if I'm a book and she's reading the words. I want to answer her every question. But I'm stumped on this one. "Can you narrow it down a bit? What kind of skills?"

"I'm looking for anything we can exploit."

"There's the element of surprise."

Callie nods. "Useful point. They won't be expecting us to show up, not with you. I'll need you to write down the name of where we're going so I can take a quick Google . . ."

I feel as if I should give myself a mark on an invisible score card. So I do.

"Um, Callie," Mag, who has remained quiet for this entire exchange, interrupts with a warning. A late one, unfortunately.

"Mag . . . Callie . . . is that you?" The guy who asks is standing on the tidy front porch of a two-story house painted light gray with Halloween-style silhouettes in the windows even though it's spring. I immediately determine this is Callie's older brother, Jared.

"Jared," Callie says. "Hey! And yes, I am me."

"And I'm me," Mag says. And studies their shoes.

"And who's your friend?" he asks, curious. But nice.

Callie glances between the two of us and grimaces, shaking her head. "Nobody. Come on. Bosch is hungry."

Nobody?

But then what do I expect her to do? Explain my dossier—or what she believes is my dossier—and how we met?

Her brother is now looking at me with a combination of curiosity and suspicion, but he moves out of Callie's way as she barrels past him into the house.

Mag says, "Hi, Jay." Then hesitates.

"Long time no see," Jared says with a hint of a smile.

"Just a week," Mag says, hiding a grin.

"Like I said." Jared stares at Mag, who bashfully shuffles past him the rest of the way inside.

There's a story between those two, which Callie doesn't seem to be aware of. Again I long to pry. But I don't.

They've abandoned me with Callie's brother. *Thanks, gang.*

I nod to him. "Hey," I say and offer my hand.

"Callie doesn't really bring guys home," he says, shaking off whatever passed between him and Mag. Or trying his hardest to. "Who are you?"

"A friend of Callie and Mag's, obviously. Should we go inside?" I say, neutrally. "You could give me a tour."

I want to see the house. All of my time spent "hanging" with humans has been spent in dimly lit bars or the occasional dank club. The fact that this is the place where Callie lives is only part of it. I'm curious to see what a home is like.

"Sure," Jared says. "Do you have a name? Where'd you guys meet?"

"I'm Luke," I say. "And if Bosch likes me, how bad can I be?"

Jared wants to know more than I'm offering, but I shrug and follow Mag and Callie inside.

The silhouette in the downstairs window is an old-fashioned iron cutout in the shape of a witch, complete with pointy hat and long nose. The door opens into a living room that I shouldn't find surprising, but do. Controlled chaos is the term. Stacks of books sit on end tables and a coffee table that's an old steamer trunk. A large TV has a videogame console hooked up to it. Shelves and shelves of more books and media surround the room. There are nerdy little touches all over, like a Star Wars–patterned throw draped across the back of the couch.

"I like your house," I say, as Callie appears in the wide entryway that leads to the rest of the place.

Behind me, Jared says, "Thanks. Our mother has a certain aesthetic—it's just her and Callie here now. Usually."

Callie has her hair tucked behind her right ear, which has turned a lovely shade of pink. "I'm just back here until I figure some things out, Jared, thanks." Her attention switches to me. "Hey, can you come with me and show me that . . . thing we talked about?"

"Of course," I say.

Mag appears behind Callie as Jared says, "What thing?"

Callie sighs. "Jared, what are you doing?"

"I know, it stinks," he says. "But I promised Mom I'd watch out for you."

Callie sighs again. "Hard as it is to believe, I'm an adult too."

Jared's eyes can't seem to avoid finding Mag, who studiously avoids meeting them. Jared has on a tucked-in collared shirt and khakis. His hair has been recently cut, impeccably neat. He gives off the air of wanting to impress someone. I'm not going out on a limb to guess it's Mag. He must've known they'd be here tonight. That's why he's home to "watch" Callie.

Callie motions for me to come with her. "This way. I promise we'll just be a few minutes."

"But—" Jared says.

"Mag's coming too. Don't worry, we're not having a ménage à trois," she says.

Jared sputters.

"Callie," Mag says, as we start up the stairs and leave a gaping brother below, "none of this is like you."

"Satan's bad influence," Callie says under her breath.

The wall alongside the creaky, wooden staircase is dotted with a mix of old posters and vintage oddities, signed photos of celebrities in costumes, and the odd family photo of Callie, Jared, and a woman who favors them both that I assume is their mom. No sign of a father in the picture, so that explains Jared's overprotective instincts. That and his torch for Mag.

"You've never brought a guy home before?" I ask, as we head up a short hallway and Callie opens a door with a Morse code poster on it.

"I have, just not recently. And you're not a guy," Callie says. "You're a demon."

"I'm still a guy."

Callie snorts.

Her bedroom is on the small side and all the books make it feel even smaller. Lots of mystical and occult-themed books, but plenty of novels with cracked spines too. There's a small desk with a semi-ancient computer on it, which she boots up now. There's also only one chair.

"You can type?" Callie asks me.

I refuse to be insulted, but it's not easy. I can time-space zappity. Yes, I am literate.

"Among many other skills." I give her a wink.

She stares at me with something like hunger, which again confirms that she's not as immune to my charms as she's pretending to be.

"I can expound on them, if you'd like," I say. "Or demonstrate . . ."

She hesitates for a breath, then shakes her head and gestures at the computer. "Can you type in the location?"

I slide into the chair.

Mag sits down on the bed. "You realize we have a problem."

Callie says, "Yes. I can't believe Jared's giving me trouble about Luke."

"That's not entirely fair," Mag says.

I decide to help them out and learn more about Callie in the meantime. "You and your brother don't get along?" I ask, as I pull up a Google window.

"No, we do," Callie says.

Mag speaks carefully. "It's funny he thinks he can tell you what to do better than you tell yourself. But in this case . . ."

"Right?" Callie asks, before frowning at the full implication of Mag's meaning. "I guess I have to rethink everything now. This . . . guardian thing. I mean, look at this. What we're doing."

She sweeps her hand to indicate me.

"I am," Mag says, not sounding happy.

"I feel so special," I say. "Here you go."

I slip out of the chair and pull it back for her with a flourish. She eyes me like it's a trick but then sinks into the seat. I slide her forward to the desk edge.

"I've got it," she says.

With nothing better to do, I ease down on the side of the bed a couple of feet from Mag. "Get used to this if you're sticking around," Mag says. "Watching Callie read is kind of a thing."

"Don't get used to it," Callie says, but she's already distracted.

"Is that how you and Jared became . . . friends?" I ask Mag quietly.

Mag ignores the question. "I'll be right back. I want to ask Jay about something." They bustle back out into the hall.

Callie doesn't bother to respond.

I can identify a brush-off when I'm given one. So I do as Mag suggested. I watch Callie read.

Callie reading is like Callie listening earlier. She is utterly focused on what's in front of her. She scrolls slowly down the page, reading until she reaches the pictures of the inspired insanity that is the estate where we're headed. She pauses at a photo of one of the Wells of Initiation, a tower cut deep into the Earth instead of atop it.

"Ugh." She shudders. "I hope we don't have to get near that place. You said the spear's under the chapel? I think I'm ready."

"Yes." I'm impressed. "You just needed that much time?"

"I'm good at remembering things."

"I have a terrible memory." *Particularly where my marching orders from Rofocale are concerned.*

"Good," Callie says, getting up. "I'll put that in your weaknesses column."

She winks at me, but before I can react she holds up her finger and bustles out of the room. I wait, scanning the shelves and teetering book stacks more closely. She comes back a few minutes later with a portable first aid kit.

"I wish I knew exactly what we're going to need," she says.

"Luck and charm," I say. "Good thing I've got the devil's own supply of both."

"That would be a lot more believable if you hadn't gotten caught in a pentagram."

I give her a smile that anyone would call dashing. One that could slay the faint of heart. I lift my eyebrows. "Got me here in your bedroom, didn't it?"

CHAPTER SEVEN

CALLIE

I ignore Luke's will-melting smile. And the way the word *bedroom* sounds when he says it. He should be illegal.

"Where'd Mag go?" I ask.

"To talk to your brother."

Reminding me of our most immediate problem: Jared. Who is being perfectly rational and doing what he's supposed to, except in this case that's not going to work.

Like I don't have enough on my hands with:

a. a flirty, delicious demon who I want to interrogate about being a liege of Hell because when will I ever get another chance but that would encourage him (and me);
b. an evil cult to thwart in some way that works out well for all involved;
c. a business to keep running this weekend or risk disappointing my mom and giving her an excuse to say no to every future event;

    d. a best friend to make sure no harm comes to since Mag's only involved in this because I am;

    e. I'm a guardian? It's not like I never fantasized about having some special secret calling in life, but that's for people in books . . . not *me*; and

    f. all of the above. But especially e. Tonight feels life-changing and as much as I've been whining about not knowing what to do with it lately, as much as the idea is tempting, I'm not sure I'm ready for my life to change.

It's not even like I'll be able to tell anyone about this. It's not like there's a paycheck in it, either. "Dear World: There was this time I ended up globe-trotting to a grandiose estate in Portugal to save the world and, oh yeah, apparently I'm on Heaven's away team . . . front a girl some credit?" That's the kind of thing that only gets you streamlined admission to a psych ward.

I design adventures for people; I don't go on them. I am the least qualified "world saver" in the history of world saving. I know. I've read a lot of history. I'm undoubtedly going to screw this up.

But.

It's not like Luke can do it. He admitted as much. I could pray—and I will—and I could wait for a sign, but shouldn't I assume this is that? I've also read enough to know it doesn't matter if you want to be chosen. There are the people who throw up their hands and let bad things happen and there are the people who stop them.

If I'm being drafted into the battle between good and evil, I want to be the second kind.

I let a breath heave in and out, which *is* what someone in a book would do. I stash the first aid kit inside my messenger bag.

"How do we get Jared to stop asking questions? Any ideas?"

"You don't," Jared says, appearing in the doorway. He crosses his arms. Mag's behind him. "Where were you thinking of going? You're supposed to stay here, helping me run the business this weekend."

Ah, great. Damn.

"Jared, it's a long story. A long, kind of inexplicable, unbelievable story. But you are perfectly fine to let us go, I swear." I cross my fingers over my heart.

When I glance over at Luke, his eyes are closed. Right, probably not a big cross fan. They pop open and he catches me looking. He winks again. Not like I didn't ask for it by winking back at him before.

But my knees still threaten to dissolve, and I turn back to Jared with the knowledge my ears are likely still the shade of overripe strawberries at the grocery.

"Callie, Jared's right," Mag says.

For a second, I wonder if I misheard.

They fold their arms, mirroring Jared. "This is all going too far. You're going to get hurt."

Mag *agrees* with Jared. They don't want us to go either.

I can only imagine the wounded expression on my face.

Jared goes on. "If Mom was here, she wouldn't let you leave. You clearly planned something you shouldn't be doing with Luke. Mag said as much. This is *exactly* why Mom asked me to come supervise this weekend. You're staying home."

"I can't believe this," I say to Mag, my emotions kicking up a betrayed fuss. Then to Jared, "Have I ever in my life done anything that you would've needed to stop?"

Jared shakes his head. "That's the point. You're overdue."

"Listen to him," Mag says.

Jared gives Mag a look I can't decode.

"I can't believe my best friend sold me out," I say.

Mag studies the floor.

I don't know what to do. Jared isn't wrong. Mom wouldn't allow this; whether I'm an adult or not, I still live under her roof at the moment.

I stop to wonder what would have happened if she'd been there tonight. If they'd taken *her*.

Horror.

No, I'm no hero. I'm at best the hero's research assistant. But I got dragged into this and there's nobody else to see it through.

"Luke?" I ask, pleading. "Can you do something about this?"

"No, he can't," Jared says. "I'm sorry, but I'm putting my foot down. You aren't going anywhere."

I take a step back. I've never seen Jared this forceful.

"That's enough," Luke says, lifting a finger and holding it in front of Jared's lips. Jared's eyes go as big and round as the supposed Area 51 flying saucer. Mag starts to step in front of him, but Luke holds his other hand up in front of them. "Both of you, stop. As Callie says, we are going to be leaving now. We will return soon enough." He looks at me. "Catch Mag."

I barely have time to react as he waves each hand, one in front of Jared's face, the other in front of Mag's, then reaches out to guide Jared to the floor as he wilts toward it. I lunge forward just in time to keep Mag from collapsing, and do the same.

My brother and my best friend lie beside each other, unconscious.

Luke stands, then makes a dusting motion with his hands. "We're good."

The average human heart beats a hundred thousand times a day, and mine must be pounding hard enough to do all of them at once. "Did you . . . break them? I . . . I love them both."

"They're asleep. That's all," Luke says. "They'll be fine when they wake up."

"When they wake up and call my mother." I still can't believe Mag sided with Jared.

Hurt as I am, I go over and pull two pillows off my bed. I kneel and slide one beneath each of their heads.

"Callisto," Luke says, watching me as I rise, "you are so *good*."

I fidget, uncomfortable. How does he know my full name? Also, why in this world is the devil's employee so determined to keep flirting with me? It must be an opposites-attract kind of thing.

Not that I'm attracted to *him*. My body has had a few immediate, intense physical responses to him. That's all.

Not even I'm buying the lies I'm telling myself.

"Are we going or what?" is my outward reaction.

"Your wish," he says, and maybe he finishes the thought, but I'll never know because he takes my right hand in both of his and my body feels like it ignites and then we aren't in my bedroom anymore, we're back in that darkness with those screams.

The black goes on and on, the walls of a vast coffin, and the shrieks are fingernails scraping my eardrums but with more than sound, with despair and pain and every emotion I ever pushed down because it was too strong for *feeling*.

When it finally ends, I'm not ready. I'm afraid to open my eyes.

I'm afraid of everything. Of what I've gotten myself into. Of whether I'll get back out.

"Callie? You should be right as rain," Luke says, and his deep voice is so voice-like, so contained in space, that I latch onto it like the lifeline it is. "Though I've never truly understood that phrase," he continues. "I suppose it depends on whether you like the rain. Do you? Like the rain?"

No matter that my lifeline is the minister of Hell.

I open my eyes. There's an avenue of statues behind Luke, grand and tall, gods and goddesses flanking a broad path amid trees. We're surrounded by hilly terrain, the moon and stars above lighting the dark so that it seems almost like day compared to that other screaming darkness.

I've never been any farther away from home than Tennessee or Ohio, or one summer, Myrtle Beach. Places we can drive in a day. Now here I am standing in Portugal.

And my best friend's not with me. Mag, who dreams of passport stamps but sided with Jared.

"Well?" Luke prompts, frowning with worry, still gripping my hand in his. "Rain, yes or no?"

I shake off thoughts of home for now. "I only like rain if I'm inside."

If I'm not mistaken, he exhales. Like he's relieved I'm okay.

I hesitate and gently extract my hand. "Why was the trip worse than before?"

"I suppose the distance." He's frowning again. "I've never . . .

I wasn't aware it would have a different effect on you. I'm usually traveling solo. Apologies if it was uncomfortable."

How can someone like him not know something like that? "That's almost like a 'sorry you were offended' apology. A nonpology."

"Apologies aren't my strong suit," Luke says, agreeably. "But I'm glad you're all right. What's the plan now?"

Duh. I must be recovered. "I get the spear ASAP. Where's this chapel?"

But it hits me the second I say it. He didn't tell them the spear was *in* the chapel. He told them the spear was *under* the chapel.

This could be a problem. I want to laugh or weep or go back into the screaming dark void. I have a mortal fear of being trapped in the darkness below . . . things. My own special claustrophobia. Tales of catacombs send me into panic sweats. The words "the deeps" are legitimately the most terrifying I've ever heard.

Though my brain knows logically the spear probably isn't *that* far down, it feels like I've just been informed I must journey to the center of a hollow Earth, where I'll likely be slowly crushed by everything that's above or, you know, trapped forever, unable to reach the surface.

Eurydice not making it out of Hades because stupid Orpheus couldn't play his freaking lyre and keep himself from looking back.

Remembering I'm here with someone from Team Hades doesn't help.

"What's wrong?" he asks.

I hate him for being perceptive.

"Other than this whole situation? Nothing. Where's the

chapel? Also . . . can you give me any more information about where I'll find it? Is there any security here?"

He motions for us to start up the path. "There is a security guy. But he's asleep in his shack, so we don't need to be too stealthy at the moment. He was reading *The Da Vinci Code* in translation and it must've knocked him right out."

"That's a little on the nose," I say, feet crunching on the pebbled path. "But you didn't answer my other question."

He exhales a sigh. "Yes, I know. I can sense the spear's presence beneath the chapel, but it's not entirely clear. Usually when I know something, I know it fully. But sacred spaces are . . . fuzzy, I guess you could say. I sense them, but they withhold some secrets. I probably wouldn't even have known the spear was there, had they not asked me to focus on it. But I can tell you the eccentric mastermind behind this place, Monteiro the Millionaire, and his set-designer architect loved to hide things. There are tunnels and secret passages all over."

Tunnels and secret passages . . . The stuff of my best work daydreams and worst actual nightmares. But if I'm a guardian, then I have this in me: the ability to deal with this. No way I'm showing weakness. Yet. "Got it."

I recognize the palace from the website. It looms over the hillside, a gray warning covered in statuary and gargoyles. Luke guides us onto a paved path, and we pass the house and head up a rise. Before long, he gestures at a much smaller, but still grandly embellished gray-and-white structure, a milky cross thrusting up against the night sky above an arched entryway shadowy as a cave.

"That's the chapel," he says.

I figured as much. "How do I get in?" I hate that it comes out as a whisper.

"Try the door," he says, irritably. Then, "What I mean to say is, I'm afraid I can't help you there. I wish I could."

The trees around us rustle in a light breeze. The air is pleasant, a faint sweetness to its scent. I wonder if there are night-blooming flowers nearby. There's a peace to standing here.

"Callie?" Luke asks. "I don't know how long we have before the cult gets here."

Or I'm scared. *Okay*, I tell myself, *you can do this.*

Time to get moving, so I do. I can practically feel the sacredness radiate from the church as I approach it. Is that because I'm a guardian? Because Luke told me what's here and I'm imagining it? I pause beneath carvings of two winged angels at the feet of the heavenly father. His hands extend in welcome.

I step through the arch, and I keep walking until my extended hand touches a door.

I press against cool, smooth wood. I'm already mentally inventorying the lock pick tools I tossed into the first aid kit, but . . .

The door opens at my push.

I don't look back to see what Luke's doing. I go forward, determined to do Orpheus one better.

Dim light filters in through stained-glass windows and I make out several rows of simple wooden chairs and an altar. The only sound is my own breathing. Taking out my phone, I thumb to the flashlight app and its glow helps steady me.

The main chapel is as filled with architectural flourishes as the outside. The floor in front of me is patterned with a giant red Knights Templar cross. Pentagrams mix in with crosses and other arcane symbols.

I make a slow circle and discover a spiral staircase to my side. It goes down.

Under the chapel.

Worth a shot.

The air gets danker the farther down I go, circling, circling, placing my feet cautiously on the steps. Then I'm in an underground chamber.

The ceiling is low, and down here, the design is plain. Black-and-white floor. A simple stone altar with two black crosses, one above and one below. Not much else.

I approach the altar, since it's the only obvious starting point.

I wish Mag was here like I wish to keep breathing; they'd say something to make me laugh, distract me from this heart-thumping terror. I discovered my fear of being trapped or crushed underneath something in fourth grade, on a church youth group trip to Mammoth Cave in western Kentucky. It's the longest known cave system in the world, and one of its earliest explorers, a slave named Stephen Bishop, described it as a "grand, gloomy and peculiar place."

Maybe that being a perfect description for this basement is why I remember it now.

On that trip we went down these long staircases with steel guardrails that I gripped with sweaty hands to get to the cave entrance. Just outside the giant mouth, gaping open like a scream, our park service guide started talking about Floyd Collins. Floyd was a white historical cave explorer and in 1925, while looking for new turf to turn into a tourist attraction he got trapped inside, a twenty-seven-pound rock fell on one of his legs. Ironically he then *became* the tourist attraction. A media circus developed over the next seventeen days as men tried to tunnel to free him. It turned into one of the biggest news stories of the time.

But the passage collapsed and when they finally made it

to him Floyd Collins had been dead for days. Eventually his body was recovered and then, horror of horrors, he ended up on display in a glass coffin.

I guess the park guide thought this was a suitably engaging story for the kiddies and we'd all be quietly rapt for the whole tour. Unfortunately for her, I started sobbing as soon as we walked inside the cave entrance and I could see the complete darkness ahead. The church leader had to take me out. Mag went on the tour, but when they came out, they just said, "Want to sit in the back on the way home?" We never sat in the back of the church van; the older kids always claimed that perk. I nodded and nothing more was said.

Here's hoping I don't end up the Floyd Collins of Portugal.

Kneeling in front of the stone altar, I set my phone down and grope around the edges looking for any promising quirks. I work my way from the bottom up, slowly but surely, not finding a single unusual seam or opening, nothing that would indicate a hidden compartment.

Until I'm almost done, that is. My searching has gone from careful to fumbling, my breathing growing shallower. I'm running out of time and the guts to stay down here.

The top surface gives the smallest bit against my frantic fingers. Or does it?

I pick up the phone and examine the altar more closely. Yes, there's a slab on top. I've dislodged it a fraction.

It can't be something so simple, can it? But maybe it can. No one's down here rummaging around during the day, nor would they have been when it was a working estate. Holding the phone to my chest with my chin, I try my best not to think of Floyd Collins. Of how all those people desperate to help were out of reach when he needed them, like Luke is for me.

The slab slides free. Inside is a gritty emptiness. The phone shows me nothing but stone.

I sweep my hand along the bottom and realize the stone doesn't quite touch the side on the right. I work the edges of my fingers around the stone there and then I pull.

It gives.

I set down the phone and work both hands into the crack in the far-too dark and finally manage to dislodge the panel.

I lift the half-inch sheet of thick stone aside. Underneath, there's an opening with a book set inside it. I reach in to pick it up and realize I'm wrong. It's not a book.

It's designed to resemble one, or, actually, more than one.

I lift the object out carefully. The wooden box is a kind popularized in the late 1800s. It's carved to look like books lying lengthwise on top of and at the bottom of a row of books showing their spines.

An Italian puzzle box.

"Thank you," I whisper, talking to the only entity I expect to be listening in here.

Shining my light over the box, I make out the words *Pilate* and *Nicodemus* painted in Latin, along with words I don't know. Strange symbols.

Right. Longinus's name didn't come from the New Testament proper. It came from an extra-Biblical text. The Gospel of Nicodemus, the Acts of Pilate.

Hesitating, I touch the top of the box and let the fact this is happening wash over me.

The knowledge I am underground comes flooding back too. Lucky me.

The box isn't that heavy. I could lug the whole thing outside. The cult is coming, after all.

But what if I get it outside and this is a decoy? That seems like the kind of thing someone who'd build an estate like this might do. I refuse to not be up to this, to fail in front of Luke. I need to prove to Mag they were wrong not to trust me. And, of course, defeat evil.

So I hold the phone under my chin again, and decide to work the puzzle. Boxes like this still exist. This place dates from around 1900 so it makes sense for it to be a classic design.

It is. I slide the carved book spine along the bottom to the left, which in turn lets me slide the panel at the far right out. I tip the box forward, and a key clunks out of the side compartment onto the stone. I move the top of the box forward to meet the rest and press the middle spine down to reveal the keyhole. I insert the key in the lock and turn it.

Bingo.

I open the lid.

A narrow something wrapped in cloth is wedged inside. I lift the object out and unwrap it. The fabric is old, rough against my fingers. What it protects is . . .

Another key, larger, old-fashioned, and iron.

Not the Holy Lance. But where there's a key, there must be a lock.

I stand and begin searching the altar again, looking for something I missed. Wedging myself between the wall and the back of the altar, the key in my fingers and my phone held by my chin, I see it.

At the very base of the altar, easy to miss, the stone is interrupted by a small wooden block with a keyhole. I shimmy down the wall, and try the key. I have to put some muscle behind it, but the block gives. The compartment inside seems empty at first, until I feel around on the bottom of it. There's a round wooden object. I stash the key in my pocket and pull on the wood.

The compartment is cleverly angled, so that as I pull and keep pulling, I have to move. Once I've got the wooden spear shaft out, it hits me at my chest. About four feet long. I step around the altar, my hand trembling around it.

I'm holding the Lance of Longinus. The Spear of Destiny.

Hesitating, I set it aside, then replace the box and the top of the altar. I don't want it to be clear someone's been here when the cult arrives. I pick the spear shaft back up.

I really must be here for a reason. Who else would know what I know? How many other people could have worked that box out so quickly?

If it's a test, maybe I passed.

I feel a little cocky about it: that I overcame my fear, that I have the Spear of Destiny in my fingers, and have, well, saved the freaking world.

Almost smiling, I turn to leave, deciding how much gloating to engage in when I get outside.

I'm blinded in a sudden flare of light. I lift my hand to block a half-dozen flashlight beams shining right at me. There's another way into the chapel basement apparently.

Of course there is. Secret passages. Tunnels.

Solomon Elerion melts out of the line of his followers. "*You*," he says.

I dive for the stairwell, gripping the lance like my life depends on it. Because now?

I'm pretty sure it does.

CHAPTER EIGHT

LUKE

This is one of the most memorable nights of my existence, and that's no small thing. Not when you consider how many times I've been to the High Unholy Days—a sort of demonic Mardi Gras that we have below.

Anyway, it turns out even the most thrilling day has room for a little something that I hate and which plagues me: boredom.

Yes, I'm bored. Waiting out here for Callie, who's been gone for-seeming-ever.

The security booth guy is still asleep and I spot an opportunity to entertain myself. It's a short walk past the palace and down the hill to the main entrance. As far as my senses detect, we're still ahead of our foes. So it's not like I'm abandoning Callie to a dire fate.

When I reach the shack, I discover a pasty, mustached gentleman so deeply asleep a thin line of drool leaks from one corner of his mouth. "Charmed, I'm sure," I say softly. It's the copy of *The Da Vinci Code* open on his chest alongside the decorative badge that makes some minor torment too tempting to pass up.

How do I know so much about pop culture? I have to study it. We all do. To corrupt humans, one must understand them, at least according to Porsoth. That includes all their current obsessions. I had to pass a test on cultural ephemera before I was cleared to go out on my first official Earth jaunt for attempted soul snagging. The administrative types don't want the Satanic horde being too obviously out of touch. You should hear the older demons moaning about having to keep up and then getting fire-and-brimstone gleeful when new Beyoncé drops.

The Knights Templar/Mason/Illuminati nonsense—well, mostly nonsense—that serves as Dan Brown's stock in trade is an oldie but a goodie.

I give the guy a hard tap on the shoulder. "It's you! Thank all that's holy!" I say, slipping into Portuguese, and perhaps overselling the enthusiasm but go big or go home. "They told me you'd have a symbol that would make you easy to identify."

The guard blinks up at me with the glazed lag between waking and sleeping.

"The book. Clever touch," I say. "I'm glad you have a sense of humor. Now, let's get going. We have to move. Now."

"What?" He's finally coming to. "What time is it?"

"Late." And then I add in my most ominous tone, "Almost too late."

More blinking. He reaches up to swipe away the drool. "Who—who are you?"

"You could say I'm . . . Robert Langdon," I say, preening a bit. "The real one." I wrinkle my nose. "Not the book version—I only inspired *him*. We should have kicked Brown out a lot earlier. He got *everything* wrong about me. I'm obviously much more competent and handsome. My name is Jacques. Pleased to meet you . . ." I offer him my hand.

The guard stands, the book falling to the floor of the shack. He frowns at me but reaches out to shake. "What are you doing here? We're closed."

"I'm here for you, mister . . ." I pause and shake my head. "I suppose your name doesn't matter. *You* are the Holy Grail. The one we've been looking for all these years."

That perks him right up. "Funny. So you're a prankster. I can get the police here with a call."

"You need proof," I say, shaking my head as if I'm the thick one. "Of course you do. We couldn't risk warning you in advance. But I'm happy to oblige."

The guard's fully awake now, and questioning everything. "You seem a little young to be the 'inspiration' for Robert Langdon."

I spread my hand across my chest as if mortally wounded. "Watch."

I wave my fingers as showily as possible, and then I make it look like I'm pulling smoke *out* of the security guard's chest. He gapes as the flow forms into a chalice. The wispy cup hovers in midair.

It's a parlor trick, but sometimes that's all you need.

"What?" He hesitates. "Me? *I'm special?*"

I solemnly nod. I'm about to send him on a wild clue chase when I hear Callie bellowing: "Luke! *LUKE, WHERE ARE YOU?*"

That does not sound good. I do a sweep, sending my senses out as far as I can. We're still alone. Just me, her, and the guard. I don't know why she's freaked out but there's no doubt she is. That makes me need to go at a run.

"Hold that thought," I say to my mark.

But his steps follow behind me as I dart back up the hill to the chapel.

Hell's bells.

Callie has got some kind of long stick extended as if to ward off the cape-wearing crew of cultists fanning out in front of the chapel. She's essentially surrounded—or she will be momentarily.

The Order of Elerion is *here*. I presume they used something in their stockpile of magical items to travel so quickly. But how do I not *feel* their presence even when I see them in front of me?

I've screwed up. Again. And I put Callie in direct danger.

"Luke!" Callie screams and searches over her shoulder.

I speed up. "I'm right here!"

"Who are they?" The security guard sounds baffled and awed. "Are they here for me too?"

That he kept up is good. Maybe he'll come in useful. It'd be the first time tonight one of my bright ideas panned out.

"Yes, but we have to save the girl first," I tell him.

I reach Callie's side and catch Solomon Elerion's sinister smile opposite us. It's like facing down a rabid hellhound when you've got the only bone in the world he wants. No masks this time, but he and his minions are no less loathsome for that. I need to get control of the situation.

When I touch Callie's arm, a heavy presence of pure power radiates over me. The same kind of sensation as when Father enters a room, with the nearly opposite effect. My knees weaken, but I want to turn my face to Callie and bask.

Light. A powerful light. It's like she's holding a small sun.

That's not a stick, it's the lance. *She has it.*

But there's something . . . off. I concentrate harder.

"Where were you?" she demands. "Zappity us out of here."

"Not so fast," Solomon says.

I stay put, meaning so does Callie. I know exactly where this damned if I do and damned if I don't situation is headed, not that she'll understand. But I can't zappity us. Not yet.

I made a deal.

There are rules to that sort of thing. The kind you don't break unless the other party releases you from the obligation, not unless you want to end up being roasted on an eternal spit by hell-flame. The kind even a Dark Prince can't duck.

"I suppose I should act surprised," Solomon says. "But I thought we might see you again. That you might be up to some sort of trick. And so we took precautions to conceal ourselves." Solomon frowns. "So . . . are you working with that guardian? Who are you, really? You came when we called, but I don't think you're Rofocale."

"Maybe the book was a fake," a woman behind Solomon says. "He doesn't seem impressive enough to hold such a position."

"It wasn't a fake. The little guardian has the spear." Solomon shrugs. "No matter. Now she will give it to us."

Callie barks out a hysterical laugh. "You've been smoking too much incense if you think I'm handing this over. No. You'll have to take it. And I don't think you can. Luke, stop them."

I close my eyes, imagining how much her hatred for me is about to grow. From a seed to a sequoia.

My words come out in a mumble. "Give it to them."

"What?" Callie asks.

"Give them the spear."

Callie's mouth works but no sound comes out. She's speechless. There's a first time for everything. Indignation makes her even lovelier.

"I'm sorry," I say. "I can't prevent them from getting it."

"He is *some* kind of devil," one of Solomon's minions says.

The security guard chooses this moment to enter the fray. Turns out he speaks English and has followed our entire conversation. "He's the exact opposite!"

I want to bark out, *Shut up*. But I need to make Callie understand. "I can't stop them from hurting you to get it," I explain. My stomach—which has withstood seminars on torture techniques and cram sessions on the minds of psychopaths and how to best manipulate them—turns at the sudden image of them hurting her while I do nothing.

And I can tell Callie isn't going to do the smart thing. Her shoulders square, her spine straightens. Her face reflects the disgust she feels for me. She won't act to save herself. I can't say anything else to help her. I wish I could read her mind, but I've seen enough to doubt she's secretly an accomplished martial artist.

A smirking Solomon lifts his hand in a lazy wave, and says, "Take it from her."

Callie bolts.

She's fast, I'll give her that.

The security guard leaps into action, and it turns out he has a Taser. Electricity jolts through the first cultist pursuing Callie, but Solomon sweeps the guard's legs out from under him. Of course, *he'd* secretly be an accomplished martial artist.

I stand, useless, watching as two more cult members retrieve Callie, prying the small-sun-as-spear away from her.

"Got it," one of them says.

I loathe people who state the obvious.

"Should we bring them?" another says.

At last, I'm able to act. "Our bargain is complete," I say to Solomon. "When we meet again, you won't be so fortunate."

I fly into motion and grab Callie's hand before she can punch me or shove me away. Before they can try to get hold of either of us. The welcoming, shrieking darkness returns, and then is replaced by a different darkness. Wet darkness. There's a *drip, drip* nearby.

And above, far above, a thin velvet glimpse of sky.

I brought us to the closest potentially safe place that popped into my head. The Well of Initiation.

"I truly am sorry," I say. "I couldn't do anything back there or I would've."

Callie says nothing.

I go on. "I do have a spot of brighter news though. Now my bargain with them's complete, but they don't *quite* have what they want." I expect her to follow up immediately, but she doesn't. "That is extremely good news." Callie stays quiet and I begin to worry the journey into the well injured her. "Are you all right?"

Finally, she speaks, "Are we in that pit?"

Not what I expected. "It's an inverted tower," I say. Then, "Yes."

"I—"

"Said you never wanted to visit it." My sigh is heavy in the night air. "But you didn't want to be taken by those guys again more, was my guess."

"Toss-up."

"Oh."

"How could you?" she says, and I'm comforted by the fire in the words. "How could you let them take it?"

"Like I said, a bargain is a bargain. Particularly an infernal one. I couldn't prevent them from getting it, not directly."

She wraps her arms around herself. "Did you know then? That I'd just be retrieving it for them? Without my help, they might've failed . . ."

"I didn't expect them to get here so fast. And they wouldn't have. Failed, I mean." I summon the heat of flame into my palm and give us some light. We're surrounded by a pool of dark water with a path laid out in stones. The tower curls up around and above us in a spiral of old stone. "Callie, I'm sorry. But . . ." I search for what would improve this situation. Surely what I discovered when I concentrated up there will buy me some forgiveness. She must not have understood what I was saying before. "There's no need to worry. It turns out Monteiro and his heaven-friendly set were cleverer than I expected—that was only the shaft. The spearhead is in his tomb. We can retrieve it before they figure it out. It won't work without the pieces joined together."

Shadows flicker, playing across her face. For a moment, they reveal something like hope, right up until she shakes her head. "Like I'm dumb enough to trust you again."

I can't stop a smile. "You trusted me?"

She growls. It makes my smile broaden, but I know I'm not doing myself any favors here.

"Why didn't you mention this two-part thing before now?" she asks.

"I honestly didn't know until I felt the spear shaft nearby."

She doesn't soften. "And why didn't you know they were here?"

"The precautions Solomon mentioned," I say, and drag my non-flaming hand through my hair. "I didn't sense them on the grounds. They have some kind of spell or item that cloaks them, even from me."

"But aren't you a fallen angel? Shouldn't you still be more powerful than them?"

I should have paid more attention to Porsoth's lessons and Rofocale's rules, to Father's legends. "I swear I'm not lying to you."

She takes that in. "How long before they figure out there's a piece missing—*if* there really is?"

"I don't know for certain, but I doubt it'll be immediate. They'll have to try using it." Surely their plan isn't to launch right into bringing about Hell on Earth. Then again . . .

"Where's this tomb?" she asks.

I can hear the wheels turning in her head. I can get this night back on course. I have to. "The cemetery is in Lisbon, about an hour by train. Should I zap us there?"

She takes a second to answer. "I need a breath. I have to think."

I can also practically see her remembering where we are as she shivers and looks around in vague panic.

"I'm guessing you don't want to think down here. Should I zap us up top first?"

She exhales a shaky breath. "Is there another way?"

I consider offering to carry her, gathering her up in my arms to make her feel safe. As appealing as the thought is, that won't go over well. "We could walk. There's a path up to the surface."

A grim nod. "Then we walk."

She must be rethinking her association with me. But . . . at least she's still talking to me for now. "Follow my path exactly." I hesitate. "Unless you want me to follow you?"

"No, I'll stay behind you."

"I am sorry you're afraid." I hold up my hand, a makeshift torch. "I didn't know."

She takes out her phone and thumbs the flashlight app bright. Technology and magic, not that far from each other these days. "I'm not afraid."

"All right."

She sighs. "You weren't lying about that at least."

"About what?" I ask, and place my foot on the first of a series of rocks that will lead us along the pool at the bottom of the well and to the winding steps cut into the Earth that lead to the top. This would be pretty in the daylight.

"Whether you can read minds," she says. "Or are all-knowing or whatever."

"Only the big guy above is all-knowing. And you do have free will. We can't see your thoughts, only certain information about things."

"Like the spear." There's a splash and I turn to see her foot plunge into the water. The night at least is warm. I reach out to help her recover her balance.

The touch is like being pulled into a planet's orbit. I want her to like me too much. I want her too much.

She sways into my grip and I consider leaning forward and—

She pulls her foot up and steps deliberately away, back onto the rock. "Thank you," she says. "Wait, no, no thank you. You're why we're down here. Let's go."

I hesitate, but decide not to press my luck. I gently release her and find the next rock. I listen hard and hear her careful progress behind me. We reach the spiral path and start climbing.

Finally, she breaks a long silence. "What is this pit anyway? Is that the kind of thing you can know?"

Yes, this I can manage. "The whole estate is meant to evoke the various schools of mysticism the owner subscribed to. A journey from innocence to experience, light to dark, Inferno to Paradiso." We're on the third level from the bottom now. "The well has nine levels. Some say they represent Dante's nine levels of Hell. There were also nine levels of paradise."

"So you feel at home down here."

Given how much she hates the place, this is not a flattering observation. "Hardly. But it's an interesting place."

We've made it all the way to the sixth level, inching along.

"I bet you think I'm an idiot," she says. "For trusting you. For believing I could do this. I'm such a screw-up."

She sounds so vulnerable. I stop moving so she'll pay attention. "No. I don't think believing in yourself is stupid. I admire it. It takes strength to try. And you haven't failed yet."

She grunts.

"I realize you probably hate me. I felt the power of the spear. Even just part of it. Giving it up . . . must have been unpleasant. It's been hidden for a very long time and *you* found it. Doesn't sound screwed up to me."

She doesn't respond, and instead speeds up and pushes past me. We've made it to the top.

I glance around and don't see any cape-wearing cultists. "Coast is clear," I say, and watch as Callie collapses on the paved ground past the inverted tower's exit.

"I just need a sec." She bends her knees and loops her arms, dropping her head between them.

Footsteps. Coming our way. *Hell's bells again.*

"Sorry, that's not going to be possible." I nudge her shoulder with my leg and offer her a hand. "On your feet."

"Why?" she asks, pushing up without taking my hand.

"Someone is coming. They should be too busy, but I can't swear it's not the cult. This way."

My spirit—voluminous, inconvenient—is buoyed by how quickly Callie climbs to her feet and joins me. If he is still around, something tells me Solomon Elerion will take pleasure in traversing the less hospitable parts of the grounds. Callie may not like dark pits, but Solomon would have a lot in common with one. *He* might feel at home there.

I prod her toward an opening in a nearby hedge that should allow us to see who's approaching without being seen.

"That stuff they were saying before," Callie whispers. "Are you who you claim?"

"Is anyone?" I ask. "This seems like existential ground for the moment."

Callie stays on the path. "I want an answer."

"I'm not playing for the heavenly side, if that's what you're asking. That much should be clear from my letting them take the spear," I say and wave for her to hurry up. "Whoever is coming is getting close. Come on."

I wish again that I had Rofocale's knowledge to get me out of this fix. I'm keenly aware that I may have underestimated the cult.

And everything else . . .

Not to mention, I've made little progress toward my own deadline.

"You know, if I did let them catch me," Callie says, "at least I'd be guaranteed proximity to the spear."

Worry stabs me with a sharp knife. "Yes, but I might not be able to help you escape."

"You didn't last time."

"Technically I did, just not right away."

"I feel like it's stupid to trust you again—there's probably not even anyone coming."

Before I can protest and do the sweep with my senses I've forgotten I could until just this moment, I breathe an actual sigh of relief at the sight of my sweaty security guard friend. He rushes up to us in wide-eyed amazement. I didn't think to question why the guard helped us before, against the cult—other than that he's a guard. If only I'd used my stronger senses, I could've avoided Callie questioning the wisdom of staying near me. Again.

"Who was that back there?" the guard asks. "What should we do?"

He believes what I told him earlier. Still.

I turn to Callie and decide to gamble. Father always says it's fun. "Are we going to Lisbon or not?"

I brace for her to say no way. I'm not sure how to convince her, and I can't blame her for doubting me. She's only being smart.

"Just there, then home," she says.

Right. She can't get back without me—at least, not in time to open the business. I forgot that small detail in my favor. I swallow my smile to keep from further irritating her.

"We're going to Lisbon? Why?" the guard asks.

"*We* are." I give him my most serious look. "But *you* must stay here and wait. It's become too dangerous to act just now." I lay my left palm on his shoulder. I switch to Portuguese. "One day I'll return, when it's safe."

The guard starts to ask a question, but I take Callie's hand in mine and we make our escape from this infernal estate.

CHAPTER NINE

CALLIE

The world turns to screams in darkness and blood rushes through my ears as Luke zappities us somewhere, presumably Lisbon.

When the seemingly endless shrieking nightmare ends, I want to either throw up or shove Luke.

I am gutted. Gutted.

I couldn't keep the Holy Lance out of the hands of the Order. Some guardian I'm turning out to be. Now here I am, half-trusting Luke again already—because he was nice to me and told me I'm not a screw-up. And also because if he's telling the truth, maybe I can salvage my inability to hold onto the spear. That part of it, at least. If only I'd ever read a handbook for a night like this . . .

"You okay?" The concern on his gorgeous face seems real.

I force myself not to soften. "Do not do that again. Give me a little warning, please."

"We had to come here sooner or later," he protests. "It was a dramatic exit for effect."

I suppress the renewed urge to shove him. *Or grab him and hold on tight.* I've been trying to avoid touching him, because despite the betrayal my brain is teaming up with my body to threaten a mutiny.

I briefly close my eyes and take a slow breath to get my focus back. A new question, one I probably should've already asked, occurs to me. "How do I know that you won't just give them this part too? Why isn't your deal still going?"

"Our deal was for them to get the spear and technically they have a part of it. Deals with Hell tend to favor us meeting the letter of the law, not the spirit—or the other way around if it works better for us."

"Typical," I say as if any of this is.

We're on a quiet street, that nearly full moon still above us. A calico cat slinks along the top of a high stone wall that stretches in either direction, interrupted only by a closed iron gate. What I don't see is a single tombstone or grave marker. Did he lie to me?

My hands go to my hips. "Where's the cemetery we're going to?"

"*Cemitério dos Prazeres*—the Cemetery of Pleasures—is just beyond the wall." Luke punctuates this with a sweep of his hand. More dramatics.

I channel my body's dumb attraction to him into a healthier emotion: frustration. "And how are we supposed to get in there, MacArthur genius of Hell? Climb?"

The smile he's giving me dims, and I almost feel bad. Almost. "Have you no faith?"

"In you? No. I thought we covered that."

A hint of the pout he wore earlier returns. "Fair enough. But I'll show you." He walks toward the entrance. "It's not like this is how I planned my evening either, you know," he says over his shoulder.

My interest spikes, despite my knowing I should stop being interested in Luke. I catch up. "What did you have planned?"

He hesitates. "Forget I said anything."

"Something demonic, I take it."

"I'm under a lot of pressure too," he says. "Believe me or don't. Either way, we'd better get a move on. I zapped us outside rather than inside in case Solomon's smarter than I think and they've somehow beaten us here."

Much like the entire evening since Solomon Elerion showed up at the Great Escape, I have no idea if I'm doing the right thing or not. But something in Luke's voice makes me think he's telling the truth. Besides it's not like I can afford to get abandoned in Lisbon or let the cult win.

Once we reach the gates, I see a broad tree-lined avenue inside that ends at what looks like a small church. Fancy mausoleums surround it on either side, casting toothy silhouettes in the night. So we *are* at the oddly named Cemetery of Pleasures. But . . .

"Can you go inside here?" I ask.

His pretty forehead creases. "Why wouldn't I be able to?"

"Sacred ground." The idea of being sent to possibly face Solomon Elerion alone again isn't a good one.

Luke takes a moment to process, then waves away my concern. "Oh no, cemeteries aren't sacred ground. Not unless it's people buried inside churches. The living made that one up to comfort themselves, but as far as reality goes the only things here are old bones and bodies. The souls are what matter in the after. The only place I can't go inside here is that chapel."

"Oh." He might actually prove useful this time. I reach out

and rattle the locked gate, the iron cool against my fingers. I consider trying the key I found in the altar, but something makes me keep it in my pocket. "We get in how?"

"I told you—easily." He flicks his hand and smoke emerges from it, shaping into the form of a key not unlike the one I have.

I know I'm supposed to be impressed, so I school my expression into boredom. The smoke key flows into the lock and then, voilà, presto, just as Luke claimed, he reaches out and lifts the catch open.

"After you," he says, pushing it wide enough for us to enter.

I ignore his smug look and walk in. He closes the gate behind us.

This is no potter's field for paupers. It's far too grand for that.

The dead are quieter than my chattering mind and we both follow their lead as we walk farther in. At the boundary of the church, Luke turns us toward the left. This is a cemetery unlike any I've ever been to—the signs make clear it's arranged into streets. Most of the graves are aboveground mausoleums and we pass one with a glass door that allows us to see two shadowed coffins inside.

A dozen escape room ideas pass through my head. I think of Mom and if she knows I'm gone yet or what happened. Of how upset Mag and Jared must be if they told her already.

Focus, Callie, don't freak yourself out. More.

"Where's the tomb we're going to?" I whisper to break my uneasy train of thought.

"Right over here," Luke says. "Looks like the coast is clear from cultists."

I should've guessed which tomb. Monteiro, true to form, has an elaborate mausoleum covered in Masonic symbols and more of his occult bent in the design. I check with the compass on my phone and confirm it faces east, like a good Masonic Temple would. There are grandly carved, if aged, columns and statuary.

A pale, dirt-flecked angel with a sword towers above us from the top spire, wings stretching out into the night. Directly in front of us is a black door, half-concealed by bare tree branches that have grown to stretch across the front. I scrape them aside.

I try to sense something holy, or even good, beyond it, but come up empty. I can't shake the suspicion that Luke is playing me. Speaking of which . . . "What are we going to do when we get the spearhead?"

Do we destroy it? Hide it again?

"Shouldn't we worry about that once we have it?" he asks.

"Okay." But I'm worrying about it now. I already lost one half of the spear to the bad guys, and I don't want it to happen again. "I take it that means you have no idea."

I hold my phone—at 20 percent and fading—up to the door to take in the detail. A beehive is carved into the surface, and the door knocker is a bee toting a skull. This guy's sense of drama makes Luke seem reserved. The bees are more Masonic stuff, a symbol of industry, busy bees. There's another old-fashioned keyhole, flourishes in the metal around it.

"The house key of the mansion opened this too," Luke says. "Same architect."

Interesting. I put my hand in my pocket, and touch the key there. But I say, "You got it on you?"

He shakes his head.

"Then smoke key, please."

Luke almost says something else, but then closes his mouth and extends his hand again. I want to see if his magic skeleton key trick works here. The smoke flows into the lock, but Luke frowns when nothing happens.

"It must be protected against magic," he says, grim. He squints. "I can try to find the key . . ."

"No need," I say, and finally remove the one I found in the basement at the chapel. "I'm pretty sure I have it. You're not the only one who can keep secrets."

His mouth opens, and I'm not sure if I'll answer his questions or not. He must not be either, because he doesn't ask them. He steps aside to give me clearer access.

"I'm impressed," he says.

I press away the need to bask in the compliment. My body suddenly becomes aware of how close we're standing and my heart flutters.

Please let this work. I fit the key into the lock and—

The door to the mausoleum opens.

"Even I almost said a silent prayer that time," he says.

Despite what Luke said about cemeteries not being sacred places, I can't help saying one for forgiveness before following him inside the dark mausoleum.

The odor of an old, undisturbed place hits my nose, and I breathe it in. The same scent as opening a long-shut closet at an estate sale. A treasure hunt of a different sort.

Luke holds up his phone to light the relatively tight quarters inside. Two large stone sarcophagi carved with more symbols are inside, presumably holding the bones of Monteiro and his wife.

"Do you think he's buried with it?" I ask.

"I don't know." Luke pauses. "You going to be okay in here?"

"I'm not afraid of the surface." I make it sound like he's being ridiculous. But I stay within reach as we go farther inside.

"Can you tell where it is?" I ask.

Luke shushes me. "It's here, but I'm trying to sense where."

He circles the sarcophagi, brushing a hand over the top of each. I force myself to stay quiet and try not to examine any shadows too closely. My phone vibrates and I discover the battery is draining fast, just 10 percent left. I've got no service here, of course. I switch it off and stash it in my pocket.

"It's you," Luke says, half accusatory.

I sigh. "What's me?"

"You're why I can't tell where it is."

Great, yet another way I'm failing. Only why would I take his word for it? "I'm not some easily fooled security guard."

"No," he says. "It's because you're too distracting. Go stand outside."

"Wha—" I sputter. "You go stand outside."

He walks in close to me. So close I can see how big his pupils are in the reflection from his phone. His free hand glides forward and lightly rests on my hip. I can hardly breathe.

"I'm trying to sense good," he says and I can't help but watch his lips. "*You* are good. And unfortunately I seem a lot more interested in you than anything else in here. I don't like that you're upset. With me. So it's hard for me to see past you and find what we're looking for."

I am struck dumb as that security guard. He removes his hand. I go to stand outside without a word and shut the door behind me.

A black cat meanders along the cemetery street outside, and I barely notice.

I'm good. I'm good and *Luke is interested in me? He's not just being a flirt?* My heart beats too hard in my chest, and I will it to stop. Well, not stop. Slow down. Heart stoppage in Lisbon in the middle of the night would not be good.

Like I am apparently.

I shake my head. The cat has circled back to me and meows.

"Tell me about it," I say.

The thing is? I wouldn't have been surprised if the cat started to talk. Instead it rubs against my legs and then bolts into the night.

What was it Luke said earlier about having problems of his own? Suddenly I can't help wondering what they are . . . Who is he, really? What *were* his plans for tonight before all this?

I'm completely aware of how dangerous these thoughts are. But there's so much comfort in knowing for sure that while I may be a mess, I'm a good person. And that I'm not the only one who feels this strangely compelling attraction when we're near each other.

The door to the mausoleum creaks open. I jump.

"Callie?" Luke asks.

"Uh, present," I say. "You find it?"

Luke steps out and pulls me around to face him. "I did, but I knew better than to try retrieving it solo."

I'm watching his lips again. They're full of danger, those lips. "Would you burst into flame or something?" I ask and hear how breathless I sound.

The slightest frown, like an injury. "No. Well, maybe. Or it might be like before. But I knew you'd want to do the recovering."

"Oh." There he goes—being thoughtful again. Was I too harsh earlier? I can be sometimes. I know that about myself.

"We better not waste time though," he says, and I nod and

step past him. My arm brushes his chest as I pass, and there's a catch in my breathing, an awareness of how close we are. My ears burn hot with embarrassment, and I reach up to make sure they're safely tucked underneath my hair.

Not that he's likely to be checking out my ears. *Especially in darkness, Callie. Get it together.*

"It was, in fact, buried with him," Luke says.

I inhale deeply to reset my breathing and roll my eyes. "This guy."

"A little much, even for my taste."

Luke holds up his phone and I see he's pushed aside the top of Monteiro's sarcophagus. I hesitate. "Is it . . ."

For all my reading, my only experiences with things truly dark before tonight have been either in books or constructing the fake version of them for the business. I've been to funerals, but sterile, brightly lit ones. The people pumped full of chemicals that make them look exactly as they did alive, only more soft-focus and formal. If they really wanted to give the impression of sleeping, why dress people up?

"Callie?" Luke asks.

"Why doesn't anyone ever get buried in pajamas? No, seriously, I can't believe that's never been a cultural thing. I want to be buried in pajamas."

Luke shakes his head on a quiet laugh. "That is not what I expected you to say right now." He moves in closer. "Which is what makes it so delightful."

I let out a nearly hysterical laugh of my own. "Ha. Delightful."

Luke takes my hand in his, and I think maybe he's going to kiss me. I broke up with my last boyfriend, Jeremy, in May. We were both always awkward about this kind of thing even after we'd been together a year. He got a job in California that started right after graduation. We said good-bye over pizza. I was . . . relieved. Since then, I've been too consumed with figuring out how to get my life together to date anyone.

The thing is no matter how much I liked the guys I've been with, I've never had a true fireworks experience, the swell of phantom music, and definitely no heart-shattering emotions. My brain won't stop observing instead of letting me be in the moment. So it hasn't been hard to put a pin in romance.

But now, right now, all I'm thinking about is kissing Luke.

I realize how weird this is given that I vowed never to trust him. But he said I distracted him because I was *good*.

He reaches up with his other hand and tucks my hair behind my ear. I see him study it. Damn him, he *did* look at my ears.

Then again, he's already damned.

"I thought so," he says. "Callie, are you embarrassed? Am I missing something?"

"Yes." Before I can talk myself out of this colossally, epically, biblically bad idea I lean in. "Kiss me."

"What?" he asks.

My ears are on fire. "Never mind."

"Not on your life. You asked me to kiss you." He sounds as surprised as I feel. "I'm happy to—"

I press my lips to his.

He's surprised, midsentence, and doesn't react right away. I am mortified. Did I misread his consent? I start to pull back and apologize . . . Until he slides his hand around to touch my cheek and kisses me back so gently I think I'm hallucinating. The kiss lasts more than the ten seconds I count in my head, and then I realize I shouldn't be counting and tell my brain to shut up and sink into the sensation.

It works.

The only thing that exists is me and Luke and the places where our bodies and our lips touch. My heart thumps hard in my chest and my skin electrifies and I want to climb inside him to get closer and closer. He deepens the kiss with a groan, and I'm pretty sure I moan, and I don't care. His hands drop to my waist and he easily lifts me and turns to place me on the closed sarcophagus without missing a beat.

He steps between my legs and I sink into him and definitely moan again and there may not be music but there are fireworks because my entire being feels like I'm exploding. His hands roam my back and one slips under my T-shirt across my skin and then . . .

Then Luke ends the kiss, puts his hand back on top of my shirt, rests his forehead on mine, and sighs.

"I don't want to stop," I say.

I can't believe I said that.

"Me either. But the cult could show up here. We shouldn't linger, no matter how tempting." He leans back enough to hold my gaze. "This night is the furthest thing from boring."

"Understatement." I smile at him. Heat crackles between us. It is not boring. In the least.

The temptation to keep going is there. If I move toward him even a fraction, I sense he'll go along, despite his objections. My body is in favor of it. But my brain kicks back into its usual mode—worry that I'm messing this up. Not to mention, he's a demon. What am I doing? And why do I like it so much?

"We should though. Stop. You're right." I press Luke away and reach up to put my hair back over my telltale ear. I slide off the sarcophagus. "Saving the world and all. Let's dig around in some old bones."

CHAPTER TEN

LUKE

allie of Good, with eyes like a fresh green field after a storm, kissed me. I made her moan. Me, the son of Lucifer Morningstar, sovereign of the kingdom of Hell. I might as well be in a boat on a sea in that storm I keep thinking about, in the flailing grasp of a kraken. I feel like the storm rages inside me.

Callie, meanwhile, is waving impatiently to get my attention. "Some light over here, please. I need to be able to see. You're not going to make things all weird, are you?"

I take comfort in the breathlessness of her voice.

She seemed to be hesitating before . . . before she *kissed me*. I assumed because she was scared. But it was because she wanted to *kiss me*.

"You're sure you want to see the bones that well?" I move to her side, doing my best to play it cool. I want to eat her overly sensible self up. "And you're the one who made it weird."

She stares at me in the dark. I hold up my hand to illuminate both her face and the open sarcophagus beside us.

"Good weird," I specify. "My all-time favorite variety of weird."

She ignores that, craning her neck to look inside the coffin. "Where is it? Did you see it?"

"Not exactly. It's wrapped up in his hand."

"Oh, right there," she says.

I scoot closer so I'm seeing the same thing that she is—and because I like being near her. Below us is Monteiro, or what's left of his bones, fairly clean, brownish, and dry, a few scraps of hair left on the skull, and those utterly creepy death's-head teeth that all corpses have. Anatomy below is very specialized with an emphasis on torture and frights and the corpse teeth have always freaked me right out. Something about the lack of gums.

I suppress a shudder. The romantic mood has officially left the mausoleum.

Monteiro's desiccated remains are arranged so that his hands fold over the wrapped item.

"Here I go." She reaches in.

Callie picks at the parcel and his finger bones loosen. A knuckle tumbles down into the sarcophagus and she makes a noise that is a cousin of horrified. But she persists and lifts the wrapped item free.

For a moment, I hold my breath. What if some trickery caused me to get the identification wrong and Callie thinks I lied to her again? I'm more invested than ever in not alienating her.

Callie bends and lays the parcel on the ground to unwrap, and I join her.

I hold steady at the good it radiates.

Inside the dusty cloth is the bronze head of a spear about

as long as her forearm. She picks it up, and I can see it has a substantial weight.

She looks at me and a smile with nearly as much light spreads across her face. "We got it. You weren't lying this time. Okay," she says and stands, "let's go home and figure out what to do now."

I don't call attention to the implied *us*. I nod. "Your wish."

She hesitates. "You'd better put back the top of the sarcophagus. And we should lock this up behind us. This was pretty simple compared to the chapel."

"Only because you had the key. You *are* good at this."

Callie gives me another beaming smile, and leaves me to finish the cleanup. I slide the heavy stone back into place, wishing Monteiro a good sleep, and go to follow her outside. That's when I feel his approach.

Rofocale is here. With the worst possible timing.

I hurry outside to attempt damage control focused on Callie, and only then recognize that I'm the one in danger of being damaged. I haven't made any progress on my task. Some might even say I've made negative progress.

"Is that Lucifer?" Callie asks, gaping up at the sky. She's stashed the spearhead in her messenger bag.

"Close enough."

At least the presence of a holy relic will protect her from any harm at seeing Rofocale in his full glory. Because I can't fault her mistake.

Rofocale is a burning man who lands with the effortless grace of an angry spark from a fire floating to the ground. He glowers at me.

"Rofocale, I can explain," I say, doing my best church-mouse meek.

"Wait, what?" Callie asks.

Oh, for all that's unholy. I said his name.

I give her a look that implores her to stay quiet. You can imagine how she takes that.

"Isn't that *your* name?" she persists. "Rofocale, minister of Hell?"

I wince. "I truly can explain," I say to Rofocale. "With, ah, your leave, I'll happily explain everything."

"Oh, I can't wait," Rofocale says, pursing his lips. His eyes gleam black with pinpoint scarlet pupils that burn like the flames surrounding his stylish, unsinged suit. I can't imagine how Callie feels, because this angry he's terrifying even to me. He goes on. "You can explain why you're standing on a street in Portugal with some good and pure soul while the cult whose souls you were supposed to collect rummage around still in possession of them *and* now the Lance of Longinus? And she's got the other part of the Lance too, so now it's possible for it to be reassembled? This should be good. I'm all ears."

"Not all ears," I quip. "There's some evil in there too."

The flames licking the air around Rofocale intensify. Still, I'm distracted by motion to my right. It's Callie, not running, like a rational human would, but placing a hand on her hip.

"Who," she asks Rofocale, "are you? The marquis or the viscount or . . ."

Rofocale's dark gaze settles on Callie, and she doesn't seem able to finish her sentence. She flinches, then gloriously pretends she didn't. I wish I didn't like her so much in this moment. I almost wish she hadn't kissed me.

Almost.

"Well?" she presses, her voice only a little shaky.

"I am Lucifuge Rofocale," he says, like he's expecting a curtsey. Which, of course, he is.

Callie turns to me. I hope to look winning as I lift my shoulders in an apologetic shrug, crinkling my face in a wince of apology.

"Then who in the hell are you?"

The person you didn't want to stop kissing, I want to say. But I'm not that stupid.

I look from Callie to Rofocale and I know this ruse is over. If I lie to her now, I'll never recover. "I'm his intern. Um, Luke. That really is my name. The one I go by."

"His intern," she repeats as she begins to pace. "His *intern*. I let an *intern* bring me to face off against an evil cult. To recover a holy weapon. I . . . I let . . ." She's thinking about the kiss, regretting it. The pain I feel at that is nearly physical. She continues. "Oh yes, I'm the worst at this. I should be kept in laboratory conditions at all times. Clearly. Being a guardian is so my calling. Just like getting a useless history degree."

"A guardian?" Rofocale asks with a double take.

Callie's pacing stops and she faces us both. "Why do you say it like that?"

"Everything's under control," I jump in, in an attempt to appease Rofocale and keep the situation from further deteriorating. "I still have plenty of time."

Tendrils of actual smoke curl from Rofocale's ears. Upset or not, Callie steps behind me.

I extend a hand to placate him. "I sense your skepticism—"

"Oh, you do?" Rofocale grits out. "How perceptive."

"It's entirely understandable, but I have a plan," I say, talking fast. "A new plan. You have to believe me. I may have miscalculated, but now I'm on top of this."

Waves of heat are wafting off Rofocale and even behind me Callie must feel toasty warm.

"Enlighten me about this plan," Rofocale says with a faux nonchalant wave of his sharp-nailed fingers. "What are its particulars?"

The question is aimed with the precision of a knife. A rumble of thunder sounds in the distance and lightning cracks across the sky. In case it wasn't already clear how unhappy I've made him.

"I'm going to retrieve the cult's souls after I help Callisto . . . get rid of the lance."

His eyes narrow. "You never were a good student. It can only be destroyed when whole."

Damnation. "Then after we steal back the shaft."

"Why would I destroy the Holy Lance?" Callie asks. "Is that even possible?"

Rofocale nods. "It is possible, and now that the halves are no longer hidden, it is likely the only way to prevent the end times. Your father is not going to be pleased if *you* trigger the apocalypse."

"He's not going to be pleased anyway. Which is why he never needs to know about any of this. I'll get the souls."

"Your time draws nigh, in case you've forgotten. Get those souls or else."

"I'm aware."

"You have considered . . . Why would they pledge themselves to you after you take the weapon? They won't need anything," Rofocale says.

"They'll want to be of service. I can promise them something else."

"Aren't they already bad?" Callie asks. "Why expend so much effort on the souls of bad people?"

"Bad and 'soul owned by Hell' are two different things." Rofocale spits the words. "As Luke here should know and you should not. Speaking of which, I should erase—"

"Don't hurt her." I say it as a command, which startles me. And Rofocale. Not in a good way. I clarify. "She's part of the new plan. You heard. I need her."

"No," she says, "I'm not helping you."

Shut up, Callie. "Please?" I ask, ignoring her. "If I fail, these are my last moonrises regardless."

Rofocale shrugs. "For now you can keep her."

"I am not for either of you to keep or release!" Callie says.

I flinch when Rofocale rolls his neck and there's another lightning strike. Closer this time.

He lasers back in on me. "I won't allow your lack of commitment and performance issues to tarnish my reputation. Don't screw this up." He rakes his fiery gaze over me. "Any more than you already have."

I sense he's about to leave. "Wait! I don't suppose you can tell me where the cultists are?"

Rofocale pauses, and I watch him search. He frowns. "I can't seem to . . ."

"No worries, they're cloaked. I'll find them," I say, sounding more confident than I am. He inclines his chin and—

"Wait!" I call, remembering my other question.

He growls, but doesn't disappear yet.

"Is it safe for her to travel in our fashion?"

"Not pleasant, but . . ." Rofocale smiles. "Sure."

In a gout of smoke and fire, he is gone, and I'm left with someone who is at least as furious at me as my boss.

"An intern!" Callie says, shaking her head with what reminds me an awful lot of disgust. "And I listened to you. I—"

You kissed me. I know. I can't stop thinking about it.

She extends her hand stiffly. "Time to go."

"Home?" I pose the question carefully.

"No," she says, "the house where they summoned you. Maybe I can find some clues there, figure out where they went."

I note the shift from "us" to just her, but decide not to question it. "I'm sorry I didn't tell you," I say, "but the cult couldn't know I wasn't him."

"I can imagine. An intern doesn't conjure the same kind of vibe at all, does it?" She shakes her head again and waves her fingers. "Let's go."

I take them in mine. I'm not ready for this to end, but it feels like an ending.

The whirring, shrieking darkness welcomes me like a friend until, after long moments, it recedes. Trees surround both sides of the narrow road, and above is the lightening blue of a country night sky almost ready for sunrise. The familiar silhouette of a certain creepy house looms ahead of us.

Callie yanks her hand away and takes off toward the house.

"What are you going to do?" I ask.

"None of your business," she says, tossing it over her shoulder. "You apparently have bigger problems. Just go take care of them. I've got this."

I'm starting to know her well enough to know that she's pretending at the level of confidence. And that she means what she says about ditching me.

"You're mad at me, I get it," I say, hurrying to keep up.

She pauses. "Take a hint," she says. "I'm not mad at you, because I don't know you. We don't know each other, and I am Team Good and you are Team Hell. I'm mad at myself for forgetting that. We had a . . . moment. But I can take the Team Good side from here."

"Point taken," I say, and I can see she's surprised. *She kissed me.* "I guess . . ."

I pull out a smile and hope it's suitably charming. I'm having trouble managing it, which isn't a problem I've encountered before. I could argue my case, that she's better off with me, that I can help her navigate these cult-infested holy waters. But . . .

I'm not sure that she *is* better off with me. For whatever reason, that matters. It's enough to give me pause.

"I suppose I'll see you again . . ." I hesitate, not sure how to finish. Then, I add, softly, "Never." My hand lifts in a good-bye sadder than I mean it to be.

Callie's reaction is to nod and resituate the strap of her messenger bag, which must be heavy with the spearhead. "Guess so. 'Nice meeting you' doesn't seem right after tonight."

"I always wondered if there was a platitude for every occasion," I say. "It seems there isn't. We've both learned something."

She half smiles. "It *has* been educational."

"See, I'm wrong again—there *is* a platitude for everything." I tilt my head. "Good-bye, Callisto. And good luck."

"Good luck to you too, Luke," she says, and might even mean it.

Then off she goes. I already miss her.

CHAPTER ELEVEN

CALLIE

march toward the house we fled earlier, where Mom and I bought the grimoire. Where Luke appeared in Rofocale's place. I refuse to let myself look back at him. There are no footsteps behind me this time, and I tell myself that I'm fine with that.

I teamed up with a demon *and* an imposter, *and* I still feel a twinge of regret about saying good-bye to him. Yes, I'm dying to know what sort of deadline Luke is on, what kind of trouble he's in, why he needs souls so badly. I like knowing things, so of course I am. But (a) I really can't trust him to tell the truth, (b) I've apparently got to figure out how to get the other half of the Holy Lance back, stat, and (c) part of me *still* wants to make out with him again.

When the option is between preventing the end times and things you shouldn't even care about, preventing the end times is the obvious choice.

Not that I'm confident I'm capable of it. But I'm not going to be like the characters in stories I want to yell at to get with the program and stop doubting themselves. So what if I can't stop doubting myself? I'll do the right thing anyway.

The first step is going back in this house and either being captured or finding some clues. Possibly both.

When I reach the front door, I find it unlocked.

Inside the lights are on, bright as a kid's birthday party. Which I didn't notice until I crossed the threshold. *Time to turn on every mental faculty and focus. Put Lying Luke in the rearview.*

Maybe a birthday party isn't the best comparison. The remnants of the ritual are strewn across the parlor—including my book. So if it was a birthday party, it was a dark and twisted theme.

Even though I know the book is a real grimoire that holds serious power, satisfaction outweighs fear as I walk over and pick it up. I might not be able to put it back to work as a prop at the Great Escape, but I'm not leaving it here for the cult to use. Then again, they must only be able to use it once. Otherwise *they'd* have taken it . . . Unless they're planning to come back.

A loud clatter sounds upstairs, followed by voices arguing, low.

Or they never left. I didn't count how many were in Portugal. The front door's still open and I could easily bail, but this is the only lead I have.

The argument is coming my way. I find a spot with a good view of the staircase and a half wall I can crouch behind. The lights upstairs are off, and two figures appear at the dark top of the staircase. One of the people is holding a flashlight that keeps me from getting a good look at them. The other hefts a baseball bat.

I know that stance. In fact, I know both of them by silhouette alone.

"Mag!" I burst out of my hiding spot. "Jared!"

Mag pushes Jared out of the way and runs down the stairs and we fling ourselves at each other. We're hugging each other awkwardly around the grimoire before I've begun to process how relieved I am. Hugging Mag grounds me instantly.

My stomach sinks with the knowledge I have to tell them how badly I'm in over my head.

"Thank god you're okay," Mag says.

"What are you doing here?" I ask.

"Looking for you," Jared says. He bops down the steps to join us, lingering at the bottom. He idly swings the bat. "You gave us a huge scare. Where's your boyfriend?"

"He's not my—" I stop. Memories of our kiss and how hot it was shimmy through my head. And bickering with Jared isn't on the menu right now. "He's gone. I asked him to leave."

Mag recoils in surprise. "Where did you go when you left? Back here? Were you here when we got here? Did you, um, see us?"

I consider how to answer this. I don't keep secrets from Mag. I'll need both their and Jared's help to see the rest of this through, more than likely. "You guys are okay?"

"Obviously," Jared says.

I turn to Mag. "Okay, so you told him—"

"Mag told me everything." Jared crosses his arms in front of his chest.

Mag nods.

"You're lucky I decided not to call Mom yet," he says.

I want to hug him. That's one piece of good news.

"I was in Portugal," I say. "Just got back. I know this sounds made up, but I had part of the Holy Lance and then the cult showed up and took it from me. So Luke and I went somewhere else and got the other part of it. Now I need to get back what they took." What I do with the spear after that is an open question, but at least my objective is clear. "Which means I have to find them. Has anyone else been here that you've seen?"

Mag and Jared exchange a speaking look that's so intimate it feels like a secret. My relief is tempered by something else. Suspicion. Worry. Uneasiness about my best friend for life and the ever after having a secret understanding about anything with my older brother.

"No, no one," Mag says, dropping one shoulder in the usual tick that means they're uncomfortable. "We're just wondering . . . is this all a practical joke? A prank gone wrong?"

My face must reflect my disbelief at the question because Jared steps in with a conciliatory shrug. "An epic one, obviously, but . . . yeah," Jared says. "That's got to be it, right? Did they drug you guys?"

I'm so confused. How could either of them believe all this is a prank?

"You guys saw what Luke did, knocking you out with a wave of his hand. Turns out he's not *exactly* who he said he was, but he does have powers. He took me to Portugal and brought me back here—in a flash. Mag, it was just like when he took us back to the Great Escape. Zappity."

Mag studies their glittery sneakers.

Jared shakes his head at me. "Like I said, he must have slipped you something. Or . . ."

"Mag," I say, "you were there tonight. The cult *kidnapped* us in a murder van. The Hand of Glory! The book!" I heft it. "You *saw* them summon Luke with it. You have to know this is real."

Mag looks up at me and nods, but carefully. "It all *seemed* real, but . . ."

"But it couldn't have been," Jared finishes their sentence.

He and Mag exchange another look.

Seriously?

"What is wrong with you two?" I say. "I know you didn't hit your heads. We kept that from happening."

"Consider what you are claiming," Jared says. "That a demonic lord from Hell got summoned by a cult who kidnapped you and then the demon took you to Portugal and back in one evening . . . It breaks every law of physics."

Wow, I'm truly bad at everything, not just being a guardian.

But this is really happening. Somehow I have to convince my big brother and my best friend we're not victim to some mass—for very small values of mass—hallucination. This night is bonkers.

Although, I suppose, technically by now it's tomorrow.

"Maybe physics doesn't explain everything," I say, a soft opening.

Jared shakes his head. "Yeah, it does. That's why it's physics—we may not have discovered all the laws that govern reality, but that doesn't mean they aren't there."

"Okay. Okay." May as well give up on that part of the argument. Jared's way too rational. "We'll tackle the ways the situation impacts the laws of reality later. But I don't know how much time we have. So." I'm going to have to go simple. "You trust me, both of you?"

There's a brief hesitation, and Mag nods. Jared glances over at them, as if to check his own reaction, then does the same.

"Then humor me," I plead. "Something else weird will happen and you'll have to believe me then that this isn't some fumes we inhaled or whatever. Just wait. In the meantime, go along with my delusions. Deal?"

The two of them don't speak, so I take that as agreement and press on. "Now, did you see anyone when you got here?"

This time, neither of them has a chance to answer.

Because the door explodes inward and a group of men and women wearing sleek matching white leather ensembles races through it. They spread out to flank us and point a variety of weapons in our direction. There's a crossbow and a katana and a knife and . . . Is that a wooden stake? What do they think we are? *Vampires?*

Are there vampires?

I'm mildly comforted when no one moves in to attack. They hold position.

"Who are you?" demands a statuesque woman with dark brown skin, red-blond braids, and a sword leveled in our direction.

"We could ask you the same thing," I say and reach out to gather Mag and Jared closer.

"We," she says, tossing her braids and tilting her face up with pride, "are guardians. Now, where is the Lance of Longinus?"

My breath grows shallow, but I manage to whisper "Told you so" to Mag and Jared. Even I didn't expect to be proven right quite this quickly. I summon the strength to say to the woman in charge, "I'm a guardian too."

I suffer under a moment of sober consideration before she throws her head back and roars with laughter.

Roars.

With.

Laughter.

Just like that, I decide there's no way I'm telling her I've got part of the Holy Lance in my bag.

CHAPTER TWELVE

LUKE

I am about to vanish. Seconds away from it. I don't want to overstay my welcome—well, I don't want to overstay it *too* much—and Callie has been magnificently clear I'm in danger of doing so.

Options array before me, the many paths I might take to wrest back control of this wayward evening. I could even plead my case to Rofocale and ask for advice on how to get those souls in time. Whether or not they belong to me won't affect Callie's chances of catching their owners and recovering that portion of the spear. I feel poised on the cusp of turning over a new, more mature leaf. An entire tree of them. I imagine Father's twisted fallen-angelic lips taking on the hint of a proud smile at my successful report.

But . . .

As I'm wandering in the waning darkness on that fiery cusp, I catch a hint of something on the wind. A squad of the righteous approacheth. Guardians are incoming.

Seeing as how Callie still thinks she is one, this meeting could go down in the proverbial flames.

So do I stay or do I go? Do I choose the mature tree or stick with devil-may-care?

Come now, you know that decision makes itself. It's just the excuse I need.

But I'm not about to announce my dark, dashing presence to them either. Guardians aren't fond of those of us from below, given that they've pledged to the archangel Michael to devote their lives to thwarting us and our sympathizers. Their sanctimony has a sickening bouquet. No thanks.

I blink and relocate from the early morning outside to the shadowy hall at the top of the stairs inside the house. The sound of . . . laughter . . . floats up from below. Am I in the wrong place? Given the last several hours, it's possible.

But I hear Mag speak up. "Stop laughing at her."

They must mean Callie.

I take it she told them she's a guardian.

Well, I can still leave. I might need the help of these guardians—by way of following them—to find the cult. Which I still have to do.

It would be by far the easiest path ahead. As far as finding the souls in question go before they show themselves again by seeking the other part of the spear, there's only one other possible way for me to locate them. And it's such an epically, hideously bad idea even I recognize that I shouldn't try it.

While I don't think Solomon Elerion has the patience to wait a day before he emerges once more out of frustration, am I willing to bet my existence on it? I am not.

I creep along the hallway. Callie, Mag, and Jared stand at the bottom of the steps, backs to me. Guardians surround them in what I suppose passes for stylish in the religious warrior garb department. I shudder.

White leather is an affront to everything unholy.

Callie has her head tilted down. She could be praying, but, no, it looks like deference. Or possibly shame. I advance the inch closer I'm willing to go as the laugher-in-chief, a tall woman with braids and the kind of relaxed grip on her sword that tells you all the ways she could destroy you with it, finally sobers.

"I'm sorry," she says. "It's just funny. What you see in front of you is an elite team chosen by God. We answer to the archangel. We were trained since childhood, our bloodlines marked by holy flame as belonging to warriors." She pauses. "I apologize if it seems rude to point out . . . But does any of that describe what you see in the mirror every morning?"

Callie's head ticks down more, and when she swipes at her cheek I catch a glimpse of bright red. She's humiliated.

Callie, humiliated? By someone who's supposed to be good? Callie is the best person I've ever encountered. That might not be saying much, but she matters to me.

I want to reveal myself and come awfully close to doing so even though it's a terrible idea. I might be able to fight back—or the leader's blessed sword might slice me in half.

Not a gamble I'm willing to take. But I think hard at Callie: *Stand up for yourself. You're not a screw-up. I would know: I am.*

"Now," the woman says, "if we've established that you have a misconception, I am Saraya, pledged to the service of Michael. I compel you to tell me who you are and what you're doing here. You don't have the stink of Elerion on you. Though you really should give me the grimoire."

"No," Callie says, some energy returning to her as she holds tight to the book. "It's mine. The Order of Elerion stole it. We came to get it back. They summoned . . ." I wait for her to say Luke and my skin itches with an unseemly eagerness to hear my name, but she doesn't. "Lucifuge Rofocale and bargained with him for the location of the Holy Lance."

Saraya the guardian's head shifts to the side as she considers this. The rest of her battle squadron remain as still and focused as statues, awaiting her decision. The discipline is frightening.

Not to mention off-putting. She and Rofocale would probably secretly get along. Little enough separates good and evil at the official level when you get down to it.

Disturbing thought, that.

"Why didn't they take you?" Saraya asks. Then she shakes her head. "We know the lance was retrieved—but how? They shouldn't have been able to get into a sacred location with souls gone to darkness."

They don't know Callie has the other half. Interesting.

Callie clears her throat. "They still have their souls. He, uh, didn't want them. Yet."

The leader's eyes narrow. She speaks to her squad. "It seems the Dark One has finally decided to start the endgame. There is no other reason an emissary would forego taking souls."

Oh no. The screams of the damned echo in my ears. They're about to escalate this situation all the way into Armageddon. It seems this evening truly wants to be the night the apocalypse begins.

I can't make a peep to correct their misconception without ending up at the pointy end of one of their weapons.

"You search the house," Saraya tells two of her people. "The site of their ritual will work for me to summon Michael. He will cleanse this place."

Callie raises her hand, and the archer among them lifts his

bow. Saraya waves for him to stand down. "What?" she asks
Callie.

"What should we do?" Callie asks.

"Leave," Saraya tells Callie. "Go back to your lives. Pray for
our strength to combat evil. We'll handle it."

I expect Callie to argue, but she only nods. "All right," she
says.

Mag and Jared exchange a look that says they're as surprised
by that as I am. But I catch the gleam in Callie's eye. She *is*
fighting back, by keeping her secret.

I have mere seconds to pop outside before the guardians discover me. The front door is shutting behind Callie, Mag, and
Jared when I reappear in front of them.

Callie sees me and her eyes widen.

I lift my finger to my lips. *Shh.*

And then I gesture for her to come with me.

Jared glances back at the door like he might summon the
pale leather cavalry. But Callie is looking at me in something
close to welcome. Her expression hardens a bit when she catches
herself, but I saw it.

She keeps walking in my direction.

"This way," I say, encouraged.

Jared asks, puzzled, "What was that back there? Some kind
of interactive theater?"

"What's his deal?" I ask Callie, gesturing to the woods.

She must be off-kilter in the worst way because she doesn't
argue, only shoves the grimoire into her bag with the spearhead
and follows my demonic cue toward the wilderness.

"Jared doesn't believe this is real," she says and finally there's
some amusement in it. "Neither does Mag anymore. Not even
after meeting the guardians, apparently."

I walk faster, hoping they'll follow suit. The woods will give us some cover from the archangel's arrival, if we make it before he gets here.

We don't.

A blast of white light with the intensity of a star flaring to life descends from above and into the house. Even a hundred feet away, we're bathed in its unearthly glow. The humans cover their eyes. I stagger back at its intensity, but refuse to be entirely undignified and fall to my knees. It's not an easy impulse to resist.

The light dissipates, but we've only got however long his visit is before it returns. "Let's go," I say and head into the cover of the trees.

"Was that . . . ?" Callie asks, hesitating.

Jared and Mag stare back at the house, gaping, and they're holding hands. An aluminum bat hangs from Jared's other one.

"I'm guessing you believe Callie now," I say to them. I answer Callie, "Yes, Michael's here. We best get going."

"The archangel Michael?" Callie asks.

"They report to him." I nod. "Come on."

"Wait," she says, "maybe I should try to talk to *him*."

"That's not such a good idea." I can only imagine how much worse hearing she's not a guardian from *him* would be.

"Maybe you're right." She doesn't sound sure. She turns to her best friend and her brother, presumably to get their opinions.

They're still hand in hand.

I consider starting some sort of ridiculous interpretive dance or bathing us all in frost-filled darkness or anything that will keep her from seeing and understanding what she's seeing. Once again, I'm too late.

Her eyes are trained on their linked hands. "Mag?" she asks with a blink. "Why are you holding Jared's hand?"

They don't let each other go. The relationship must be more advanced than I assumed. They both look at Callie and, if anything, Jared holds onto Mag's fingers tighter.

"Don't freak out," Jared says. "We're in love."

"You're in love. The two of you." Callie sounds so calm. "Are in love."

Mag wears a careful expression. "I knew you'd react like this."

Honestly, Callie's much calmer than I expected. She folds her arms. "How should I react?"

"I wanted to tell you," Mag says with a pleading note that tells me the calm is actually the worst possible reaction. "I was going to tell you this weekend. You could be happy for us?"

"You're in love with my older brother and you kept it a secret and I'm supposed to be happy for you?" Callie shakes her head like she's trying to clear it.

"Yes," Mag says.

"Is this night happening? Because now I think it might be a hallucination after all." Callie is a tightly controlled bundle of betrayal. "I'm not happy, that's the last thing I am."

"Hey, sis," Jared protests.

I look at him and put my fingers over my lips.

"First off," Callie continues, "you're already doubting your own eyes and ears and experience. You knew I was telling the truth, but after talking to Jared, you doubted yourself. You don't doubt yourself. Ever."

Mag's mouth opens and closes. This has taken them by surprise.

"It's not like that," they say, finally. There is heat to it. "I can't believe you just said that."

Callie's jaw clenches, but then she continues. "And number two, worst of all, you lied to me. I feel so stupid. How long have you been lying?"

Mag says nothing.

"And you," Callie says to Jared, "you're my brother and now you just stole my best friend."

"I didn't. Callie, come on, be reasonable."

"I am. I'm saying how it is. Two people I trusted have been lying to me. I'm sure you'll be happy together." Callie sounds heartbroken amid her hurt and I feel for her, I do, but we need to get farther into the welcome cover of the forest. Before I can begin the process of urging her on, she shakes her head again. "Never mind. I have the rest of the Spear of Destiny to re-cover." She swipes away a tear and takes a deep inhale and exhale. "You two go run the Great Escape. Hopefully Mom will never have to know about any of this."

"Callie, we're not leaving you here alone," Mag says.

"What Mag said," Jared adds. "And, sis, I'd never feel this way about you dating one of my friends. Just give it a minute. Adjust to the idea."

Callie's smile is filled with bitterness. "Go home. And I'm not alone. Luke, come on."

She marches into the forest. I shrug at them. "You know it's going to take longer than a minute for her to deal with this," I say quietly.

Mag nods. "Yeah, I do. Maybe forever."

"She's not going to give up on doing this. You know that too."

Mag and Jared exchange a look. Mag says, "I may not be thrilled with her right now, but if anything happens to her . . ."

"I'll look after her," I promise. Not that my promises hold

much weight when they aren't sealed with a bargain. But they don't know that.

Jared still has Mag's hand in his. "You really think this is okay?" he asks.

"Someone has to run the place or your mom *will* come home early," Mag says. "This'll give Callie time to cool down. I hope."

This crisis averted—at least the crisis of losing Callie for good—I give them a half bow. "We'll be back by tomorrow at the latest."

"Wait," Jared protests.

I dash between the trees to catch up to her, leaving a confusing trail of fog in my wake to discourage them from following us.

Callie stalks forward in silence. Branches scrape her arms and it's as if she doesn't even notice them. The matter I have to broach with her is delicate, to say the least, and though it can't wait it also probably can't withstand her current betrayed fury. I keep my peace. Let her be the first to speak.

After five minutes' trek through the woods, Callie comes to an abrupt halt, turns, and stares at me. "I forgot to ask . . . Why are you still here?"

There are several reasons, but the biggest one is: you. Fear the guardians would crush your spirit. Fear I might actually never see you again. This is not a question I feel comfortable answering.

"What'd you think of the guardians?" I catch myself. "The other guardians, I mean."

Callie is quiet for so long I don't think she'll answer.

"Like a bug on their windshield. So, if I wasn't picked out in childhood that's how it is? I just pretend I don't know? Go back to doing nothing? I was right about needing to see Michael . . ." She gazes back the way we came, but she doesn't move.

"I wouldn't let it bother you," I say. "You don't need to petition Michael. What you need is to prove them wrong, show them up. Those guardians are practically salivating now that they think Rofocale is trying to start the apocalypse. Which means we're the best chance of recovering the lance before—no pun intended—all hell breaks loose."

"You're asking me to trust you again." She huffs a breath. "Not sure I can trust anyone again right now."

"You can. Mag loves you. And you love them and Jared, whether you feel like it right now or not."

Callie sighs. "I could've reacted better."

"Yes."

"But they could have told me."

"Also yes."

A wind whips through the treetops, and a few weak spring leaves give up the ghost and flutter down around us. The light of sunrise that filters through the trees might as well come straight from Heaven. Even I can appreciate its beauty.

And I'm going to take her as far from that as possible.

"Look, there's only one way for me to get around not being able to tell where the cult is," I say. "For me to help you find them and the lance again. I'll need to use a tool that belongs to, ah, one of my superiors."

It's Father's, but I'm not telling her *that*.

"What tool?" Callie asks.

"It's a globe that can be used to locate anyone on Earth," I say. "A sort of spy-globe called the World Watcher."

"A spy-globe," she says. "Is the idea you go look on it, then come back to me?"

This is *such* a bad idea. I should've known I'd end up pursuing it the second it occurred to me. The globe is Lucifer's sole property. But aren't I supposed to inherit it someday? I could go on my own but . . . I don't want to. For all I know if I leave her here she marches back in and gets Michael to talk to her without cooking her eyeballs in the process and I don't want that yet.

I still have time to get the cult's souls. I don't want the guardians to get away with treating her like that.

Silly, but there it is.

And not nearly as ridiculous as what I'm proposing. "It will save time if you come with me."

"Spit it out, Luke."

"We need to go home. To my home."

Callie's lovely mouth opens, closes, then opens again. "You want me to go to Hell!"

"You'll be my very special, very secret guest."

She stares at me for a long moment and I wait for her to say no. She's only being sensible.

"Okay," she says.

I can't believe she agreed so easily. This plan will inevitably fall apart, but why bother fighting it when you've got stubborn people and demons to contend with, especially if one of them is your own self?

No use waiting now that I have the buy-in. We leave now or I sense it's back to see-you-never.

"This way." I lead her deeper and deeper into the wood,

which grows darker, wilder, less beautiful and peaceful and worldly with each step.

Callie rubs her hands along her bare arms. She's noticed the temperature drop. The thin places that serve as entrances from Earth to Hell don't leak with heat. They are forgotten and dark. They are cold.

"I could warm you up." I stop to make the offer, giving it my best purr.

She hesitates . . . briefly. "Don't even think about it."

I can guess by the way her pupils contract *she's* thinking about it now. I'll take it.

"Why can't you just zap us there?" she asks.

"When we've been traveling that way, it's unpleasant for you, yes?" I press aside a branch and gesture for her to pass before I release it. I wave a hand and make the air around her a fraction warmer. Not so she'll object, but enough to make her more comfortable. A pity I can't use the method I meant at first.

"Understatement," Callie says.

"So," I say, "the reason that mode is so unpleasant is because I was taking us through the kind of . . . outskirts, the borders . . . of Hell. We were passing close to the boundaries of its lands, through which we could easily travel to any spot on Earth. But we didn't cross those boundaries."

"Oh." Callie breathes the word. "Now we will?"

"Yes, but using one of the Earthly entrances will allow us to journey into Hell without the same risks to you." Only because I'm with her, but there's no reason to spell that out. I've never been the best student of Hell's rules, as Porsoth would tell you, and he's not even the worst of the long-winded, often foul-smelling tutors in my past. But even I know something this basic. Humans with intact souls, particularly good ones, would experience a sudden journey of the zappity variety from the mortal plane into my father's castle as death itself. When mortals visit and manage to leave, they follow specific rules.

Lucky for me, any wood or river or cave can lead back to a gate home, if you know how to follow it. After a few more minutes, like dark magic, the gate appears up ahead.

"We're taking the path less chosen, you might say." I watch a leopard slink through the foliage to my right, trailed by a wolf who nips at its shoulder. To my left is a lion.

Dante had some things right.

Callie spots the gate.

The entrance stretches high above us, almost disappearing into the canopy of trees, its dingy bones knit together with magic. Hanging in the center is a large horned demon's skull, flanked by the bone-wings of a misshapen bat, the whole thing a mockery of an angel. Beneath it in curving words is a twist to the message that's usually credited:

Abandon all heart, you who enter Hell.

"Enough with the platitudes," she says. Before adding, "I'll see you in Hell," and striding forward.

My heart does that thing again, where I'm aware of its beating.

Dante also had some things wrong.

"I'll be able to make you less noticeable," I say, rushing to catch her, and my heart, that puzzling creature, now drums inside my chest as if I'm nervous. I suppose that means I am. "But try not to call attention to yourself. We need to get in and out as quietly as possible."

I offer Callie my hand and to my surprise she takes it. There's the slightest tremble when our fingers join.

"Don't be afraid," I say. "I'll protect you."

"Oh god," she says, and I really should caution her about speaking so freely after we're inside, "I actually found that comforting."

I laugh and take a step. So does she. Well, the stepping part.

"Here we go," I say. "Next stop, home sweet Hell."

Behind us, the lion roars a farewell.

PART TWO

THE DESCENT

"Little Alice fell
d
o
w
n
the hOle,
bumped her head
and bruised her soul."

ALICE'S ADVENTURES IN WONDERLAND, LEWIS CARROLL

Mephistopheles: That's Lilith.

Faust: Who?

Mephistopheles: First wife to Adam.
Pay attention to her lovely hair,
The only adornment she need wear.
When she traps a young man in her snare,
She won't soon let him from her care.

FAUST: THE FIRST PART OF THE TRAGEDY, GOETHE

CHAPTER THIRTEEN

CALLIE

 shockwave of heat slams into me when we hit the other side of the tall, creepy gate. I go from shivering to sweating in a few breaths.

Bless or curse my brain, it chooses to latch on to the fact that there's a lion behind us.

My random recall ability and the fact I've read Dante kicks in. Otherwise my main reference point for what a lion sounds like involves the MGM credits lion and so I don't think I'd immediately connect the dots and know: LION. BEHIND US.

But the *Inferno* starts with the Pilgrim encountering three beasts on a strange wooded slope: a leopard, a she-wolf, and a lion.

It seems they aren't just literary symbols to argue over. They're *real*. As real as the Hell we walk into.

"Don't worry," Luke says. "Growly back there won't come in after us."

"That's not what I'm worried about." I hold up a hand to silence his response so I can get a look at our surroundings.

Hell is a shadowed land under a roiling storm-gray sky. A strange palace sprawls some distance in front of us, the stones fashioned into the shape of a giant bare-limbed black tree. Thorn hedges with branches that look like bones protect it. At least, I hope they only look like bones.

They're probably actual bones.

Everything in the landscape is in the same muted palette highlighted only by the occasional burst of orange-red flame. The rest is blackened, sharp, deadly.

But there is a dark beauty to this place. A designer's eye I appreciate. It's like visiting the biggest, most elaborate escape room of all time.

Assuming you manage to escape.

I realize I'm more than a little excited.

I shouldn't be excited about going to *Hell.* Avoiding this destination has literally been the focus of most Sunday mornings and half the Wednesday nights of my life.

And yet.

How many people get to journey through here while still alive? And how many of them are obsessed with reading about everything occult?

There's also the fact that the immense weirdness of being *here* takes my mind off the fact that I'm no longer a team of two who shares everything with my best friend. That my best friend is now in another team of two. With my brother.

That Mag has been lying to me . . . For too long. Any length of time is too long. I picture Mag and Jared talking about me late at night in one of their apartments, while I sleep unknowing in my childhood bedroom. They discuss how awful and judgmental I am, how they have to keep things secret from me. I have enough to worry about as it is, they say, figuring my life out. They cuddle first on couches, then in beds, falling for each other while I have zero clue. Everyone I love is leaving me in their dust.

Losing the ability to trust the one person I trust absolutely is too much to bear. Over my brother. My beloved-by-all brother who always wanted to be a lawyer and is well on his way. I didn't have a hint, not an inkling, they were hooking up. When did this happen? Why didn't they just tell me?

I shouldn't fixate on this when I have much, much bigger things to tackle.

"What now?" I ask Luke, who is watching me far too closely.

He hesitates. "You want to talk about it? Why finding out about the two of them bothers you so much?"

"No. I want to get to this spy-globe of yours and save the day." *And if it wasn't so hot here, I would rethink taking you up on that warming offer. The idea almost melted off my clothes.*

I reach up and make sure my hair's over my ears and I suspect he caught the motion. He doesn't comment on it though. He gestures at the first ring of thick hedge ahead. "Mind the thorns," he says.

"After you," I say.

"I don't blame you for wanting the view," he says with one of his winks and moves forward before I can protest.

I have to admit he's not exactly wrong. He's walking sin and those jeans show it off.

There is a path, however slim, through the hedge—which turns out to definitely be bones growing thorns, by the way—or maybe it makes a path for Luke. I stay close to him so as not to test the theory, which unfortunately means my view doesn't last.

"You grew up here, I guess?" I ask, making conversation as

sweat slides down my temples. Unfortunately, my inability to both walk through the hedge and talk at the same time means I snag my bare arm on a nasty gray thorn. "Ouch!"

Blood wells and the thorn bulges, growing, trying to follow me as I almost back into another part of the hedge. I freeze in blind terror, nowhere to go. I wait for death by a thousand thorns.

Luke whirls and, after a moment's hesitation, steps in close and holds his arms out on either side of us. The thorns recede.

I'm breathing hard. His attention fastens on my pricked arm, a drop of blood sliding off . . .

He thrusts his palm out to catch it. He hesitates, then wipes it on the inside lining of his leather jacket.

The thought of that stretching thorn and what it might be capable of makes me tremble. "I'd say that's gross, but I have a feeling you just did me a favor."

The saved-my-life kind.

Luke's brow furrows and then he quickly takes off the jacket, drops it at our feet, and rips a sleeve off his T-shirt. He gestures for me to hold my arm up to him. He wraps the cloth around the spot with the puncture and ties it loosely.

"Blood attracts attention here. We don't want that."

I can tell he means to resume his jaunty, devil-may-care tone, but it barely works. He's rattled. "I'll take your word for it."

"Just be careful." Our eyes link, hold. "Try not to touch any-thing."

Intern, he's an intern. I will try my best not to touch you again. Especially not with my lips.

"Will do," I say. "Or will not do. You know what I mean."

He picks up his jacket and puts it back on, and we start to-ward the castle. I don't make any further attempts at conversation. Instead I concentrate on every footstep, every movement, knowing any misstep might be my last.

It's Hell.

After slow-going through the hedges, we finally get close enough to our destination that the giant castle's tree-shaped shadow falls over us. Luke turns and I know from one look at his face that we are in grave danger here. Or I am, anyway.

Of course, I am. The thorn proved that.

Though I'm reminded that Luke's dark internship overlord isn't happy with him and I still don't know why. Sure seemed like it was about more than the cultists.

"Once we're inside the Gray Keep, stay with me. Whatever you do, don't talk to anyone else." Luke waits for my nod. Rules and Luke haven't seemed to go together, so that he's issuing them now tells me a lot. "I'll make you less noticeable than usual. Best case, we're in and out so quickly no one sees you at all and only guards see me."

Best case hasn't been happening for us much. "What do I do if someone *does* see me?"

I'm getting way too good at reading him. I can tell from his expression that he hasn't developed a contingency plan for that.

"Let me handle it," he says.

The fate of the world, your chance to prove yourself, et cetera. I don't argue, but I have no plans of ceding my ability to make decisions to a demonic intern. No matter how hot he is.

"The Gray Keep?" I ask.

"Think of the castle as Hell's HQ."

Which reminds me of all the *Far Side* cartoons my mom loves best. We grew up on them, Jared and me. Another sting at the thought of Jared. I wonder if I'm about to discover that besides Luke demons are slightly pudgy in floppy suits and the devil has pointy ears and a pitchfork. Maybe Gary Larson entered here the same way I'm doing and came back to do cartoon reportage.

I doubt it.

Then we're moving again. Just past the end of the thorn hedge, there's a moat that isn't obvious until we stop at a black cliff's sharp edge. There's no hint at how far down the bottom might be. The sound of something like a mix of bubbling water and roaring fire comes from below. Even hotter air than that around us wafts up from the absolute darkness, bringing the sulfur smell of rotten eggs and smoke.

Across the moat is the Gray Keep.

We're to the right of the broad trunk-shaped portion of the building, and how the branching limbs stay in place is an architectural mystery. But that question can wait. The current problem is how we get in. The place is made of seemingly impenetrable, unreachable-from-here-anyway smooth obsidian walls.

I start, "How do we—"

Luke holds out his hand and a portion of the wall breaks free in response, lowering to provide a smooth black bridge with jagged stone teeth lining the sides. He looks at me, lifts his fingers to his lips in a *shh*, and starts across.

I follow, staying close.

Then I see why the cue for silence. Two demons lurch toward us from inside a corridor of the keep, their semihuman silhouettes odd.

That's *before* I get a good look at them.

Scratch odd and substitute something that means so far

beyond odd I need to invent an entirely new word. One of the most interesting books in my occult collection is a cheap reprint of the *Dictionnaire Infernal*. I own it for the illustrations added in 1863. I always assumed they were fanciful nightmares.

Given the twisted smirking red face and curling pair of elf ears on a being with hissing snakes for feet coming at us, it feels like the images way undersold reality. Beside him is a male figure with impossibly long, thin legs and a crocodile's head, bat wings extending from his shoulders. Both wear what seem like a parody of old-timey evening clothes. A silk vest for the red-faced, snake-footed elf, a full jacket that hangs to the knee for the crocodile-bat man.

They catch sight of Luke and bow. The crocodile-bat speaks, "Greetings, P—"

"Lord Geonald, Lord Sethany," Luke says, hurrying to one side of the bridge. I stay in his shadow. "In his dark glory . . ."

"Let us reside," they answer in chorus.

We're past them quickly, with no indication they've spotted me. Luke said he'd make me harder to notice and maybe he actually told the truth.

The palace isn't as hot as the outdoors, just unpleasantly warm, like sitting too close to a fireplace. A long carpet with a swirl of a red-and-black pattern runs the length of the black stone corridor in front of us. Paintings that look like portraits by Bosch (the painter, not my sweet dog) punctuate the walls. Candles with black tapers burn in skull-shaped sconces along the walls.

"Those were demons?" I wipe sweat from my forehead. "Like you?"

Luke pauses to lift his eyebrows. "Not everyone can be as attractive as me."

I snort.

He assumes that familiar wounded pout, and there's no way I'll let him see how right he is by reacting. Didn't that kiss reveal too much already?

"Do most demons look like that? Your boss didn't."

"Not as such. They're among the old ones in the aristocracy who like the drama of a 'perverted form.' It's all about the pageantry with them." He shrugs. "The demonic horde takes all types."

I catch on one of his words. "Are you aristocracy?"

It only makes sense, I guess. They bowed to him. Otherwise how would he know so much about the castle?

After a moment's hesitation, he says, "We better hurry up."

"Shady non-answer noted," I say.

Luke strides ahead, so I have no choice but to drop it if I want to keep up. Several paces along, voices reach us from around the corner at the end of the hallway. Whoever they belong to is barely out of view and coming our way.

Luke looks around and his panic would be funny, if it wasn't so real.

"It's Rofocale. In here," he says, grabbing my arm and thrusting me toward a wall—which I stumble through and land on the other side of before I can even blink.

I'm alone.

In the most wonderful and magical place I've ever seen in my life: Hell's library.

The shelves stretch up and up and up. I count thirteen levels of stacks, with a stained-glass mural ceiling that riffs on Michelangelo's Sistine Chapel, only in this image Lucifer's arm stretches out to offer a black book to a horde of angels. The smell of old books is intoxicating, paper and dust and . . .

presumably all the occult knowledge that's forbidden for someone like me to know.

I walk toward the shelves closest to me and inhale deeply. I may be in Hell, but it feels almost like Heaven right now.

I run my hand along the spines. I choose a volume with brilliant gold lettering on black leather and slide it free, nearly bowing under its weight. My shoulder is already aching from the weight of the spearhead and grimoire in my bag, so I sink to the floor to take a look at the new book. Laying it flat, I admire the tracery of gold symbols embroidered into the cover.

Finally, I open it.

For a second, I think it's Latin, and I don't know much Latin. Then I realize the words are almost blurred, nearly hovering above the page. I can't read them.

I crawl to the shelf and pull down three more books. I open them and . . . The same thing happens.

"Oh, hell," I say, because there's a panic drum in my chest. Surely, it's *just* Hell. Luke told me not to touch anything.

But what if I can't read anymore? What if I've permanently stolen my favorite thing in the world from myself? With no way to get it back? Something makes me certain that there will be no workarounds. No audio books, no learning Braille. Hell has gotten into my head and made it so I'll never read again. Books have been stolen from me forever.

There have been plenty of times in history when someone like me wouldn't be able to read. But I am me. I can't imagine it.

Except now I can, and it's the worst thing as I visualize it spiraling out into my daily life. It might sound silly, but if I can't read, if there are no more stories, no more random facts to be learned, how will I continue to be *me*?

Wait. Wait, I need to get a grip. I haven't slept in way too long and I'm overtired. Possibly, it's only Hell's collection that's a problem, not intended for my mortal eyes.

I slip the grimoire from my bag. This is the test. This is how I'll know. The pages and the way they look is burned in my memory, even if I can't read the language.

I open the cover.

The words hover and blur. It's exactly the same as the rest. Whispering laughter wraps around me even though I don't see anyone.

I try to steady my breathing. That doesn't work. Before I know it my chest heaves with sobs and my eyes burn with tears and I'm pulling more books from the shelves. I know I have to stop, get control of myself. But I can't.

Maybe the next book will make sense or the next . . .

Or maybe I'll be trapped here and go mad. What a fool I was to come to this place.

CHAPTER FOURTEEN

LUKE

Rofocale and Porsoth spot me immediately, and Porsoth's busted expression makes it clear I'm the subject of their intense corridor confab. I hope Callie remembers what I said about keeping her hands to herself until I can steer these two in another direction, far away from me.

"Master!" Porsoth says with a pleased vibrato squeal. "You've returned!" He raises an owlish brow at Rofocale. "And so soon! I told you Luke would surprise you."

It's hard to believe Porsoth used to be considered one of Hell's most fearsome demons. His exploits were legend. He's always been so kind and deferential to me, so more or less accommodating of my slacking off instead of applying myself to my studies. The exact opposite of Rofocale. The only torture I can imagine Porsoth accomplishing is assigning an overlong reading list.

"He constantly surprises me," Rofocale allows, making it clear he means in unpleasant ways. "It *is* soon for you to return . . ."

He scans me from head to toe. "And you're still as soulless as when I last saw you. What are you doing back here?"

Rofocale *would* ask the right question. I choose the obvious course of action: I lie.

"I, ah, came to seek Porsoth's counsel," I say.

"You did?" Porsoth smooths a wing down his black scholar's robe. He's the shocked one now, though he recovers quickly. "I mean, why, of course you did. How can I assist?"

Rofocale, however, isn't buying what I'm selling. "Luke, what are you truly doing back here? Don't obfuscate."

"Fine." I heave a weary sigh, as if I'm sick of the worst being assumed. Poor me. "I came to geolocate the Order of Elerion with a tool Father loaned me."

Rofocale's brows arch over his red-pupiled eyes. "You told your father about this situation?"

I shrug.

His gaze narrows, but he doesn't call me out. If I'm telling the truth and he doesn't believe me, then it might offend Father. Obviously I'm not anywhere close to veracity's neighborhood, and in point of fact I fully intend to break into Father's throne room and use the World Watcher with him none the wiser. Forever and ever, lament.

Here's hoping Rofocale never finds that out.

"We'll leave you to get on with it, then," Rofocale says at last. "Tick tock, after all."

"Most people use digital clocks these days," I say because I can't help myself. "But I get the point."

Porsoth gives me a pleading glance. He clearly wants me to beg him to stay, to ask his counsel. I'm honestly tempted. He is our wisest scholar.

But involving him might eventually end up with him in the

boiling water of deadly old Dad's wrath. Better for him to not know what I'm up to. Then he can't be blamed.

I wave. "I'm on top of it all now, I promise."

With a skeptical sniff, Rofocale continues up the hall and, after a breath's hesitation, Porsoth goes after him. I wait until they're out of sight and I step through the wall.

"Oh, Callie, no," I say.

She's on the floor, a heap of books scattered around her in disarray. The library wraiths are going to lose their know-it-all cool at the mess, but that's not my main concern. My concern is that Callie already seems to have. Hell doesn't need much of an invitation to torment a human. She must have given it one.

It's my fault for leaving her alone here. I should've known something like this would happen.

"Callie?" I try again.

She doesn't even look up at my voice. Her chin is tucked to her chest. She clutches the grimoire that brought us together to her stomach and rocks back and forth. Her eyes are shut tight.

"Look at me." I approach her cautiously, crouching nearby. I put a hand lightly on her shoulder. "Callie, look at me."

"You're not real, none of this is real," she says.

"It is," I say. "But it'll be okay. I promise."

She shakes her head. "If it's real, I don't want to be."

This is not the Callisto I've come to know and . . . appreciate. She's a human and this is Hell and I abandoned her not just anywhere, but in the one place I knew she'd most love.

Of course, it turned on her. *Of course* it did. Just my latest screw-up.

I scoop up a nearby book and understand immediately what the library has done. I shake my head. I can't help but be impressed. This is what I meant when I said Hell understands us better than we do ourselves. It's an ingenious way to torture Callie, making her unable to read.

"Leave her alone," I say.

"It's not real, not real," she says.

I've got to get her to a place where she can listen. I reach out and smooth her hair back from her cheek. Her eyes are closed and she's still shaking her head.

At sea, I latch onto a drastic measure. I need her to feel something besides this sorrow.

I lean in, placing my hands carefully on either side of her face. And then I slowly duck my head and press my lips to hers. There's a change in her breathing, a pause, and her lips move against mine.

Softly at first, but soon enough with greater heat. I forget why we're doing this. Or, rather, why we're doing this no longer matters.

I am home, and I don't hate it. I am home.

Callie makes one of those little moans like she did earlier and it undoes me. I scoop her forward onto my lap, and her legs part effortlessly, straddling me. My turn to moan as she rocks her hips against me and I go instantly hard. Her hair falls around us as I kiss the tender skin of her throat and coax another, deeper sound from her.

I could play the game of trading wordless pleasure with her forever. But it doesn't feel like a game.

I remember why I started this.

It's going to take more than this to put her to rights. With great difficulty, I stop for a second.

A second in which she apparently remembers what's happening and pulls back, her hands on my chest. "Luke—what?

Oh no," she says, sweeping her gaze to the books around us. "It was real."

She slides from my lap. Her kiss-swollen lips aren't enough to take away my guilt at seeing her red-from-crying eyes. I left her here. That's why this happened.

But I also know *why* I left her here. Maybe that can fix this.

"Hold on," I say, sending a command to my body to cool down. It obeys. A perk of demonhood. "Just hold on. It's going to be okay. I promise. I'll prove it. Gather your things and come with me."

I wish I could help her, but I'm afraid to touch her bag with the portion of the Holy Lance inside it. She moves slowly but does as I say, slinging the bag over a shoulder once the grimoire is back inside.

When I extend my hand, Callie blinks, then takes it. The fact that she sniffles and follows me into the hallway without protest is telling. "I have something to show you, and you need some rest," I tell her. "You've been up all night."

"But—do we have time?"

I'm the one who's short on time. "We'll make it. There's nothing much Elerion can do while you have the spearhead here."

Thankfully, Porsoth and Rofocale are nowhere in sight. There's a hidden door that opens into a spiral staircase of gray stone not much farther up the hallway and I keep her hand in mine as we climb up two floors. To my apartments.

The smooth wall parts to admit us. I'm unaccountably nervous about what she'll think of the place.

It's a sprawling assortment of rooms, a branch of the Gray Keep's tree. We walk into a large open great room filled with sumptuous, pillowy seating. A chandelier with black candles and a thousand dark crystals sparkles to life as we enter, imbuing the place with extra glamour. Off the entry area, there are several rooms through arched entrances and along corridors: a small kitchen, a study area I've turned into another lounging spot, a set of baths, and, obviously, my bed chamber.

"I know it's not fancy," I say.

"It is extremely fancy." She frowns a touch. "You are an aristocrat, aren't you? This is where you live? Alone?"

I left Father's enormous wing of apartments five years ago at seventeen, which, as Father put it, is "almost a man."

I nod.

"This way." I lead her up a short hall and through the arched entrance to my bedroom. I've never noticed exactly how large my bed is before, the chamber's dominant feature. Covered by the silkiest gray sheets and blanket and too many pillows.

She shifts from foot to foot. "I know that, um, back there, I climbed all over you like a tree."

"Anytime," I say.

"But, um . . ." She stares at the bed.

"Oh no! That's not why I brought you here." Is there a tinge of disappointment on her face? I keep going. This isn't about me. It's for her. "You need to rest. But first, like I said, I've got proof that you're fine now."

Her face nearly crumples as she remembers her panic, but she manages to recover. "What if I'm not though?"

I stride to the side of the bed where a stack of unread books assigned by Porsoth are arrayed in a messy tower. I pluck off the top one and sit down.

"I'll show you," I say. "Come, sit. I won't bite . . . unless you ask nicely."

She sticks her tongue out at me. It is, in fact, one of the

most welcome things I've ever seen. A glimpse of her back to normal.

Callie settles next to me, and I shift toward her. "What was your favorite story growing up?"

"Alice. *Alice's Adventures in Wonderland*. What if I've lost it forever?" She squeezes her eyes shut. "What if I'll never read it again? I'll never . . ."

"No," I say, stroking a hand along the cover to turn this book into another, "look at this. This is better. This is the Wonderland tale that Carroll never finished, but dreamed of and began later. It was his toll to cross over. I've conjured it here, now, just for you."

Her eyes blink open. She releases a breath. "Luke, I touched a book. In the library. You told me not to touch anything and I . . ."

I reach out and brush a strand of hair off her cheek. *She kissed me again.*

"Try now," I say.

There's an illustration in this book that as far as I know only exists here. It's Alice among demons, Porsoth-like cousins. The text explains that Alice went down the wrong rabbit hole and visited the underworld. She makes it out alive after a daylong journey.

I hope it'll comfort Callie. Not just being able to read it, but the story itself.

You're going to make it out too.

"I . . ." Callie drops her hesitation and snatches the new book from me. She skims the page. "I can read this," she says and her green eyes only tear away from it back to me after a long moment.

"I know." I sigh. "I'm sorry I left you alone there."

"I'm okay," she says and looks from the book back to me. "This is a new Wonderland story. Is this real? Lewis Carroll really wrote this?"

"Yes," I say and stand. I move over to a stiff-backed chair in the corner. No rest for the wicked. "Read it. Get some sleep. I'll wake you in a bit."

She hesitates, but then she slides back and props a pillow behind her and holds the book up to see better. I watch her and remember that Mag said I'd better get used to watching her read.

I could and that frightens me. As she turns the pages, her blinks come slower and the book finally falls to the side of her lap. She's fast asleep.

I walk over as stealthily as possible and fold the cover from the other side of the bed over her. Then I ease down next to her, if two feet away, and pick up Lewis Carroll, intending to reread one of my own childhood favorites . . . I watch her instead, the gentle rise and fall of her chest, passing expressions and mumbles in her sleep.

She's more fascinating than any story.

I like this human far too much for my own good.

On those nights I bother with sleep—I don't need it, strictly speaking, but it's one of life's great pleasures, after all—I wake in a slow, grumbly process. But for Callie, wakefulness comes between one breath and the next, sooner than I'd hoped. Her eyes pop open after a short nap and she bolts upright.

I'm reclined on my side, still watching her. I stay where I am, and wait for her to turn and see me.

Which she does. She glances down at the book at my side.

She reaches out and strokes her fingers across it with a faint smile. "Thank you for this."

I prepare for her next remark to be something about how we have to get going, or maybe about how I've been pulling an Edward watching her sleep (she knew I was in the room, so I was *not*).

She looks up, her eyes meeting mine, and the heat in them is familiar. "What was it you said about biting?"

I only thought I was awake. Turns out my body was asleep until right now. "That you have to ask nicely."

She climbs free of the bedcover I folded over her and keeps coming. I shift to my back so she can straddle me again.

Leaning forward, she nips at my lips, gently, catching one between her teeth. "That nice enough?" she asks, barely pulling back.

I answer by sliding my hands down her body, which makes her pant and I'm nearly undone. I relish the feel of how she arches into my hands, the perfect more-than-handfuls of her breasts, and then her hips against mine as we rock together. She leans down and our lips meet again, open and hungry. We're both breathing hard.

I groan and flip her over beneath me and then I ever-so-gently bite her neck. In a second, the noise she makes changes this from Hell to something like how I imagine Above.

We try to get as much of each other as possible. A nip thrown in now and then for good measure. She strips off my shirt with the missing sleeve and her hands on my skin is a gift I never knew to ask for.

Callie's hitting a fever pitch when she says, "I can't believe I'm doing this—I can't believe . . . I don't usually."

"Enough of that," I say.

"What?"

"Talking."

But I sense where this is headed. She'll start overthinking or she's already beginning to leave this moment and panic about how long we've paused here. I know we can't spend the time I want, but I won't let her be unsatisfied.

My fingers move to the button of her jeans. "Is this all right?" I ask.

She moans and nods, lets me help her shuck them. Her ears are bright red and her cheeks are flushed and before she can decide not to take this moment of pleasure I cup her over her panties and watch as her head tilts back. I slide them aside.

Callie takes her pleasure the same way she reads, it turns out. Completely absorbed, utterly transported. Her gasping scream might be my greatest accomplishment.

After Callie's used my bath chamber and shyly smiled at me, and I'm adorned with a fresh T-shirt, we head back to the stairwell to access one of the many back entrances to Father's throne room. At the age of five, I made it my business to begin finding as many as possible. Currently, I know fifty-one ways to reach Father's sanctum.

Although I wouldn't be surprised to discover there are still a hundred more hidden windows or doors or tunnels I'm unaware of. Given what I know about Callie and her phobia of being trapped under things, I choose the most direct route from my apartments to there.

We go up another level and approach a statue made of red marble in a wall sconce. The figure is a female demon in a shadowed cloak with a torch thrust high.

I flourish at the statue. "You'll like this. Pull the torch."

Callie hesitates. "What about not touching anything?"

I raise my eyebrows. "Little late for that, isn't it?"

She blushes.

I raise my voice: "Leave her be." I nod for Callie to go ahead.

My heart does that weird existing thing in my chest as she tentatively does so. She tugs on the torch and, when it starts to give, puts some elbow into it. The shelves beside the figure slide away to reveal a secret passage.

I'm rewarded with a grin. "A torch that's a lever," Callie says. "We should do one of those."

A cloud passes over her face and I guess it's due to images of her fraught home and family situation. She must wonder if she'll ever experience normal again.

"Something just occurred to you," I say. "What is it?"

"My mom left me in charge. More or less. I wonder what she's going to think if she finds out that I left, what happened."

"I think she'll understand." The woman in the pictures at Callie's house did not look like someone who'd be overly harsh. "And you should, do a torch secret passage. But now onward."

We step into the narrow passage and the shelves automatically seal up behind us. All we have to do is locate the Order of Elerion using the spy-globe and be on our way.

"Where are w—" she starts.

I put a finger to my lips. "Quietly now."

Father should be out and about at this time, but he's not exactly what you'd call predictable. He doesn't like people poking around in his things or his space. Servants only invade the throne room or his quarters when he summons them.

The passage grows ever narrower, and behind me Callie

takes a handful of my jacket in her fist to stay close. Ahead is the veil of darkness that marks an actual entrance to dear old Dad's sanctuary and ruling chamber.

"Don't be afraid," I say.

When I step into the dark, she holds on tight. It's quiet and black for a moment, and then we're through into the thin light of the deserted room.

I try to imagine the opulence in front of us from her point of view. My rooms are pitiable by comparison. An enormous obsidian throne dominates. The floors and long mosaic windows are a symphony of images in gray and white and black, demons and angels engaged in bitter combat and some lustier pursuits. There's a sprawling table representing Father's theater of war with tiny figures representing souls and demons and guardians and angels.

There's a hard beauty to it all, as there is to everything Father touches.

Even me? But, no, he'd never say that.

"Wow." Callie breathes and steps around me.

"Yeah. It's a definite look. No one will ever say he's not on brand." The World Watcher, Father's best spy toy, is behind the throne, where no one but he accesses it.

No one would trespass here in his unsacred space, the fear would be too great.

Or so he assumes.

I can't keep a grin off my lips at the knowledge I'm doing exactly that. "This way," I say and stride forward.

The shadow behind the throne throws me off for a moment. But then it's reality that does.

Because there's nothing. The spy-globe, which has never moved in the entirety of my childhood, is nowhere to be seen.

"No no no," I chant, stumbling across empty tile where the globe should be.

"What's wrong?" Callie asks.

I rake a hand through my hair, trying to quell the panic. This was an insane plan, but it was my *only* plan. And Rofocale's not wrong. Time's running out. Possibly for all of us.

This is the worst turn of events I can imagine.

"No, no, no."

"Luke, you're freaking me out," Callie says. "Talk to me. What's the problem?"

I do my best to summon an explanation that won't make her hate me again. Nothing comes.

"Why, hello there," a new voice smooth as gravel says. Father's. "I see we have company."

I was wrong about the globe not being here as worst case. This is the worst case.

It occurs to me that I made a crucial error before I ever met Callie. I never stopped to question why Father suddenly wanted an update on me, why the deadline for a report on my progress obtaining souls. He's been monitoring me this entire time. I'd bet on it.

Which means that I'm in deep, *deep* trouble.

"Look at me, son," he commands.

I catch a glimpse of Callie's frozen face as I turn. If I'm in trouble, so is she. Deep, *deep* trouble. It's a small comfort that she isn't experiencing any visible ill effects from being in the presence of Father in his seat of power. The holy relic she's carrying must offer her protection normal humans usually don't have.

"Fancy meeting you here," I say meekly and stand waiting under his scrutiny.

His white-tinged-with-gray wings extend out on either side of him, something he does when he wants to take up more space. His deeper-gray suit is slightly wrinkled and yet still the most stylish thing in creation. His face is craggy and almost human when he wants it to be, but the tiny nubs of horns nestled in his blond hair give him away (well, and the wings). Right now, he looks faintly amused—the worst among many bad possibilities.

Father pretending he's amused is him at his most dangerous. He's a charming devil, original sin made flesh but with a sentimental, nearly ethical streak that makes him unpredictable. He's obsessed with all the things so-called "great men" are: reputation, legacy, appearances, and his offspring's achievements as a reflection of those.

You might say I've been an epic disappointment. He certainly says it.

So whatever he truly is in this moment, amused isn't it.

"Did you think I wouldn't know when a piece of the Holy Lance entered my kingdom?" He tosses off the question and stalks back around the throne, throwing a hand up in a wave for me to follow.

Callie catches my arm. "Is that . . ."

"The devil. Yes. Be quiet and careful. Let me take the lead." Though, honestly, I'd be happy to give it up to her. I think she's going to argue for just that, but she bites her lip and nods.

"Coming?" Father calls out.

"Yes, sir," I say and Callie comes along. "Stay behind me," I murmur to her at the last moment. She doesn't protest. We take up a spot in front of the massive black throne, but not too close.

Father has taken his seat. The throne was constructed with

low arms so his wings sprawl out on either side. He leans back, and from his relaxed posture, he looks like he hasn't a care in the underworld. Deception is his special gift.

"Now, son." His words are lazy. "This should be good. Explain to me how you've finally given me an apocalypse eve and it's not even my birthday." He squints. "Or yours. You haven't even managed to grow your wings and then this. This is some talent you have for . . . fucking up."

While not untrue, it stings. But then Callie clears her throat.

No. I look at her and try to communicate silently. *Don't do it. Stay quiet.*

She raises her hand, because it's Callie. Despite everything, I can't help a little flutter at how brave and polite she is. She's raising her hand to *speak to the devil in his throne room.*

I'm terrified for her. For me.

"Yes, human," Father says.

She clutches her bag close to her side, no doubt drawing strength from the spearhead's presence there. "Why do you keep calling Luke *son*? Is this like when waiters call me *sweetie* and *honey*, because I hate that."

Father takes a second to digest the question, then throws his head back with laughter.

CHAPTER FIFTEEN

CALLIE

People have *got* to stop laughing at me when I say completely logical things. I'm beginning to feel like the Greek myths' Cassandra, cursed to know and tell the truth but no one believes her—only in my case it's cursed to be taken as hysterical when I'm being 100 percent serious.

The devil sits there with his legs casually sprawled and his stunning wings wide and just keeps laughing.

"Excuse me," I say to the manspreading devil.

Luke is no help. I've never seen him like this. Cowed. I think he might be trembling.

"What's so funny?" I press, but to no effect. I have no choice. I pull out my best imitation of Mom on the rare occasions when she's annoyed and issue a command: "Stop it."

The magic of a mom voice always works. He sobers.

I instantly regret pushing my luck. He grows fearsome between one breath and the next, radiating big *I could crush you like a bug and then do it again and again for a thousand years* energy.

Problem is, the devil seems like a complete jerk. I can't help but *like* Luke at this point. He rescued me from not being able to read. He gave me a Lewis Carroll story no one else on Earth knows exists. He also gave me the best, most brain-melting orgasm of my life. He's helping me save the world. It may be stupid, but I want to stand up for him.

When the devil speaks, it's not to me but to Luke. "She doesn't know who you are."

There's a resolve in Luke's expression. "She knows me better than you, than anyone, and it only took her a day."

The devil shakes his head, eyes glowing like coals. Luke has made him angry. Yes, Luke *is* trembling. I step next to him, and slip my hand in his to lend him strength.

I don't know if it's true that I know Luke better than anyone else, but, no matter what, it's sad that he'd say so. Heartbreaking, honestly. I see him clearly for the first time. He's lonely. Alone. Feels like he's screwing up constantly. I can relate.

No wonder he wanted to tag along with me initially. That he's been eager to help me despite playing for Team Dark Side.

I can't forgive everything he's done, the lies he's told. I get it, though. I get *him*.

"I'm Lucifer Morningstar." As he peers down his nose at me, Lucifer's eyes are sharp, hard chips of broken glass. "*He* is my son. Meet Luke Astaroth Morningstar, crown prince of Hell, my heir." He stops and considers. "At least, *if* he secures a soul before tomorrow's moonrise. Otherwise . . ."

A prince. Or *the* prince of darkness.

So much for my seeing Luke clearly. I hesitate . . . Maybe I still do.

"And that explains the apartment." I turn to Luke, who's studiously avoiding looking at me. "You couldn't have mentioned this when I found out you weren't Rofocale? You told me you were an intern."

"You pretended to be Rofocale?" This revelation has taken Lucifer Morningstar by surprise.

"I am an intern," Luke says and finally meets my eyes. "Callie, I'm sorry I lied."

I wave my hand in dismissal. "We have bigger problems."

Because what does it matter? We have an apocalypse to stop. If anything, this is good news. Right? Right. I ignore the tiny twinge at being lied to again. That's not important right now.

"You're sorry you lied?" Lucifer asks him. He's staring at our linked hands. "Oh, I see. I always liked a challenge myself."

That one takes me a second to process. "Ew," I say. "I take it #MeToo hasn't made it to Hell, but no thanks."

"I didn't mean like that," Lucifer snaps. "I meant your soul."

He leans slightly forward, the shadow of his wings moving.

The devil's wings rustling turns out to be the eeriest sound I've ever heard.

"I see what this is now," he says. "Son, want to ask what you came here to ask?"

Luke hesitates. Again, unusual for him. He hasn't been much for hesitation in our time together.

"Yes?" his father prompts.

Luke clasps his hands in front of himself. "I'd like to use the World Watcher to locate the Order of Elerion. I plan to secure their souls in order to meet your deadline."

"Now, was that so difficult?" Lucifer asks. He settles back on his towering throne. "Too bad it's not here. But there's an available human soul right next to you."

The gray light outside streams through the stained-glass battle scenes. I might as well be in them. This is a battle.

"Not really," I inform him. "I'm a guardian."

"A guardian? No, you're not." Lucifer dismisses the possibility.

That guardian warrior's laughter echoes through my head. I raise my brows at Luke. "You lied about that too?"

He lifts his shoulders in a pained shrug. "I didn't know—"

"So, you see," Lucifer interrupts, silencing Luke, "why my son needs the discipline and focus of a challenge to rise to. You'll do."

The hits just keep on coming. I'm not a guardian. My teammate is the heir of Hell.

But, again . . . so what? I have half the Holy Lance in my messenger bag and the world needs saving. *So what* if I wasn't born with the right pedigree? If Luke made it all up for whatever reason . . .

The actual guardians—which I'm apparently not—believe this has all been done in a calculated fashion by Lucifer. Luke's right. They're not going to buy the truth that it's an accident. Occam's razor is the principle that says the simplest explanation is most likely to be the right one. The simplest explanation here may be wrong, but it's the one they've jumped to.

The upshot is that I'm as able to stop this situation from spiraling into complete destruction as anyone. I might not be the most qualified, but what choice do I have?

"I don't care." I act like it's an easy decision. "I'm still seeing this through, guardian or not."

"Callie . . ." Luke starts.

"We're fine," I say and mean it. "As long as you can convince him to let us use that globe. We need to find the cult."

"Ahem," Lucifer says and his amusement is clearly a front. "It's not here, as I said and you've seen. It's with your mother,

Luke. If you want to use the globe, you'll have to go see Lilith. And there are some rules: no more traveling by our method with the girl. You'll have to make the journey. It should give you the time you need."

Luke asks exactly what I'm thinking. "What's the catch?"

"I want you to get *her* soul by the deadline." Lucifer smiles. "Any worthy son of mine should be able to pull it off."

The horror on Luke's face is almost funny. "Father, no."

"I've made up my mind." Lucifer's smile widens, baring his teeth like a formerly angelic wolf.

My immortal soul. The one thing I've been taught to guard against Hell my entire life. My palms go cold even as my heart pounds. I refuse to let Lucifer see my fear.

I shrug. "We're done here?"

Lucifer's grin vanishes and I give an inward fist-pump. Just then, there's a commotion and Luke and I turn to face it.

A demon in a long black cape like a Supreme Court justice's rushes into the throne room. He has an owl's head and wings but his *hooves* clatter on the floor. "Sire, I'm afraid there's a problem with Luke—" The owl demon stops talking when he sees us.

"I tried to prevent him from interrupting you," Rofocale explains, hurrying in behind him.

"He's a loyal sort, our Porsoth," Lucifer says, and nods for them to approach. "He can accompany the prince and his conquest on their journey."

"I am *not*," I say, but I might as well be shouting into a void for all the attention anyone pays.

"Happily, sire," the demon named Porsoth says. Then, to Luke, "Where are we going?"

"To Lilith's," Luke says. "I could use your help."

Odd that he calls his mom by her given name, but then, maybe that's how they do things here. I recognize it—Adam's notorious first wife, replaced because she refused to be subservient to him. And, considered a men's-soul-sucking demon afterward. I've always liked the idea of Lilith. Now I'm going to meet her. Maybe she can tell me how to stand up to these guys and win.

Porsoth's owlish throat works as he swallows, and there's pride on his strange features. "Of course." He bows his head to Luke. "You shall have my aid."

"You are all dismissed," Lucifer says with a wave. "Except you, Rofocale. You stay. We need to discuss combat strategy and . . . other things. Luke, don't fail me. You won't like the results if you do."

I want to argue that he can't simply flap his hand around and get rid of us, but Luke and our new companion, Porsoth the Supreme Court–garbed demonic owl-pig, have already started to leave. I stand my ground for one more moment.

"We're going to surprise you," I say.

Lucifer looks past me to Rofocale, but I know he heard.

I follow Luke. Something tells me he's not going to like the new plan forming in my head.

Which is only fair, since I don't like it either.

Luke is quiet as we head into another long, dark, goth magnifique corridor. That's not a good sign. Then again, he's been tasked with taking my soul.

The owl in the robe is monologuing and it's not even a little comforting. "This is going to be one for the history books. Or that will *end* the history books, which is a shame since we'll hardly have time to enjoy writing them, or reading them. Oh, his damnable word! Luke! I worry—"

"Who are you again?" I ask him.

The owl stops and ruffles his feathers. "Luke hasn't mentioned me?"

"He's a little self-absorbed." The response is meant to needle Luke on purpose, but he doesn't even seem to notice. This is heading into Mayday territory. Maybe I should grab him and kiss him. Hey, it worked on me.

The owl blinks at me and then snorts a laugh that he attempts to hide. "He is. That he is! But you can't say that! He's the heir."

The owl snorts again, barely containing the laughter.

"I can say it, though," I say smugly. "I just did."

The owl nods. "I can't argue with that logic."

I gamble and extend my hand. If this creature's coming with us, I may as well get to know more about him. "I'm Callie, nonguardian tasked with saving the world."

"I'm Porsoth, formerly the minder of the befouled pit of eternal grievance, the abject terror of the black-hearted, and now Luke's tutor." That last one sounds convincing, the others not so much. From beneath the robe, he extends a wing with a skinny hand at the end of it and we shake.

I take him in. "And you're an owl."

"I'm a half-owl, half-porcine demon with some humanoid features in this, a variant of my natural form. I can change it if this isn't becoming."

I've insulted him. "No, that's not what I mean. It's just this is all like Hogwarts, but bigger and more . . ." I search for a non-insulting phrase.

"Demonic!" Porsoth cries after a beat, seemingly delighted.

"I always wanted the owls to stage an uprising in those books. What's your house?" He blinks again. "Gryffindor, am I right?"

Sure, I'm discussing Hogwarts houses with demons. My entire life has led to this.

"Me? Ravenclaw, all the way." I squint. "And you'd be Slytherin, I guess."

"If I must," he says and sighs. "But I'm a Ravenclaw at heart too. Don't tell."

"Our secret." An idea occurs to me. "You guys weren't involved with all that nonsense from her, right?"

"Wouldn't touch it." Porsoth shudders.

I hazard a look over at Luke and find him staring into space. Porsoth follows my gaze. As we watch, Luke paces from one side of the corridor to the other and back again.

"Luke?" I ask. "You okay?"

"I'll convince him to drop it, don't worry," he says, continuing to walk. "He can't mean for me to actually do it."

"What?" I ask.

He halts and faces me. "Your soul. I know I can't take it. You're good. He must be joking."

May as well get this over with. "You can and you will. We're making a deal."

Porsoth inhales sharply.

Luke goes motionless. "No, Callie, you don't understand. Deals with our kind are serious business. You can't just back out of them."

"I understand."

"No, you don't. If we make a deal, it can't be broken." Luke pauses. "Not without severe consequences."

I've made up my mind. I can't do this alone. I need to be certain Luke will see it through. Lucifer Morningstar gave me a way to accomplish my task, and I have to be brave enough to take it. This is my chance to matter. Even if there's hell to pay for it later.

"I do understand." I approach him, set a hand on his arm. "How could I live with myself—how could I expect to get into Heaven anyway—if I did nothing? If I stopped here and now."

"You'd find a way," he says, but I can hear the weakness in it. He knows it's a lie.

"You said I know you better than anyone, and you must know a little about me by now."

"And that's why I can't."

I suck in a long breath and let it out in a sigh. "Here's the deal. You promise to help me recover the rest of the lance and end this race to Armageddon, and, in exchange, if we succeed then . . ." It hurts to say it, but I have to. "You get my soul." I raise my hands and wipe off imaginary dust. "It's the only way I can trust you going forward. You'll have a real interest in helping me."

Luke is serious as a cemetery. "Callie, you don't understand."

"I do. I know what I'm saying. The library, remember."

And what came after . . .

"But . . ." He searches for words.

"Enough. We have to get going to Lilith's ASAP."

Luke continues to stare at me, tilting his head slightly. I wish I could read his mind.

"Or do we need to shake on it?" I ask. He didn't do that with Solomon Elerion, but then, he was trapped in a pentagram at the time. "Porsoth?" I turn to the demon when Luke doesn't respond.

"It's best if you do," Porsoth says. "But are you absolutely sure—"

"If this is what you want, I agree. It's a deal." Luke extends his hand. "I help you, you help me."

I take his hand and we shake on it, sealing the deal.

"Now," I ask, pretending I haven't agreed to give up my soul, "which way to Lilith's?"

CHAPTER SIXTEEN

LUKE

The corridors of the Keep are closing in on me. I long to be beyond these walls, in the foul air, gray sky above. But I also know that once we're out there—me, Porsoth, and a *human who is good* and who I like way too much and has *just made a deal to give me her soul*—it won't feel any safer.

Callie can't fully understand what she's agreed to, no matter what she says. I should have said no, but . . .

Assume we do save the world, and then I never see her again. The selfish part of me knows this means that I will. I tell myself I'll find a way out of it, get Father to change his mind. But if not, that secret part of me, which for the first time in my life I feel actual guilt for having, isn't hating the idea of Callie living here forever.

I'd get to be her hero on the regular.

Of course, there's as much chance that we fail miserably. But I'm not going to tell her that.

And changing Father's mind about anything is easier said

than done. He wants me to fail as much as he wants me to succeed. He's been watching and waiting for a chance like this. He's not the king imp of the perverse for nothing. I don't want to be like him, but I fear that I am. Or worse, him but lesser.

The part about still not sprouting my wings was fresh-ground salt in a tender wound. He'll cast me out, as his father cast him from Heaven, or worse, unmake me, if I disappoint him too badly.

"Luke?" Callie asks, and I realize I've gotten lost in the labyrinthine spiral of my family dynamics.

"Right. This way," I say and indicate the corridor in front of us. "No time like the present."

She gives me a skeptical look, but when I don't answer and start up the hall, she comes along. Porsoth's hooves click on the stone.

"Luke's Slytherin all the way, right?" I hear Callie ask Porsoth.

"Perhaps." Porsoth hedges. "Definitely *not* a Ravenclaw."

"I'm a Slytherpuff," I toss over my shoulder.

"That's not a thing," Callie says.

"Sure, it is," I counter.

Callie sniffs.

She asks Porsoth how he became a tutor and I'm familiar enough with the story to tune it out. I'm stuck on the fact that Mother has the World Watcher, something which has never before happened, and why is that again? It has to be that Father knew I'd need it. How I didn't connect the dots that he'd use it to spy on his only begotten (for now) son is another indication of how little I've been paying attention.

When I tune back in, Porsoth is eliding the true details of the fact being my tutor is a huge step down that he was given only out of admiration for the fearsome position he used to hold. Slowly, he went from all-day and all-night torture and mayhem to more and more time in the Keep's library followed by a discovery of prophetic scrolls some whispered that he planted himself so he could use them as an excuse to move into the Keep full-time to study them. I've never asked.

That Porsoth and Callie are fast friends shouldn't surprise me. In truth, it doesn't. I *am* surprised she seems to take promising her soul more in stride than her brother and best friend having become a secret couple.

A mystery I'll have plenty of time to fathom. Mother's abode isn't exactly next door.

"Is Lucifer always like that?" Callie asks.

"Rather," is Porsoth's diplomatic reply.

Sometimes he's far more awful, I add silently.

"What about . . ."

I can feel her eyes burning into the back of my head. "I'm right here," I say.

"Yes, him too, rather," Porsoth says. And then adds, "Sorry, Prince. I overstep."

"It's okay. Callie has this effect on people."

"Me? Look in the mirror."

We reach the end of the corridor and a legion of skull-pale, bat-winged, long-clawed demonic troops is marching toward us. That was fast. But when you can issue telepathic commands, there's no need for a delay. Father must have called them to report for duty before we left Earth. Along with keeping Rofocale back, it's confirmation that he's taking the threat of Armageddon seriously.

He has no faith in me.

"Stay close," I say, finding Callie's hand with mine to ensure she does. I keep her tucked into my right side, away from the demon soldiers, who reek of sulfur and ash. They leer at Callie as they pass by and I'm grateful there are no grotesque catcalls, only silent salivation.

Even the worst among leerers salute me as they continue to eyeball Callie like exactly what she is: a prized soul in a very bad place. To her credit, Callie keeps her expression neutral and waits patiently.

At last, the gauntlet passes and we start to walk again. An exit to Father's palace looms before us in moments, drawbridge already lowered. I see the guards there call a halt to the next batch of soldiers heading into the Keep. We get priority.

"What do you think?" I pause to ask, squinting back over my shoulder in the direction of the troops. Porsoth senses it's a question for him.

"Word is traveling. It always goes fast in Hell," Porsoth says. "They don't seem particularly excited about the end days. Very interested in her, which means word of her is also moving quickly."

I noted that too, and I don't care for it.

"I'm right here," Callie says. "You can use my name."

Chanting from the charred plains outside reaches us, the rhythmic clash of shields and swords clinking in a pre-battle symphony. Along with shrieking howls that would curdle any decent human's or angel's blood.

"That will be the Howling Demons," I inform Callie.

"They *do* sound excited," Porsoth says.

"Stick close to me as we go out," I tell her.

"Got it," she says, lifting our still-linked hands. "You don't need to keep saying it. Trust me, I'm not in a hurry to go traipsing around the underworld solo with half of a powerful religious artifact."

I lightly squeeze her hand in mine.

We hit the drawbridge constructed of yellowed bones, and the Howling Demons are an impressive sight to pair with the sound of their arrival. Bloodred armor molded like scales covers their entire bodies. They weave and chant and screech and manage to still look terrifying doing it instead of silly.

Callie's mouth has fallen open.

"Make that: if you leave me alone out here, I'll kill you," she says.

"We won't," Porsoth puts in. "I swear it to you."

She's gotten to him too. That was fast.

"Speaking of, we've got a decision to make." I raise my voice to be heard over the chanting troops. They're still a few dozen yards out. "We can't go instantly, so we'll have to trek. There's north and the Cocytus or east to the Phlegethon—"

"No, north is out," Porsoth says. "And east. Not fit for a living human of this caliber."

"The rivers are real?" Callie asks.

"Very. South is out too, no Acheron or Lethe," I say. "She doesn't like subterranean passages, so that leaves . . ."

"West and the Styx," Porsoth says. "Do you think she can make it across?"

I meet Callie's eyes. "How do you feel about dragons?"

She blinks, taken aback. But, "Love 'em," she says.

I bet she hopes we're joking.

Porsoth and I trade shrugs. We don't have much choice.

"The Styx it is," I say. "It's the closest route to Mother's anyway."

The Howling Demons get close enough to spot Callie and begin bowing and jeering.

"It's her, the girl bringing our damnation!" one calls.

"Good sport, human!"

"Torture you soon!"

Callie stands motionless for a moment, then lifts her hand and raises her middle finger.

The Howling Demons wail louder in delight and outrage and she doesn't so much as flinch as she lowers her hand and looks expectantly at me.

"Lead on to the Styx," she says.

I hesitate to think it, but I may be falling in love with her.

The plains around us are a smoking wreck, the pitiable cries of the damned languishing here a constant chorus. Callie's triumphant departure got stepped on by the endless willingness of the Howling to keep earning their name. I presume they entered the Keep, but maybe they're still out there chanting. We eventually outdistanced their raucous farewell.

"What did these people do? Is it like in Dante, all one type of sin to a place?" Callie asks.

She means the wailing, moaning souls that surround us. We're no longer holding hands, but she stays close to my side anyway. The other advantage of this route is the comparatively gentler scenery.

"Not necessarily. They've done different things," I say. "Dante was what you'd call an oversimplifier."

"And a bit of a pompous ass," Porsoth says. "We made him do some time as a donkey. He didn't enjoy it. He really had no reason to complain—we eventually turned him back."

"But these people," Callie returns to her question, "what did they do?"

I consider. There are detailed responses I could give for each and every one of them. The pale shade of a man who stole from a widow in medieval France. The woman who took her next-door neighbor's child and raised him as her own in '70s SoCal. And a host of far greater and lesser sins.

But the truth is . . . "They were human. That's the real answer."

Callie stares off into the moaning distance. "But that's not what they're being punished for."

"Isn't it?" I ask.

Porsoth has gone quiet, but he lets out something like a hoot. "If you'd been this thoughtful with your studies, who knows what you'd have accomplished by now?"

"Do they deserve it though?" Callie is stuck on this. "I need to believe they do."

I wish I could say yes, but I've lied to her enough.

"I don't know." I've never confronted this, but it's also true. Maybe it's even the real reason I haven't secured any souls. And now I'm about to take the one beside me, knowing it'll be luck and Father's caprice if I'm able to keep her from crying out in pain like the people on these suffering plains.

"It's a corrupt system," I say finally.

"I get that," she says. "But it has to be for the ultimate good, doesn't it? All of this?"

Callie, trying to find a way to make sense of Hell's existence. She should've been born here, not me.

"A corrupt system for a corrupt world." Porsoth sounds resigned. "I admit, I'm no longer sure which world makes more sense, that of humans or ours, the divine and infernal. It's why

I truly left my old life to educate our next generation. I needed something to hope for."

I'm rocked back on my heels. *I'm* Porsoth's hope for a better future? I don't know whether to laugh at him or myself or the futility of everything.

"What a disappointment I must be," is what I manage to say. Suddenly, I don't feel like laughing at all.

"My hope is still right here," Porsoth taps his wing across his chest.

I swallow hard over a lump in my throat that feels the size of a stone fist.

"What do I need to know about the Styx?" Callie asks, presumably picking up on the heaviness in the air. The subject change is well timed.

"Nothing we can tell you will prepare you," Porsoth says.

Callie frowns. "That's spectacularly unhelpful."

"He's being literal," I say. "It's not like the stories. To cross the Styx, it's not the same cost for the ferry every time. She will demand a toll and you'll have to pay it." I am worried about this part, but it's the least deadly option to travel to Lilith's within the time we have.

"That's just great. But I'm already in Hell, so why do I have to pay a toll anyway?"

"Because you're seeking to travel freely within it. At some point, everyone who enters must pay a toll of one kind or another."

"Got it." Callie accepts this. "Then tell me about Lilith. Your mother. Did you grow up with her?"

I've been waiting for this. I recall Callie's tidy home, packed with love and trinkets and photographs. How cozy it is. I want to sweep a hand out around us at the smoking rubble and remind her that this is where I grew up. Mother is Mother and I'm important to her as a chess piece with Father.

"Lilith is interesting," Porsoth says. "A human who became an immortal. The terror of those who cross her, but not without a human heart for those she loves."

"It's just that she keeps the human heart in a jar and shows it to them," I say.

Porsoth clucks, but doesn't argue.

"You didn't live with her?" Callie asks.

"Father sent me to stay with her when he was angry with me," I say. "I spent two years with her once when I was six."

"He must have visited?" Callie asks, surprised.

"When he was ready for me to return to the Keep, he sent a messenger." I pick up the new quality in her silence. I can't bear to look at her to confirm it. "Do not dare pity me, the prince of Hell."

Callie is quiet for a moment, then. "I wouldn't dream of it. Privileged punk."

I absorb it and snort a laugh. Porsoth laughs too, but I know none of us are amused by anything except how clever Callie has been to take the moment and remove its sting. Her soul sings to me like the beat of my own heart and I want it to be mine.

Something I've never felt before.

Maybe Father was right. I just needed the temptation of a truly evil act to realize my full potential. He'll be so proud.

"Not much farther now," I say. "Let's hope Styx is in a good mood."

"It happened once," Porsoth says thoughtfully. "In one of the years we got all those Roman soldiers in. She took a fancy to them."

Callie stops and gazes up at the blackening sky. "You're saying this Styx is a person who hasn't been in a good mood for three thousand years? And she gets to decide my toll?"

Porsoth and I nod.

"Just checking to make sure I had that right," Callie says and walks on.

"Hey." I stop her with the word. "You can do this."

She smiles and my breath vanishes. "You do know that in mythology the goddess named Styx was Nike's mother, don't you? Did you basically quote a Nike ad at me as an inside joke?"

"That's 'just do it,'" Porsoth says. When Callie gives him a look, he says, "We keep up with the times."

"My version is way better than a shoes slogan," I say. I had no idea about Styx's daughter Nike. "It has you in it."

Callie peers up at the sky again as if waiting for it to fall. She hefts her messenger bag with its precious cargo—I offered to carry it, but she said no. I didn't argue.

She takes another step and says, "I guess we'll see."

CHAPTER SEVENTEEN

CALLIE

There's a point at which the mind is confronted with so many unreal things that are undeniably real you just start to roll with it. This is my theory on why I'm still walking upright, putting one foot in front of the other on ash-coated ground while surrounded by damned souls, in the company of the prince of Hell and a scholarly, morally conflicted demonic owl-pig-humanoid I'm fast becoming buddies with. Why I can manage philosophical conversations about the reasons this twisted reality exists.

One thing I'm figuring out is that I'm not sure I believe any of this makes sense—and that doesn't matter.

It's real anyway. I have to deal with the prospect of spending eternity here. Of being one of these damned souls.

Mag—who I'm still mad at for falling for my brother and *not telling me*, but who I miss like a limb and wish was here so I could ask them what I'm doing, what I *should* do—is going to want to kill me. But they'll have to line up after my mother. That's only in the *best*-case scenario.

So.

One foot in front of the other, on toward the Styx and her mystery toll.

Even though I have no clue whether it'll be useful or not, I review everything I remember about the Styx. Originally the name of a Titan's daughter who also ruled the river, like I told Luke, with four kids including Nike. The Styx was the river that the Greek gods used to swear oaths on. Sometimes it was poison and sometimes it gave powers. It was the river Achilles got dipped in, except for the heel his mother held him by (and can you blame her for not thinking a vulnerable heel would get him? Just wear shoes). In stories, it's often the border between our world and the underworld. Which doesn't seem to be how it works, at least not now.

But it's the border to cross to where I *have* to go, apparently, because of MaHGA (Make Hell Great Again), Lucifer's new travel rule. In most myths, the ferryman is Charon and takes a coin that people leave on the tongues of the dead as payment for the crossing. If only.

The first sign of water is a rivulet black as an oil slick but without any of the rainbows in its gleam. Dull-as-death water. Then, there are more, puddles and streaks. Slowly, they grow into black streams that it's hard to avoid stepping in.

"Careful," Luke says, grabbing my arm when I almost blunder into a wide furrow filling with more water.

"How?" I ask, troubled.

Ahead, what moments before appeared as marsh is crisscrossed with streams rushing toward the shores of a tumbling, flowing broad body of dark water. I can't even be thankful the cries of the damned are quieter. That the smoke stinging my nostrils is fainter.

"Call a bridge to the bank, Prince," Porsoth says. "It will hold for you and we will follow."

"Yes, that'll work." Luke hesitates. "Porsoth . . ."

"I'll be right by her side," he responds.

I'm touched.

Luke looks at me. "You've got this. I mean it."

He's dreaming, but I nod. I like that he seems to believe in me.

He faces the river and extends his hand. The stream in front of him parts and the mud-gray earth rises up until a bridge made of bones extends forward all the way to the bank of the Styx. It hits me again: *I'm in Hell. With its hot prince.*

Luke steps onto the bridge and it holds. Porsoth extends his wing to me, and I grip it as gently as I can manage through my absolute terror of being swallowed by the black water. This is where the rolling with it kicks in.

Porsoth and I step with caution after Luke. As predicted, the bridge supports us.

I wish for Luke to walk faster, certain the bones will shatter under my feet at any moment. But that's not his style. He saunters along, only pausing to check for us over his shoulder once or twice. His leather jacket makes him seem like he's shooting some strange video for Hell's favorite band.

The bridge widens as we near the banks, so we can stand beside one another. The churning black water is entirely opaque this close up, nearly viscous. The sound of its flow is like the devil's laughter. Otherwise, there's silence.

Nothing happens.

"Mother Styx," Luke says, at last, and there's a respectful solemnity to it, "I have one who requires passage."

The water burbles and I keep watching, expecting it to part

like the earth did before, for the Styx to rise up in some form or another. But she comes from above.

The shadow of wings widens as the river falls over us. I gape as the gleaming black-scaled dragon alights on the tumble of river water as if it's solid rock. Her body and wings are sleek, a pterosaur stretched to Godzilla size. She stares down at us, her vaguely reptilian, vaguely human face giving no hint of her reaction to our arrival.

They weren't exaggerating about the dragon thing. My throat dries up. I struggle to calm my breath.

This is happening.

Deal. With. It. Callie.

"Porsoth the merciless," the giant reptile says, her voice like a scrape to my eardrums, "who has lowered you this way?"

Porsoth's head ticks down with what must be shame.

"It can't have been this human," Styx continues. "Tell me and I shall slay them, for I can imagine no greater tragedy."

I shouldn't push my luck, but I open my mouth just as Luke catches my eye and shakes his head.

"Leave him be," Luke says. "He's a loyal servant of the king."

"The king," Styx spits. The water bubbles and rolls on either side of her, but stays steady under her talons. "Princeling, never forget that your father was a twinkle in the eye above when I was old and tired. Is it he who has done this?"

"Be that as it may," Luke says, "we stand in his kingdom and we seek passage to my mother's house."

"Ah." Styx uncoils her neck and dips it lower to examine me.

I don't shrink away, but I want to. Oh, I want to. I swallow, on the off chance I have to say something.

Styx goes on. "But you do not need my passage, the human does."

"Yes." Luke's answer is clipped. "What's to be the toll?"

There's a rumble from deep in the dragon's throat that I take to be a sign of her consideration.

"I hear she's a clever one. She could ask me a query and if I cannot answer, then she may have safe passage across my river."

"Probably the best we'll get," Luke says to me, voice low.

The offer seems too good to be true. *This* is something I can do. Trivia! I half-expected she'd ask for the spearhead.

I search my mind for a good question.

"Do you accept?" Styx growls at me.

"Yes," I say quickly.

She sits back onto the churning water. "Then, ask."

Usually I can't stop my brain from throwing up weird, random facts. Now, when I most need the ocean of them, they dry up to a single drop. I try to come up with something other than my first idea. Anything.

But nothing else comes.

"I said ask." Styx's patience is wearing thin.

"Callie, go on," Luke says.

Porsoth must sense what's happening because he says to Luke, "Give her a moment."

"No moments. Ask," Styx insists.

I still have this lone question in my head. It's not a great one, but why would the goddess Styx know the answer? I don't have a choice. I have to go with it.

I clasp my hands in front of me and look straight at her and ask, "What is the episode of *Star Trek* where Kirk and Uhura kiss?"

Luke gapes at me. Porsoth sighs heavily.

The dragon is silent and when she opens her mouth steam

hisses out and her long sharp teeth show and I recognize that she's grinning.

"'Plato's Children.'" Her long reptilian head shakes, her face a frown. "I expected more."

"Me too," Luke says and that hurts.

I failed. I didn't win passage. I lost a *trivia competition* with an old one.

"Let me try again," I say and even I hear the pleading note. "Give me another toll."

"Callie, you don't know what you're saying." Porsoth's words are a warning.

I'm fully aware this is probably not smart. "I don't have the option of failure. We have to get to Lilith's."

Luke takes a step closer to me. "We need to get out of here," he says.

"No, I need another toll," I say to Styx.

Styx stretches her long neck again and gazes up at the sky. "Oh, you humans with your ceaseless scheming."

"Callie," Luke says, "let's go."

The dragon lowers her head. "And yet a favor to the prince might be to my benefit. I'd like to see how this all turns out, so . . . I'll let you pass for what's in your bag."

I clutch it. "You can't have the spear. That would make this whole thing pointless."

"Not the spear," she says with a hiss. "The *grimoire*."

I should say yes. Why do I need it? I don't. But something inside me balks. Hard.

"What about another round of trivia?" I try.

"The grimoire," she repeats.

"What's the problem?" Luke asks, forehead crumpled in a frown. I know he's right.

"I can't explain it." I shrug helplessly. "I don't want to give it up."

"We all have to do things we don't want to do sometimes," Porsoth says. "Sometimes for thousands of years."

"Thousands of years," Luke repeats. "That's it." He lifts his hand. "How about if Callie gives you the grimoire—"

"No!" I don't know why I protest that way. But I couldn't stop if I wanted to.

Luke continues. "How about if Callie gives you the grimoire at the end of her mortal life span?"

After he's said it, Luke checks in with me. "Okay? You're not going to need it in the afterlife."

The something that balked inside me seems to find this acceptable. "Oh. Okay."

"Very clever," Porsoth says with approval. "That hadn't occurred to me."

Luke ignores him and turns back to Styx. "Do we have a deal?"

"Do we have a deal, do we . . ." Styx plays coy. I expect her to start swimming in the river, doing some dragon backstroke, making us wait for an answer.

"Do we?" Luke says.

Styx's pointy chin inclines. "Only for you. What's a mortal life span to me? A nap."

"So we get to pass?" I ask. And under my breath, "That was both better and worse than I expected."

Luke waits. "We're not across yet."

"You may pass." Having made the declaration, Styx sweeps one long wing out over the water, holding it level, stretching from one bank to the other. Her wing is our passage across.

She could move it at any moment and get the grimoire with no waiting.

"No," I say. "It's a trick. She'll drop me in."

The wing snaps tight, but stays extended.

"Styx has granted us passage," Luke says and offers his arm. "She won't revoke it."

I hesitate, because Luke does also get my soul if we don't make it. But the world ends and so he'll still be in trouble with his dad. Foolish though it probably is, I'm not worried that he's betraying me.

At least, not at this very moment.

"Trust me," Luke says.

"I don't trust her."

Luke considers and smiles at me. "That must mean you trust me."

Crap. "I didn't say that."

"Let's go before her mood changes," Porsoth says.

I hook my arm through Luke's like we're on some silly promenade and not about to cross a deadly poison river on the wing of the cranky goddess who rules it. Across the leathery dragon wing we go, step by step, steady as if we're on solid ground, on toward Lilith's house.

"I'll be waiting here for you and your pretty book, human," are Styx's last rough, whispered words. They drift to me on the stale air.

It's not as close as I thought it would be. I can barely keep my eyes open.

That's despite being surrounded by a black forest, dead trees with grabbing branches, and more of those hedges with long, flesh-seeking thorns. The place on my arm where I got stuck by one earlier aches as if it's calling out to this new batch.

"She needs to rest."

Porsoth sounds fussy. I can't help liking him.

"I know," Luke says and gives me a concerned once-over. "She's running on twenty minutes of sleep."

And I can't help liking Luke *way* too much.

I don't bother to point out I'm right here and they could talk *to* me. Saying the words would take too much effort. The idea of curling up for a nap on the charred ground is almost tempting. Thorns or no thorns.

"It's not much farther," Luke says. "We can afford another little rest for you at Mother's."

I try to nod, but suspect I'm only looking at him. I've never been one to skip a night of sleep, because if I do I'm useless for days afterward. But Mag has always been able to manage an all-night movie or study fest without a yawn.

I don't want to be angry at Mag anymore. I don't want them to be angry at me either.

I may cry.

But that seems like a lot of effort at the moment too. Still, my lower lip trembles and my eyes start to burn.

Luke stares at me with a concerned squint. Porsoth pushes aside a branch, then stops. "What is it, Prince?"

"Apologies," Luke says to me.

Before I can ask for what, he's scooping me up in his arms. My first thought is that I fit there, nearly perfectly. I could protest, but why? I curl in toward his chest, keeping my arms where they aren't in danger of thorns.

As Luke stalks forward, the last thing I see before I fall asleep is Porsoth, blinking those big owl eyes at me cradled against Luke's chest.

I dream in shadows. It's like zappity land, but more feverish. Screams and wails. Images of thorns sinking deep into my skin. Styx baring her teeth. Solomon Elerion baring his.

Those guardians dressed in white, laughing, always laughing. Lucifer laughing too.

When I come to, the gritty scent of ash assaulting my nose, I don't immediately signal that I'm awake.

"You can't walk in there carrying her, you know," Porsoth is saying. "Your mother is territorial. And unpredictable. She might torture the girl."

"More likely, she'll torture me. I just wanted Callie to get a chance to sleep before . . . everything."

Porsoth doesn't respond.

Luke speaks again, quietly. "I didn't want her soul."

"You can't lie to me. I've known you too long. I see how you look at her."

"Fair enough. I do want it." Luke sighs. "But I wish I didn't."

"Your father used to say the same thing about Lilith."

"I guess I *am* like him," Luke says.

I can't stand that he'd think that for a moment, even though he's going to take my soul. "Good . . . evening?" I say with a stagey yawn and wriggle enough that Luke puts me down. We're surrounded by a charred wood, trees like skeletons and ash everywhere.

Luke studies me. His blue eyes are too perceptive. "Sleep well?"

I give no indication I've overheard anything they said. "I think so. Where are we?"

"Close. I was just about to wake you up," he says.

I feel like he wants to say more, but he doesn't.

"We're practically on her doorstep," Porsoth says.

I wish desperately for a toothbrush, and there's really no choice about the other necessity I have to do. I look around panicked, because it's not like there's a safe spot. I toe the ashy ground with my now-filthy sneakers. At least I'm not on my period. "I need to pee."

"Oh."

"I guess demons don't have to?" I say. Then I realize that I'm way too close to inquiring about the mechanics of demon bodies. "Never mind. I'll hold it."

"We love all things bodily," Porsoth says. "Especially waste."

"Speak for yourself," Luke says.

My ears are burning.

He goes on, wearing a sexy little half-smile. "The sad thing is, you're probably wishing he meant that in the dirty way right now, aren't you?"

"Kind of," I admit. "Somehow that's less gross. Which."

"I'll keep watch for you," Luke says. He hesitates and reaches into his leather jacket and pulls out a monogrammed handkerchief with a little flame and the initials L.A.M. on it, then hands it to me.

"No need to return it," he says.

A woman with an artful tangle of black hair, a wild grin, and cold, kohl-lined eyes emerges from the forest. "How cozy," she says. "But I'll be happy to make you all comfortable. My son, I can guess why you're here, but I'm way more interested in the company you're keeping."

She walks straight to me, and takes my arm. "I'm Lilith," she says. "And you must be Callie. You're in danger of making a huge mistake."

I paste on a smile, dream of peeing, and stuff Luke's handkerchief in my pocket. I make a mental note to ask who does Hell's monogramming later.

"What mistake is that?" I ask.

"Why," Lilith's grin widens, "trusting my son."

"But I don't."

I hear a soft intake of breath and know it's from Luke.

Lilith makes a *tsk* sound, dismissing me. "Men will disappoint you every time. But it's not too late. Come with me. We'll talk . . ."

I can't imagine Luke's face right now. I also can't bring myself to look at him. I have to do what his mom asks.

I wonder if she senses that I can close my eyes and still imagine his arms cradled around me. The truth is, I felt safe there. I think I was.

But do I trust him? With anything besides my soul? With my *heart*?

I'm not *that* foolish.

Or that brave.

CHAPTER EIGHTEEN

LUKE

Mother pauses her educational monologue about the deficits of men in general and me in particular when we reach her overgrown house, the cottage frame completely hidden by wild black vines with small dark blooms. This is one of the few spots in Hell where things grow.

Lilith herds Callie through the open door. Once inside, we're crowded into the common room stuffed full of herbs and random objects amassed over the centuries. Mother is a bit of a pack rat.

I see Callie hesitate, wanting to examine everything, starting with the stuffed alligator extended from the ceiling. But she's hustled into the nearest bath chamber.

"I've set out everything you need, my dear girl," Lilith says, more warmly than I will ever merit. "I watched your approach."

Mother shuts the door to the bathing room before Callie gets in a word. She has yet to greet Porsoth.

She watched me carrying Callie. I've no doubt when she

turns to catch my eye. My mother's smile is eager. She doesn't get many visitors out here, and she's long since ceased being entertained by expeditions onto Earth. I asked her once if she ever got lonely and she laughed and said, "How can I be lonely when I have the best of company at all times?"

Mother and I have some personality traits in common. We both wear our confidence like armor, confident in the magnetism of our charisma. I'm not nearly as judgmental as she is, though.

"Your father paid me a visit. He was in rare form," she says. "Did he meet her?"

"I imagine he told you all about the deadline he gave me when he loaned you the World Watcher. Where is it, by the way? And why did you ask for it?"

Mother extends a hand and tweaks my chin. "Not yet. Tell me what you mean for that girl." She pauses. "I like her. You should leave her be."

"We're a little past that."

Mother's cool eyes do what she's best at: judging me. She finds me lacking too, but in a different way than Father. All she sees when she looks at me is him, and her own mistakes in that particular arena. He lured her here with the promise of immortality, a family, power. Bonus that her creator would not be a fan of the address. And here she is, her son (when she'd prefer a daughter) raised half a kingdom away by her enemy/paramour, who she must still attend state occasions beside, her domain this cottage queendom with a smaller border than she wants.

"I didn't think you'd turn out to be so much like him," she says.

I shrug as if it doesn't bother me. He'd disagree; I don't get to. Given how many stings I've suffered lately I tell myself that I barely feel this one.

I get back to the point. "We need to use the device without further delay."

"He is correct," Porsoth puts in. Then adds, "And you could be kinder to him."

Mother rolls her eyes in cartoonish fashion. "Did I ask for your advice? Men are used to the entire world being kind to them. Anything else is a corrective."

"Be that as it may," Porsoth says.

The bath chamber door opens and Callie emerges. She's cleaned up a little more and tidied her hair, but her shoes are still gray with ash and her T-shirt smudged with a long day and evening. She looks wonderful.

And concerned.

"Where's this magic spyglass?" she asks.

"Spy-globe," Mother and I say at the same time.

Mother's lips quirk on one side with amusement. I do think she loves me, somewhere, way down in the darkest deeps inside her.

"I'll show you when I'm ready," she says. "Food?"

Callie looks at me like she's ready to murder my mother. I cough to hide a laugh. "Sure, we could eat," I say.

When Callie stalks over to me with her murder-eyes, I say as softly as I can, "Trust me, we're not leaving without food."

"Right," Callie says with a frown. "She's a mom. I am starving."

"Me too."

Callie's frown deepens. "Is it safe for me to eat afterlife food?"

What a curious question. "Why wouldn't it be?"

"You know, in the old stories about Faeryland and other realms, sometimes if you eat the food, then you have to stay there."

"Luke rather skipped those tales," Porsoth says.

Mother appears close beside us. "Do I look like a faery?"

Why I assumed these two busybodies would give us a second's privacy, I don't know.

"Don't answer that." I put my hand on Callie's arm. "I didn't skip all the reading. No pomegranate, okay? She's not staying . . ." *Yet.* I don't add the *yet*, but I can hear its echo.

Callie's muscles stiffen slightly under my fingers. She hears it too.

"I know your father told you to get her soul." Mother glances between us and what she sees must tell her everything. She puts a hand dramatically to her heart. "No. You wouldn't. No son of mine would do such a thing . . ."

"She volunteered it." Porsoth uses his full demonic voice, something I've only heard once or twice. There's a sonic boom quality to it. We all tremble like leaves in its wake.

Mother recovers first and prepares to argue. "But—"

Callie holds up a hand to stop her. "It's true. I'm on a mission. I needed Luke's help, and now I have it."

Mother shakes her head. "I have failed. And I do like her."

So do I. I want to say the words, flirty and light to disperse the darkness in the horrified way my mother is staring at me. But I doubt that's a magic trick I'm capable of pulling off.

"Some people would be glad to hear their son won't be ended inside twenty-four hours," I say instead.

"Not everything is about you." Mother rakes a hand down my cheek, then Callie's, almost tender, and crosses the jam-packed room to a small kitchen. There's a soup pot on, and when she removes the lid the entire house fills with a rich, spicy, delicious smell.

"Porsoth, if you're done showing off, set out the bowls." She gestures to the open-faced cabinets above the counter.

Porsoth says nothing, and I wonder if he regrets speaking as he did to her. I liked it. It reminds me that his legend is based on fact.

"He did nothing wrong," Callie says with a wink to Porsoth. Before anyone can stop her, she's plucking down the bowls.

Callie plainly agrees with me that it's nice to see Porsoth asserting himself.

Mother ladles soup into the first of the bowls. "He has tormented more souls than you've met in your life, or will," she says to Callie. "Do not sleep in the room with a wolf just because he is old and tired."

"Is it okay if I eat in the room with one?" Callie asks. "I promise I'm as hungry as the wolf."

I start singing the chorus for "Hungry Like the Wolf," that old '80s song, and when Callie laughs in surprise I soak it in.

Mother notices me noticing Callie.

But, "Simon Le Bon, now there's someone who owes me a visit," is all Mother says.

Porsoth sets the soup in front of me, and I tuck in like a good son. At this point, I only hope we get out of this cottage before my deadline passes. I'd at least like to do something nice for Callie—like help her save the world—before I betray her forever for my own ill-gotten gain.

Now I know just how rotten I am for agreeing to take her

soul, based on Mother's reaction. I have that to thank her for, I guess.

I don't bother.

"Mother, the World Watcher. *Please*."

She hesitates, but rises from the table. "I suppose you must. You'll visit me again?" The question is for Callie, not me.

Callie nods, but doesn't commit out loud. Good thinking. My mother's house might bring her a measure of freedom in the future. But it will come at a cost.

"Why did you borrow it?" I ask Mother.

"He told me to," she said. "I agreed, because I wanted to see you, son."

I bask in the crumb, not quite able to speak. This confirms my thinking that Father knew far more than I assumed about my activities, or lack thereof.

"Can we see it?" Callie asks, and lays a gentle hand on my arm. Comforting me.

I am a terrible person for accepting it.

"Outside," Mother says, intent on Callie's hand.

Then she leads us through the cramped common room and another door to her bed chamber. I carefully do not look around once I take in the giant bed with carved details painted black with sheets to match. I've never been in this room before. I do not want to think about what's gone on in here. No, thank you.

A wide set of doors is open to her back garden, inset with stones. Here, more things bloom. Strange blooms, stranger plants. They're alive, truly alive. They wave as if to greet my mother and she lifts a hand, soothing.

The World Watcher sits among this odd tableau, almost as if the garden was designed to create a space for it. Or maybe the Watcher is one of those things that makes every space seemed designed to house it.

Callie gapes. The globe stands two storeys tall with a million other colors shining beneath a golden sheen. It's much larger than all of us, and a set of spiral steps curls around it to allow the viewer to climb up to any vantage point and spin it to view the desired place.

"Show me what to do," Callie says.

I slide her hand into mine and she allows it without a hint of protest. I feel more than I have before. More than a heart beating in my chest, more than the air in my lungs. So much more that I don't want to examine it. We change that which we observe—isn't that something I'm supposed to have read about?

"Solomon Elerion," I say, "you black-souled heathen, here we come."

Mother and Porsoth watch, silent for once, as I lead Callie to the stairs and up and up around them. I navigate by feeling. I send out the question *where where where* as we continue up the steps, picturing Solomon, and finally a signal faint but discernible to my gut tells me when to *stop*.

We're past the middle point of the globe. I have to drop Callie's fingers to pinpoint the spot and I feel the loss.

I place my hands flat against the curving slope of the globe and I give it a turn.

As places and faces rush past in a mad whirl on the spinning globe, Callie gapes and says, "Oh my go—"

"Not here," I remind her, barely in time to prevent whatever saying that word here would've caused.

"Goodness," she finishes on a breath, correcting course.

I can understand why she forgot herself and why she thought of the Above. The globe is magnificent because it's the world. It shows the brutal beauty of Earth. Every living thing in war and in peace, in sickness and in health, in flesh and in bone. It's a touch overwhelming to focus on. I do it anyway, because it's the only way to locate our quarry.

I place my hands back on the surface to stop its movement at the moment that feels *right* and squint beneath the glossy surface layer.

"There," I say. "There they are."

Callie cranes her neck to confirm.

Solomon is in a circle of his followers, another pentagram drawn beneath him. He's stalking back and forth across it, clearly upset and in the middle of a tirade.

"Looks like he's figured out it doesn't work," I say.

"Yup." There's a note of satisfaction in Callie's tone. "Are they back at the house?"

"I don't think so—it would probably reject them now that Michael's been there."

She squints harder and then gasps. "Widen the angle."

"What is it?"

"Please," Callie says roughly.

I mentally command the globe to do as she says, giving us a wider view of the room.

The space has every appearance of an occult lair. I'm about to use my powers to find out where it is, but Callie speaks first, strangled. "I know where they are."

She doesn't sound like herself.

"Where?" I gaze at Callie, concerned.

Callie peers back at the globe, and then sinks to sit on the step. "They're at the Great Escape."

I look harder. I see what she sees. Along one wall of that spooky room—which I now see has a flair of arrangement and design that is more perfect than a real occult lair would be, like the theme park version—stand her brother, Jared, and best friend, Mag. Both of them have their hands bound behind them.

I state the obvious. "They have your family."

Callie climbs to her feet. "We have to get back there. Now."

PART THREE

APOCALYPSE RIGHT NOW

"I could tell you my adventures—beginning from this morning," said Alice a little timidly; "but it's no use going back to yesterday, because I was a different person then."

ALICE'S ADVENTURES IN WONDERLAND, LEWIS CARROLL

"Better to reign in Hell, than serve in Heaven."

PARADISE LOST, JOHN MILTON

CHAPTER NINETEEN

CALLIE

While we were lingering around Lilith's kitchen table, eating soup and listening to her theories about mankind, Solomon Elerion got Jared and Mag. Mag, whose last words with me were . . . not good. Whose only wish was never to be in the cult's grasp again.

I have to save them both, and that feels somehow harder and more urgent than saving the world. Also, my mother truly is going to want to murder me.

"Zappity us out of here," I tell Luke.

His expression reminds me.

"You can't." I want to jump off the edge of this staircase next to this miracle globe and fly, because there's no time to lose. But apparently making good time is not an option.

"I can't," Luke says. "He'll know. It'll make things worse."

I let a dry laugh escape. "How can things be any worse?"

But I know. The people I love are the tip of a very large iceberg. All those demon troops weren't traveling to the Gray Keep for their health. This could go very wrong.

Maybe I'm not such a good person. Because the only thing on my mind is getting to the Great Escape and helping *my* people, two of the humans I love most.

I start walking down, because every step is taking me somewhere and I have to pray it's closer to home.

Lilith is waiting for us at the bottom of the stairs. The smirk on her lips is an unwelcome sight. "Now you're beginning to understand what being a pawn in the games of Heaven and Hell truly means. You will never be the center, Callie. The story will always be about the men. You'll only be a casualty."

She could be right. But I can't accept it. "They won't be. How do I get back there? To them?"

"Let us hide you," she says. "It's all starting. It's too late."

"I still have half the spear, so it is definitely not too late." *Please, let me be right.*

"Even so . . ." Lilith shrugs.

I turn to Luke, helpless and without time for Lilith's negging. I know this is bad. I don't need her rubbing it in.

"Mother," he says and spreads out his hands. "Callie's not like us. She's not going to run away. She's going to run into danger. And I'm going with her. Now, is there a shorter way to get there or not?"

"You know there is," Lilith says, pouty.

"I do?" Luke asks, making clear he doesn't.

Porsoth finally speaks. "This was in your assigned reading three years ago."

"Humor me," Luke says.

"Please?" I ask.

Porsoth bobs his head. "Lilith's house is specifically located in a territory that borders the entire human world. You can go anywhere there from here."

Finally something goes our way. Only . . .

I pound back up the stairs to the spot we'd occupied. Luke's right behind me. Solomon Elerion and Jared and Mag are still right there, where they were before. Not for much longer.

They're still in the Chamber of Black Magic, but they're being shuffled out the door. Solomon is ordering them taken somewhere.

"Follow them," I say. "We need to see where they go."

Luke touches the globe and it tracks their movements. We catch a glimpse of guards posted at the front of the shop—armed—as the rest of Solomon and his grim band march my best friend and my brother up the back stairs and to the control room.

"'No one will get to them up here,'" Luke says, and I realize he's repeating what Solomon is saying that I can't hear. For me, it's like watching a silent movie.

Luke turns to me. "Is he right? How do we reach them?"

A terrible, perfect idea occurs to me. "Come on." I drag him down the steps with me and we stop in front of Lilith and Porsoth. "You said we can go anywhere from here, right? How specific? How targeted?" I ask.

"What do you mean?" she returns with a frown. A vine curls around her arm, as if the garden is petting her.

"Are we talking a block or a building? The bathroom or some random place inside? How specific can it be?"

"Anywhere you can visualize."

Ha. This is funny in the not-funny way. "Great. Because I'm going to visualize the most awful place I know, a place I've never actually been, and you're going to send us there."

Lilith barely reacts. "If that's what you want."

My heart pounds in my chest so hard I can barely keep

standing here. The idea of where we're going makes my knees want to give out, me to give in.

Mag. Jared.

Hang on, I'm coming.

"Callie?" Luke asks.

"It is," I tell her.

She reaches out a hand, one to me, the other to Luke. He takes it without hesitation. He doesn't even ask what my idea is first.

Porsoth coughs and raises a wing. "If I may, I'd like to go too."

I imagine where we're headed. "There won't be room." When Porsoth opens his beak to object, I say, "But you could wait outside, be our backup. Can you manage that?" I ask Lilith.

She shrugs. "Of course."

Frantically, I inventory the contents of my bag. I have to keep the spearhead, obviously, but there's my book. I don't want the grimoire anywhere near Solomon Elerion again. I swallow and pull it out and extend it to Porsoth. "Would you be able to look after this for me while we"—I search for the right word and find it, and my heart beats even harder—"fight?"

"It would be my honor," Porsoth says.

I pass it to him and he disappears it into what I presume is a magic pocket in that scholar's robe he wears.

"You'll wait across the road from the Great Escape," I tell him.

"And us? Where will we be?" Luke asks, frowning at me, still concerned.

"You'll be right next to me, keeping me from hyperventilating. Hopefully."

I reach for Lilith's other hand and then I imagine the space

I mean for us to go to. Small and dark and secret, filled with stairs and nothing much else.

With a murmured word and a breath, she sends us there.

Under the Chamber of Black Magic.

The exit I designed from my own nightmares.

Jared. Mag. I repeat the names like a charm to protect me.

The secret passageway is dark except for tiny pinprick lights to reveal the stairs on either side of us. One set goes up into the outer hallway, the other up into the chamber.

I struggle to breathe. This is so much worse than the chapel in Portugal. Floyd Collins flits through my mind, but there's plenty of other famous dead people who shared my weird fear or one of its variations.

"Callie, you okay?" Luke whispers.

"Give me a sec," I choke out.

Fairy-tale writer Hans Christian Andersen was so afraid he'd be buried alive that he liked to leave notes around when he slept saying things like, "I only appear to be dead." He was also deathly afraid of pork—I wonder, with a hysterical impulse to laugh, what he'd think of Porsoth. The urge to laugh passes.

My heart feels like it wants to stop. The tight space presses in. I can sense the building above us, ready to collapse.

Get it together, Callie.

Jared. Mag.

Luke puts a hand on my arm. "Steady there."

"Trying," I say, keeping my voice down.

"Can I ask something?" Luke says.

He's attempting to be helpful. Maybe he will. "Go."

"I thought you were really upset at Mag and your brother."

"Yes?"

"But you immediately flew into action to save them . . ."

That's not a question, but it is an easy response. "It doesn't matter if I'm upset at them or about them—they're my people. I'd do anything for them. To keep them safe."

"So you're not still mad?"

"No, I'm curious and it still hurts, that they kept it from me." I pause and my heart thumps as I imagine the building collapsing on top of us. "But the truth is, I know I could've been better. Mag said they planned to tell me this weekend." My voice sounds thin. "Can I ask you a question?"

"Shoot," Luke says.

"Tell me more about the not-having-wings thing. Why is it a big deal?"

Luke hesitates. Guess I chose the sorest of sore spots. But then he answers.

"You may have gathered I'm something of a massive screw-up where things infernal are concerned."

He's attempting to keep his voice light, but I hear the pain beneath it. When did I get to know him well enough for that?

"Debatable," I say to be kind. It's what I'd want someone to say to me.

"Thanks, I think." He pauses then goes on. "Wings are a birthright of mine. Most demons and angels grow them within the first few years of taking breath. It's part of our nature. When you realize what you are, you get wings. So."

"So, you haven't figured it all out yet?" I squint in the dark and wish I could see his gorgeous face. "So what?"

"Or I'm too broken or weak to accept it. Maybe the truth is that I'm a complete failure." He breathes out. "Feel better? That's what Porsoth calls a Patsy Cline moment."

I take the bait. "A Patsy Cline moment?"

"Famous country singer."

"Walking encyclopedia of random facts here. I'm aware."

"Right. Well, all her biggest songs are so sad—'Crazy,' 'I Fall to Pieces,' or my favorite, 'Walking After Midnight,' in which a woman is literally depressed and walking by the roadside at midnight. And she's done it more than once."

I half laugh despite myself. I've almost forgotten the building looming over top of us. Almost. "What's the moment part?"

"When you realize no matter how bad you've got it, Patsy Cline had it worse." He nudges me with his shoulder. "I'm your wingless Patsy Cline in this scenario."

In this darkness, something small glows inside of me. Enough to light the way forward. "I wish we had time for me to kiss you again."

"Maybe we do," he says.

"Later. If we make it through this. Let's get out of here first."

He reaches up, slides a hand over my cheek and touches my lips with his fingers. I nearly change my mind. My entire body stretches toward that sensation.

"It's a promise." He sighs, drops his hand, and apologetically asks, "Do you have a plan? For right now?"

"Take our chances by sneaking out into the Chamber of Black Magic and then hope we have time to make it to upstairs before anyone sees us on camera?"

"All right, I'll go first. Which way?"

I feel around for his hand and then point to the right. "Those stairs. The hatch should push open from in here. The coffin that blocks it was still locked to the wall when we looked."

He goes to take back his hand, but I hang on. "Do you mind?"

"Not even a little." He drops his arm so he's holding my

hand behind him and we inch forward and then upward. With each step, I repeat my mantra—Jared, Mag, Mag, Jared—to keep from curling into a ball.

Jared. Mag.

I'm coming, hang on.

"Are you ready?" Luke quietly asks when we can't go any farther.

No.

Yes.

Ready to be out of this place. At least if whatever's on the other side makes me scream, it won't be irrational.

"Do it."

Luke releases my hand and I don't protest this time. He needs both of his to press up the hatch. The hinge is too new to creak, even if we did distress the floor on the other side to look like old stone.

The light in the chamber is dim, so I don't even squint as he slowly presses the hatch up. He holds where he is and I understand he wants me to climb out first. I do.

There's no one in here now, and I eye the stand where my book—the bargain real grimoire that started this mess—would usually be. Luke slides out of the exit behind me and replaces the hatch.

I take a breath and we face each other. "Good plan," he says. "What next?"

"That part is a little more fly by the seat of our pants. We have to go out there."

He glances around us. "You should take something from in here to defend yourself."

"I've got you," I say, attempting a joke.

"Just in case," he says, taking it seriously.

I cast a quick gaze around and reject things too clunky or heavy and settle on a long brass candlestick. The idea of hitting someone with it is so foreign I have trouble visualizing it, but it does make me feel better. I think it came from the same estate sale as the grimoire.

Luke and I cross to the door customers use to enter the room. We're taking all the paths that should be easy, the reset paths. Escape rooms are only hard to escape if you enter them from the right direction.

Or they should be.

For all I know we've already been seen on camera.

I glance up into the corner and see words appear on the screen: They r up front

A clue. Mag and Jared just gave me a clue. Or it's a trap?

I point up at the corner and Luke takes the words in too. Then I go to the door and push it open.

And *crap*, there are two unmasked Order of Elerion members hanging out in the fake graveyard vestibule, having a low, heated conversation.

Not so heated they don't immediately notice us though.

We stare at each other. They're about to scream for help, I know it. I consider about-facing back through the door, but if the rest *are* up front then we'd be trapped in the underground exit. No, thanks.

The robed creep in front advances and I heft my candlestick, but Luke steps in my path and I abort my swing just in time. He lifts his hands like he did with Jared and Mag, and the cult members fold to the ground in sleep as before. We don't bother to give them a soft landing.

They thud when they hit the floor.

I whirl to check the corner cam: Hurry

"Can you do that to all of them?" I ask Luke.

"Maybe? But I'm guessing Solomon will be protected by something."

Still, it's encouraging. I grab Luke's arm with my free one and tug him toward the outer door that opens into the main hallway. This is the point at which we'll be most exposed. They can easily block us in.

On the other hand, my people are at the end of it. We need to make it that far and then . . .

I'll figure out something.

"Callie?" Luke asks.

He gestures at the corner screen, which still has the same message, now with an exclamation point: Hurry!

Right.

I turn ye olde–fashioned knob and press the door to the hallway open, hearing how loud the creak is. No one comes.

They probably think we're the two prone bodies behind us, if they hear the sound at all. There's another argument going on up front and it includes the unwelcome timbre of Solomon Elerion's voice. He's talking about the spear.

I make myself not listen. If he says something about Mag or Jared, like that he's hurt either of them, I'll lose it.

I clutch my bag tight to my side with my free hand and grip the candlestick with the other as I dart into the hallway and toward the stairs to the control room. Luke's behind me, barely detectable, his footsteps quiet compared to mine. I'm doing my best, but stealth is not my forte.

"Boss, hey," I hear behind us. "Boss! They're here!"

In a blink, we're surrounded by a fog thick as gauzy cotton. Fear comes with it.

"It's mine," Luke says.

"Good thinking." I pull him forward, navigating from memory. We make it to the steps and pound up them and if we hadn't been given away already then Bosch's howl from inside the office door would have.

I bang on it. "It's me, open up."

"They were bound," Luke says. "In the vision."

"How were they messaging us then?"

"I don't know."

He waves his hand, and the fog around us forms into one of those magic keys. The wispy teeth slither into the lock and the door releases with a click. We lunge through and Bosch climbs onto me, all paws and snoot and licks.

The sound of our pursuers gets closer. Luke shuts and re-locks the door. I find a chair and prop it under the knob for extra security.

Only then do we stop and take a pause. I wanted to see Mag and Jared so badly, but this is going to be complicated. I shouldn't have thrown a fit about their relationship.

When I turn, I find Mag and Jared glued to each other's sides, hands bound behind them and standing in front of the computer console. The two have clearly been working together to do the messages. Jared must have guided Mag as they touch-typed backward. Impressive.

Seeing them is such a relief—Jared, Mag, *and* Bosch—that I nearly lose my breath.

Mag stares back at me defiantly, still angry at me. They have every right to be.

"We need everyone free," Luke interrupts. "We can't stay here indefinitely."

Bosch has moved on from me and is dancing joyfully around Luke's legs.

I head toward Mag and Jared and my brother says, "Untie Mag first."

"Why not both of you at the same time?" Luke asks.

Luke shifts toward my brother, lifting a brow in question. Jared nods, giving him the wariest look in his brother tool kit.

"Oh, right," Jared says. "Fine."

After tugging uselessly at Mag's restraints and then finally rummaging around in the desk to find some scissors, I saw at the thick rope.

Someone pounds on the door, but it holds.

"Aren't you going to say anything to me?" I ask Mag.

"Like what?" they say.

I take a shaky breath. I rushed back here to save these two. Who are acting like I've committed a crime.

"Like that you accept my apology for being so judgmental before and freaking out. I was wrong. I'm sorry I overreacted."

The ropes come free at that moment and Mag shakes out their arms for a second before flinging them around me.

We don't have time for a long hug, but it's an important one. "I really am sorry," I say.

"Me too," Mag says.

"Ahem," Jared says. Luke's almost done with his bonds.

I pull back. "Sorry I was a jerk to you too. You're my brother and I love you. But you better not screw this up."

"I'm trying not to," Jared says.

"Apology accepted," Mag says. "And I really am sorry I didn't tell you sooner."

"It's okay. We'll talk later." Presuming there is one. "Have you guys heard from Mom?"

"I texted her things were cool and have been ignoring her

calls," Jared says. "I'm a little surprised she's not here already, honestly. What's the plan? Is my car still out front?"

I shrug helplessly. "I don't know."

He frowns. "How can you not know?"

The only way to say it is to say it. "We sort of, ah, came from Hell. Into the Chamber of Black Magic. We got zapped there with a spell."

My brother opens his mouth to say something and then shakes his head.

"But you're terrified of being in places like that," Mag says.

I'm proud of myself for coping. "The things we do for love."

The pounding on the door intensifies.

"Can he zappity us out of here?" Mag asks with a head tilt toward Luke.

Up to now, Luke has mostly been taking in our conversation. I wonder how it feels for him, seeing mostly non-dysfunctional family and friends talk to each other, even in a completely dysfunctional situation.

"Forbidden at the moment. Getting here was a special case." He continues. "But we do need a way out. You don't have a panic room or a secret passage to the outside or something handy like that?"

I can tell from the way he says it that he already knows we don't.

"Listen up," Solomon Elerion says, loud and creepy from the other side of the door. "I don't understand why you're so determined to mess this up, little guardian. Or how you got a demon to help you. The others are doing what they're supposed to do: preparing for the war to come. We know you have obtained the piece that we need. You could just hand over the spearhead of the Holy Lance."

"Never," I call out.

Everyone nods in agreement.

"That's too bad," says Solomon. "I suppose we'll just have to burn this place to the ground with all of you inside it. The portion of the spear won't be touched by the flame. It's inconvenient for us, a tragedy for you, but what choice do we have?"

Luke's face turns grim.

I try to decide if it's too early to panic.

Then Solomon decides to add to his threat. "I'll give you five minutes to decide. If you choose to hold on to what should rightfully be ours, this place and all of you except the demon will be gone by dawn. Ash."

Bosch whines.

I'm definitely going with panic.

CHAPTER TWENTY

LUKE

allie doesn't move. Not a blink, not a muscle. This is the stillest I've ever seen her, and that includes while she slept as I carried her through Hell's forests.

"Callie." I say her name gently. "Don't freeze. We've come this far."

She jolts into motion and pulls out her phone. "I'm calling the cops."

A good idea in theory, but it won't work. "Too slow, since he'll undoubtedly have some sort of magical accelerant. And they're not well equipped to deal with supernatural threats."

She doesn't say anything for a long moment. "After all this, everything we've been through, Solomon Elerion's going to win. Hell's going to win."

"You're not going to ask if I can try to use magic on him?" I can't believe what I'm hearing. She sounds close to throwing in the proverbial towel.

"Can you?" she asks.

"Probably not," I admit. "They seem to have gotten their

hands on a lot of forms of protection from the demonic and I'm not exactly on speaking terms with the angelic."

"At least we're together," Mag says. "Callie . . . you're still . . . you haven't turned to the dark side?"

"She's good." I say it firmly. "And she's not giving up."

Callie looks at me with a plea. "I'm not?"

"We have a deal," I say. "I promised you I'd help you stop all this. But . . ."

"I don't like whatever's coming after this *but*," Mag says.

"Me either." I stay focused on Callie.

"Three minutes," Solomon Elerion calls out.

"Tell us your plan." Jared motions a hand for me to spill it.

I can imagine the response I'm going to get, *but* we're out of options. "I will give him the portion of the spear once you're all safely out of here."

"No." Callie says it like she's in mourning.

"Yes. Once you're all safe, *then* we will get the spear back."

She shakes her head. "How?"

"We'll figure it out. Together."

"Two minutes." Solomon's enjoying this, the douchebag of darkness, relishing his countdown.

Callie starts to pace, which is difficult to do with Bosch literally dogging her steps. It'd be endearing if we weren't in such a dire position. I wish I thought I could protect them all from the flames—the one thing I *should* be able to do—but I'm not willing to underestimate Solomon again. Or, rather, I'm not willing to gamble these humans' lives by doing it. I've sworn to take enough from Callie as it is.

Jared holds up a hand. "This is the Holy Lance we're talking about. What will it allow them to do?"

"Whatever they wish," I say. "But they want to please my father, so there's that limitation. The forces from Above will ride into battle in an attempt to stop them. They think this was all my father's plan, when really it was an accident. The forces of Below will respond in kind. We'll have a short window."

In theory, I'm answering the question, but my words are for Callie. We might be able to pull this off. There is a chance. Slim, yes, but present nonetheless.

"Your father?" Mag asks.

"Oh, right," Callie says. "This is Luke Morningstar, Lucifer's son. Prince of Hell."

I wave a hand dismissively at the honorific.

Mag glances at me with new curiosity. "Wow. Okay." They hug their arms around their torso. "Look, I know I should be the kind of person who would sacrifice myself and you guys without a thought . . . I don't think I am."

"Me either," Callie says.

I hope she knows that's not true. She'd sacrifice herself in a heartbeat. I won't let her.

Not until it benefits me.

"Upstairs and downstairs love to put humans in positions like this," I say, reassuringly. "That doesn't mean it's a fair choice. What kind of person lets those they love go without a fight? And he's going to get what he wants either way. There's no point in dying to prove that you're a good person. If we fail, it'll all be pain and misery soon enough."

"Is that supposed to be comforting?" Mag asks.

"Sorry." I shrug. The situation is what it is.

"I say we do it, Luke's plan," Jared says. "What isn't a gamble right now?"

Callie has stopped walking. "You're right. It's our only call." She pins me with a gaze. "You *promise* we'll keep fighting to stop all this? After?"

"I already made you that promise," I say, thinking again about the one she made in return. And, if I'm being honest, thinking about her lips on mine back in my bed. "I meant it then, and I mean it now."

"One minute," Solomon calls.

Callie nods to me. Her eyes are as deep as the part of the ocean where the krakens live.

"Solomon?" I ask.

"Yes?"

"Let's make a deal."

Solomon hesitates for only a moment. "I'm listening."

Even someone like me who didn't pay enough attention to their tutor knows how to make an ironclad deal with a human. This is the easy part.

"You allow safe passage to all three of the humans in this room and swear that no harm will come to them by you or your people's hand or efforts."

"And . . ." Solomon drags out the word.

"And in exchange, I will give you the spearhead of the Holy Lance."

There's quiet as Solomon considers or confers with his cultists. Callie has her hands clasped nervously under her chin, waiting beside me.

"In the interest of time, I accept your terms," Solomon Elerion says. "We have a deal."

I say the words fast, before he can change his mind: "It is spoken, it is sealed."

I trust Solomon Elerion about as far as I trust myself, which is saying something. We're in negative numbers territory here.

This is what we're doing though.

"Then let's get this show on the road," Solomon says. "We've wasted enough time on your games."

Callie has a death grip on her bag and I can't blame her. I extend my hand and hide my reaction to how hard it is for her to hand over the lance to me.

For all I know, I'll burst into flame upon touching the thing. I don't think it would kill me, not that I did that reading either, but it would certainly remind everyone here why Callie should never have been within a million miles of my side. Not that they need it.

It would also remind Callie.

"What's wrong?" she asks.

And it seems I've lost even my ability to put a good face on. Fantastic news.

"You have to ask?" I say.

"Fair," she says. "It's going to be okay, right?"

She wants my reassurance. She continues to wait for it. I feel a twinge at the back of my throat and nod. "We got this. No problem. Easy peasy. Don't—"

"That's enough. I knew it was bad." She reaches into the bag and pulls out the spearpoint with its dinged metal and aura of good. Light and peace wash over me and it's no trouble at all to accept it.

Until my skin touches the surface . . .

Unholy Hell, every point of contact burns against my skin like it'll smoke away every sin, every error, every piece of me. I don't let her see my pain. But it's not easy to hide.

Maybe it *will* kill me. Which means time is even more of the essence.

"Time to go," I manage.

Callie hesitates and I nearly scream. "Should I go first?" she asks.

"I'll go first," her brother says. There's no arguing with that tone. "If they don't hold up their end . . ."

"They will," I say through gritted teeth. "It's kind of a thing. Deals and demons. If they break it, it'll hurt them more than it will anyone else."

"I'm still going first," Jared says.

"I'll go with you." Mag leans toward Jared, and if they think we can't hear what they say next, they're wrong. "They might want a moment."

"What?" Jared asks quietly.

Mag elbows him. "Shut it. I think maybe . . ." They crook their head from me to Luke. "They're . . ."

"Really?" Jared scoffs. Which hardly seems fair given his secret romance with Callie's BFF.

"We don't have time for this," Callie says and her ears must be bright red with embarrassment.

I do my best to keep from screaming in agony.

"Are you coming out or not?" Solomon Elerion says from behind the door. "Those are the terms."

Callie and I move aside so Jared and Mag can get to the door. He removes the chair from under the knob, but pauses before he unlocks it. "Callie?"

"Yeah?"

"I love you too, little sister." He undoes the lock and opens the door.

Mag is right behind him. Callie lingers next to me, Bosch at her side.

Cultists line the stairs below Solomon. He leans forward to find me with those black empty eyes of his. He grins.

"No exchange until they're out," I remind him. I swallow against the pain. I hope holding the lance hurts him the way it does me.

Mag and Jared go through the door holding hands, him slightly in front.

Then it's only Callie and her faithful hound left with me. She fishes a leash off the desk and clips it to Bosch's collar.

"You promise you'll come right out?" she asks.

She's worried about me.

The blinding pain is getting to you, she's probably just worried about getting the spear back.

"Promise." My knees have a distressing weakness to them and I envision my coming collapse. *Go, Callie, go.* I don't want her to see me fall.

She hesitates.

Solomon Elerion snarls at her, "Come on. Hurry it up."

There's a first time for everything: I agree with him. *My thoughts exactly.*

Callie frowns at him, then at me. She leads Bosch to me and tilts her head up to kiss my lips softly.

"Promise still holds," she says.

I almost forget about the searing pain.

"How sweet," Solomon mocks. "I see now why your pet demon was so concerned about securing your fate."

Callie straightens and walks Bosch past Solomon.

I work to press aside the pain, to find the power inside me

that will let me know about this place, about who's in it. Yes, Solomon's people are still shielded. It's not them I care about. I feel the moment Callie leaves the building.

"They're out," I say.

Solomon steps over the threshold into the room. "Hand it ov—"

I thrust the spearhead at him and drag in a breath. My mind starts to clear the second it's out of my hands, the fire fading.

"Well, well," he says, but I made a promise. I don't even stick around to see how holding it affects him.

In a beat of my heart, he's talking to nothing but empty air and I'm outside across the street, where everyone is waiting safely.

Porsoth's appearance is causing quite the stir. Jared is wide-eyed and circling him. Mag is telling him, "Stop that. It's rude."

"Praise to darkness," Porsoth declares when he spots me, flinging himself in my direction. "You survived!"

Callie raises both eyebrows. "He seemed to think that holding even part of the lance might've injured you."

"Not injured," Porsoth says. "He could have been *unmade*."

"Me?" I play it off, despite the word *unmade* echoing through every fiber of my still-existent being. I open my arms to accentuate my fine form. Bosch thinks I'm trying to play with her and leaps around me. "See for yourself."

"I suppose those rumors were just that," Porsoth says. "Gossiping demons. Or perhaps it must be the full lance to manifest the full powers . . ." He raises a wing to stroke his chin.

Mag shakes their head. "I just don't know if I was ready for a demon pig-owl."

"How could you be?" Callie says and there's a lightness in her that comes from her and Mag being on speaking terms again. "Don't worry. Think of him as a demonic Ravenclaw owl-pig."

"How do you know?" Mag says. "Maybe he's a Hufflepuff or a Slytherin."

"We discussed it," Callie says.

"Oh, all right," Mag says.

Jared sighs. "I guess I'll have to read those books finally, won't I?"

Callie's mouth even crooks up on one side, almost smiling. "That's up to Mag," she says.

"If you want," Mag says, then holds up a finger in his direction. "But whatever you do, *don't* follow the author on Twitter."

Callie shifts so she's closer to me. "You're okay?"

I nod.

Porsoth is ignoring all this, deep in thought.

There's blue sky above us, sunshine bright enough to kill the hungover. Until there isn't. Clouds appear as if out of nowhere, dark and foreboding. They race across the sky, slippery shadows. An enormous burst of lightning crackles above, tracing a pointer to the Great Escape.

I expect Father to show up in front of us. This is the kind of entrance he prefers.

"I take it this is not good," Mag says.

Callie agrees. "Omens are extremely consistent across various religious texts. Darkening skies is one of the classics."

"They've reunited the spear." Porsoth lowers his wing. "The end times begin."

"No," Callie says, staring at the sky, "they do not."

That's my girl.

Only in your dreams.

She did make it sound like there would be more to come

later when she kissed me. I file that away for further consideration. "What are you thinking?"

"Porsoth says the spear wants to be in the presence of good, that it won't be happy about this." Callie closes her eyes, obviously thinking hard. They pop open. "The terms of your deal—Solomon can't hurt us."

She's on to something. "Correct. He and his followers can't hurt any of you, at least not directly. You could be hurt by the battle and the end of the world, but he can't use the spear to hurt you either. What do you want to do?"

"Trap him in the Great Escape and save the world."

I have to laugh. "Oh, is that all?"

Jared gapes. "This doesn't seem like you, Callie."

I expect Callie to give him what-for, since it seems *100 percent* the Callie I've come to know. But instead she shrugs. "I don't understand it either. Apparently it is like me now."

"Does this have something to do with that guardian stuff?" Jared asks. He wears a skeptical expression. "They didn't seem too welcoming."

Callie shrugs again. "That's because it turns out I'm not one."

"You lied to her about that too?" Mag is offended on Callie's behalf.

"We're past that," Callie says. "I decided I don't care. Because—"

Callie's interrupted by familiar shrieks and screams. Hell's first legion and the Howling Demons have arrived on the field. Rofocale is at the head of the company, riding a hoofed black beast somewhere between a monster and a horse up the highway. Steam emerges from its nostrils.

Trumpets sound from the other direction. The Above's brass

section, I suppose, and the aforementioned guardians show up in their deadly white leather ensembles with a portion of the angelic warrior host behind them.

Horns begin to honk in the distance as traffic backs up behind what the citizens of Lexington must assume are cosplayers gone rogue.

"Because?" Mag asks weakly.

Callie turns to Mag and Jared. "Because I'm the only one around to try. Who's willing to help me?"

I'm the first one to raise my hand, but not the last.

CHAPTER TWENTY-ONE

CALLIE

I prepare to go back across the street to face off with what Porsoth has told me to expect is a now nearly all-powerful Solomon Elerion. Mag's to my left. Luke stands on my right. Both of their presences are one of the few things that keep me standing. Jared has already gone back to loop around the alley two buildings over to the back entrance.

It's a long shot, this whole plan, but one we have to take.

Never has someone been in so far over their head as me—and I've brought people I love along. We are trapped between Heaven and Hell's armies on state highway 25. The business my mother worked so hard to build is presently headquarters for a cult that is this close to ending the whole world.

Neither of the armies has made a charge forward yet, though there's speeches and cheers and jeers happening on both sides. The whole scene is a little like being in the middle of the most surreal Super Bowl halftime show ever.

People love to predict the end of the world, especially cult leaders. Seems like it would be bad for business, setting a date. Risky. What if you're wrong?

But it happens over and over again.

By all accounts when you read about doomsday cults, the followers are disappointed when no catastrophe comes. Sometimes they take matters into their own hands, Jim Jones or Heaven's Gate style, choosing murder or suicide or some combination. Ending the world one way or another because *they* want it to end.

A lot of people seem to *want* to believe in the end. That this, *their* life span, is when it all goes kaboom. But there has to be a better way to feel special.

Baffling as I find it, didn't I spend many church services reading Revelations and jokingly referring to it as the coolest book of the Bible? I did. There's a thrill to reading about the Mark of the Beast and the Antichrist and the Four Horsemen of the Apocalypse. The devil in his pit. The lake of fire.

But when our preacher used to long for it, called Armageddon a happy day, I never believed that. To want the world to end before other people are ready for it to strikes me as selfish.

Plus, I'm not ready for it to end.

"You'll keep Bosch over here," I say to Porsoth, who remains on grimoire protection and backup duty. "She'll want to follow us."

How could anyone want the world to end with so many good dogs in it?

"I will protect her with my life." Porsoth makes it a solemn vow, and Bosch, sitting patiently at his hooved feet, is clearly on board.

I do remember his demon voice though, heavy with vibrato and threat. Appearances, deceiving, and here we go . . .

"Jared should be in place by now," Luke says, echoing my thoughts.

The three of us walk forward, one deliberate step at a time. I do my best to ignore the roiling sky above.

Mag's nerves are practically radiating, and distracting them seems like a good idea. Also, who knows how this is going to end? They're my best friend forevermore. I want to know about their falling in love.

"How did it start with you and Jared?" I ask.

Mag is quiet.

"I'm not judging," I say, "just making conversation."

"He asked for my help," Mag responds slowly. "One of his classes was doing a unit on copyright and a case related to digital art came up. He asked me to coffee to talk about it, crediting and not crediting, that kind of thing. All the stealing that goes on."

Whatever I expected, this wasn't it. "So you were helping him with his homework?"

Mag shrugs. "Yes and no. Three hours passed, and we were still talking, so we went next door to get a drink. And then he made this admission to me, when he was walking me to my car later."

"What was it?" I'm riveted.

Mag can't keep a smile off their lips. "Turns out he has always had a crush on me."

"What?" I can't believe it.

"I know, right? He just never worked up the courage to say anything."

"That's disgustingly sweet. Okay, I approve. You decided to go out and . . . ?"

"I told him I had to think about it, because I didn't want to hurt you. But then I kept thinking about him and how easy he was to talk to and, I'm sorry, but how cute he is . . . I said yes to a date. Then another. We didn't know if it would work out, so we decided to wait and see. I hated lying to you. But we . . . we just feel right." Mag lifts their hands to indicate it got away from them. "We never found the right time to tell you. Jared wanted to, but I was afraid and so I was definitely going to do it this weekend . . ."

"What else do you like best about him?"

Mag answers quickly. "Honestly? He listens. That's how it started, not just us talking, but him listening. I told him how it feels, the way people look at me, the things they say that they don't expect me to hear or see . . ."

"Who?" I ask, as always ready to call out anyone who hurts my friend.

"That's the thing," Mag says. "He listens. Sometimes that's all I want. Sometimes I don't want anyone to do anything except hear about it."

Oh. "I'm not good at that, am I?"

"No, you're really not, and that's okay," Mag says. "But Jared is."

I catch Mag's eye. Mine are stinging a little with the emotion of everything. "I trust you with my life. I don't want you to be afraid to tell me *anything* ever again."

Mag smiles, glittery lipstick catching the light. "So . . ." they say, "what about you two?"

"What—" *Oh.* Mag means me and Luke.

I don't know how to describe my feelings for him. I'm not sure why I kissed him inside just then. I only know I wanted to in case Solomon somehow broke the deal. I didn't want to risk never getting to do that again.

"We've been through a lot," I say.

"What she means is, she met my parents." Luke's voice is a little strained, almost like he's embarrassed or worried about how I might respond. Is that even possible? His heart-stoppingly attractive face stays calm as still waters.

"And a dragon," I say, casual. "Who is also a goddess."

"Wait." Mag stops, eyes wide, absorbing what Luke and I have said. "You met his parents?"

Okay, so some things are not capable of being discussed casually. Dragon goddesses, Lilith, and Lucifer Morningstar among them.

We're almost across the road now, and there's no time to get into all that. Luke saves the need. "I feel like we're all learning and growing so much. But look alive, there's bad guys in the lobby."

I swallow. "We are so screwed."

"If anyone can manage this, it's you," Luke says.

The jury is out on whether it's possible at this point. Though I didn't actually mean to say that out loud, the (mostly) confidence helps. Whether the cult will buy this last-gasp effort now that they have what they want—let's just say that the jury's out on that too.

"Is it wrong that I'm planning to enjoy it, if at all possible?" Luke asks with a grin.

I could say yes, but . . . "*If* it goes well, hopefully you can."

Not that anything much has gone well. Not that I'm counting on this to. There's a first—and maybe last, period, the end times—for everything.

"Here goes the world's best chance," I say.

The three of us take the last cautious steps to the front door. I figure the cult members on duty will open it to greet us, probably by telling us to get the hell out of Dodge. But I have to knock on the glass where our logo is imprinted.

Mag and Luke wait right behind me.

There's some conferring inside and then a robed guy pushes open the door, barely, and says, "What do you want?"

"Hello to you too," I say. "I'd like to speak with Solomon."

The guy begins to snarl what is surely a no, so I add: "We're interested in joining your cause. He'll want to see us."

He hesitates, then says, "Wait here."

The door shuts.

Luke puts a steadying hand against my back. "You did good," he says. "Very convincing."

"I'm not a dog. I don't need pats." What can I say? I get cranky when I'm nervous.

He must sense the lie in the second part, because he keeps his hand in place for a long moment. I lean back a little, into his touch.

"Thank you," I say.

The door opens. "You have five minutes," the jerk says.

The other cloaked cultist up front is a woman. She smirks and says, "You should have said *another* five minutes."

The jerk guy frowns in acknowledgment that her way would have been pithier.

"Where is he?" I ask.

They make no move to escort us. That's fine by me. I got a

whiff of the door opener when we passed and I don't think he's had a shower since this all started either. I got to clean up with first Luke's and then Lilith's finest array of hellish plant-based soaps or I'd be just as gross.

"Second room," the woman finally says.

Solomon's in Tesla's Lab. *Good.*

I thought he might use that one, because despite the more appropriate décor of the Chamber of Black Magic, Tesla's Lab is far more open and roomy for conducting evil shenanigans with the Spear of Destiny to brandish.

The hallway is clear, other than us. Luke conjures some sneaky shadows around Mag. While he and I enter Tesla's Lab through the outer area, they keep going, slipping along the hallway to let Jared in the back without tripping the alarm.

The door to the room is open—the cultists probably forced it. Which gives me an idea.

I stride over and lift the knocker. One, two, three. *Bang, bang, bang.* The keys topple from the ceiling, and I snatch them from the air and pocket them.

Luke lifts an eyebrow at me.

"Keys can come in useful," I whisper.

"Enter," Solomon says without a hint of trouble. He probably assumes we're more of his henchmen and -women.

A cultist appears in the doorway. At least they're not wearing plague doctor masks anymore. "It's *them,*" the man says.

"It's us," Luke says with a rakish grin and maneuvers past the cultist. I follow suit.

Solomon and the bulk of his followers have rearranged the lab to be their makeshift stomping grounds. The lovingly placed furniture is jammed against one wall. No one could ever follow the clues to get out of here now. If we make it through this, Mom is never going to leave me in charge of anything again.

The cultists surrounding Solomon melt back when he greets us. "To what do I owe the imposition?"

Solomon holding the Holy Lance is the most deeply wrong thing I've ever seen. There's a faint cloud around him—a dark halo—that must be from its power. Restored, reunified, it must be five feet long, the wooden shaft ending in the metallic spear point, and even at thousands of years of age looks like exactly what it was and is: a weapon.

Luke and I glance at each other.

"You passed the test," I say as grandly as possible.

"Flying colors," Luke adds.

Solomon levels the lance at us and it's only remembering that he can't *hurt* me that keeps me from running in the other direction. That and the con we're trying to sell him.

"I'm not really a guardian," I confess. "I'm allied with Luke here, whose father is—"

"Lucifer Morningstar, sovereign king of Hell." Luke shrugs as if it's no big deal. "He needed to make sure you were up to the task you've set for yourself."

Solomon absorbs this. I wonder if Luke has any anxiety about what happens next, or if it's only me that does. Maybe he doesn't *get* anxious. No, that can't be it. Everyone does. He must be excellent at hiding it, is all. Probably comes with the demonic starter pack.

Or with a dad like his you don't show weakness to.

Suddenly, I'm grateful that ours ran out on Mom and only bothers to send a card with fifty bucks every year on our birthdays.

Solomon slowly shakes his head and then he chuckles. Save

me from people who chuckle. "That's why we got you instead of Rofocale, the minister. He sent his son."

"The crown prince," Luke says. "You *could* have been a touch more polite . . ."

Solomon waits, bowing his head slightly. Does that mean he's buying it? The rest of the cultists do the same.

Luke dusts off his hands. "But bygones. We have bigger worlds to fry."

"Sir, it's happening," one of the cultists says and holds up a phone.

Solomon lifts his hand and bares his teeth in that awful smile. "Speaking of that . . ."

"What's happening?" I ask. My pulse quickens. Are we too late?

"Our first move," Solomon says. "The weather today is cloudy with a chance of fire and brimstone."

"Where?" Luke asks and feigns appreciation. I hope he is, anyway.

"Here." Elerion lifts one hand from the lance and sweeps it around us.

"The angelic host outside will *love* that." Luke whistles.

This is not good. We have to get the Holy Lance back, stat.

Luke must read my mind. He stretches and does a sort of yawn with an eyebrow arched. "You should let Callie have a go with that thing, as a favor to me. Father loves her."

Solomon Elerion hesitates.

The clatter from the hallway reaches us. We all swivel toward it.

I figure we're made and dive toward Solomon. I get one hand on the Holy Lance and it glows. Not pure white, not the darkness from before, but a mix of both as we struggle.

"Get her off," Solomon says.

His cultists come at me and Luke begins knocking them out one by one with a hand in front of their faces. Since they can't manage to grab me, presumably because of Solomon's promise that I won't be hurt, Luke's strategy is effective. Although some of them manage to evade him, and the room descends into general mayhem.

Especially when Jared jogs through the door, Mag right behind him.

Solomon wrestles free from me and backs off to stand against us.

"I should've known," he says.

"Yeah, you should've," Luke says and knocks out the last cultist with a lifted palm. "Too bad you made that deal."

"The deal doesn't say anything about hurting you." Solomon lifts the spear and points it at Luke.

My body thrums with the knowledge: *He's not wrong.* He wouldn't be that brave, would he? To threaten the devil's son?

"Luke wasn't lying about who he says he is," I say.

"Then his father would probably thank me." Solomon frowns as if thinking. "I don't think this is fitting company for a prince of Hell. So, what will it be?"

"He's not wrong," Luke says to me. "He can't hurt you and that's what matters."

I can't believe what I'm hearing. "No way. You promised to help me. Jared, catch!"

I toss the keys from the ceiling to Jared and lunge forward again.

I don't go for the spear. Solomon is still holding it up, which leaves a crucial part of his anatomy unprotected. Jared darts around me and jabs the keys toward his face, raking them down one cheek, then dancing away.

Solomon's roar of pain leaves me able to spike my knee hard right into his crotch. He moans and shoves me back before his knees crumple and . . .

The spear flies free.

"Luke!" I shout.

Luke doesn't move for a long second and then he rushes in and grabs the lance with both hands.

The glow turns a soft red. Luke's face tells me everything I need to know about how it feels for him to hold it.

He's in agony. His scream confirms it.

He said it didn't hurt him before . . . *Another lie* . . . But why? Why didn't he tell me?

Solomon gets up and stalks toward Luke but Jared throws himself at the cult leader's feet, hanging on to halt his movement as he attempts to keep walking. I start wide to get to Luke.

Solomon attempts to push Jared off him, which must not count as hurting. The two grapple.

"Get away from them!" Mag has found the painting meant to be Tesla's beloved pigeon in the mess against the wall. They rush forward, gripping it in both hands, and bash it over Solomon's head.

Which goes clean through. I'm impressed.

He staggers and—

He falls, his head sticking through the painting.

I finish my journey to Luke as quickly as possible and pry at the Holy Lance. His eyes are closed and he hangs on like his life depends on it. "No, I won't give it to you. No."

"It's me," I say. "Callie."

Luke sucks in a gasp of air as his fingers release. His legs give out and he crumples to the floor.

Then I'm flying backward with the Holy Lance in my hands, the relic emitting a light so bright it seems to come from inside me and outside at once. We did it. We got the lance away from Solomon Elerion and his awful order. I didn't honestly get to this point in my brain, because I wasn't sure we'd be able to do it.

Definitely not this fast.

There's one question in my mind: What do I do now?

CHAPTER TWENTY-TWO

LUKE

The pain is inescapable, my body untethered from anything but its howling madness. The flaming river Phlegethon flows through my veins, fills my lungs, and there's no escape. I burn from the inside out.

Finally, I could truly make Porsoth happy. I could write a whole treatise about the target level of suffering to inflict. My hands on the spear have yielded an exact prescription for maximum torture.

Over the course of what could be eons but is probably at most a minute or two, the sensation of not death, but suffering that seems to have no end, begins to, well, end. Or taper off, at least. The sensation fades like a scream getting farther away.

I'm back on the floor in my shell of a body. Which might be a burned-out husk, but I'm in it. I wonder if I look as exhausted as I am.

I'm weak. Too weak to open my eyes. Survival is a question.

If I do, I'll never forget the utter wrong of my hands on the lance. A good so powerful when it came into contact with me, it tried to obliterate me.

"Luke, are you all right?" Callie asks. "I need some help here."

A cool palm touches my cheek and I gasp, blistered by a sense of calm and light. I drag my eyes open.

I back away when I see that she has the spear in her other hand. She looks like an avenging angel. A faint white halo surrounds her, along with an image of a Tesla coil on the ceiling. Nice decorating touch.

"Luke, it's me," she says.

"I know," I say and let my eyes drift closed again. "Just stay back."

"Do you think he's dying?" Jared asks, and I hear the underlying *Is that a bad thing?* in his tone. Nice solidarity, bro.

"He's not dying," Callie snaps back.

I wonder what they'll think when they find out about her soul. That it's pledged to me and darkness. What if Father tortures Callie the way I was just tortured?

I can't bear it.

"Luke, I need your help. Please wake up."

She's pleading. My weak heart responds to it.

"What help?" I manage to get the words out. She appeared fine to me. Glowing, actually. The picture of health and vitality and unstoppable power.

"We should tie up Solomon Elerion," Mag says.

"I can't believe you put that painting right over his head," Jared says.

Mag sniffs. "Tesla's pigeon is too good for him."

Callie responds to them. "Just check for a Hand of Glory. If they don't have one, we'll lock them inside the room."

"Good idea," Jared says.

"I have my moments," Callie returns.

They don't need me. Just like I thought. Callie's got her own little army, practically as good as the two outside. Certainly more fun to hang out with.

Hands shake my shoulders. "Luke, wake up. I've put down the lance. I need you."

I force my eyes open again and stare up into Callie's. There's a storm brewing there. Doubt. And yes, need.

"What's next?" she asks. "What do I do now?"

It becomes clear that she's being absolutely honest.

She has no idea what happens next. And she thinks that I do. She needs *me*. Or believes she does, anyway.

There's truly a first time for everything.

I manage to push myself up to a seated position and extend a hand to her. She helps me to my feet. I wobble.

Once we're both relatively convinced I'm not about to fall, she lets go and picks up the Holy Lance. There's that glow again. Callie of Good.

Jared holds his phone up so we can see the screen. A headline shouts apocalyptic news, along with a photo of gouts of flame. "I don't want to interrupt, but there's apparently fire and brimstone storms going on all over the place outside," he says.

"He said that was their first move," Callie said. "Any ideas?" she asks me.

"Start there." I gasp the words. I suck in a breath, and say the next stronger. "Stop it."

I don't bother—because I don't feel up to it yet—to explain that one apocalypse will likely trigger, to put a point on it, all of them. Most religious traditions are more intertwined behind the scenes than people realize. This is an extinction-level event in the making.

But it's not like Callie needs more pressure at the moment.

"Right." Callie frowns at the Holy Lance in her hands. "And I do that how?"

I can't help smiling at her. "You're way smarter than him and he managed to make it work. Just will it."

Callie's frown deepens as she examines me. "Are you going to be okay?"

Again with the worrying about me. I'm not used to it. I don't know how to wave that off. I feel something akin to devastated. My throat chokes back up.

"Right as rain," I grit out.

"I hope you like rain," she says and our gazes hold. I remember standing in the night in Lisbon together what feels like a lifetime ago, when she was in pain from traveling in my manner. Now I can barely stand from the assault of good, but I aim to aid her. How far we've come.

Literally and figuratively.

That might be a hint of tears at the back of my eyes. I inhale sharply.

Gather your wits about you, Luke.

"Callie?" Mag interrupts our staring contest. "Fire and brimstone—"

"Raining from the sky," Jared finishes. "Better get on that."

Callie squints at me. "When all this is over, you're getting a milkshake." I'm puzzled, until she specifies. "Best treatment for most non-fatal injuries."

"Milkshakes are Mom's cure-all," Jared says. "She's going to kill us, you know."

"I know." Callie sets her shoulders. "Okay, I'm going to try this."

"Should we get out of here first, in case he wakes up?" I ask.

I'm getting stronger by the second, so maybe this milkshake cure idea has something to it. But I still don't want to deal with Solomon Elerion again anytime soon. Not if it can be avoided.

"Yes," Jared agrees.

Mag locks the door we came in, the one that opens into that little vestibule. Meanwhile, Jared flicks open a portion of wall to reveal a hidden keypad, then punches in a series of numbers. That triggers the exit door to the hallway to open.

Callie hugs the lance to her with one arm, and reaches her opposite hand to me. "Lean on me," she says.

I can't resist, even with the possibility I might burn.

Surprisingly, touching her when she's also touching the lance doesn't hurt. It's nice. That sense of peace and calm radiates through me.

Maybe not *all* good things hurt me.

"Wow, Luke, that is some major moony look," Mag says.

"I do not," I protest, "have a moony look. Impossible."

"You kinda do," Callie says. She shrugs the shoulder nearest me. "I don't mind."

"Let's go," I say with an eye roll I don't mean.

We shuffle through the exit into the hallway. Jared secures the door behind us.

"Oh my god," Mag says, pointing toward the front windows.

The scene outside is much, much worse than seeing it in a photo on a small phone screen. If Mag hadn't been able to say that word without making thing worse, I'd wonder if I was back home.

Fire rains down in heavy gouts amid angry gray clouds that

I'm betting fill the air with the reek of sulfur. The whole thing is akin to a volcanic eruption, but coming from above. Most of the fire burns out on the way down, but that just means we probably won't die in fire caused by it. Yet.

"I always thought *fire and brimstone* was just an expression," Callie says.

I see her face tighten into resolve. She marches toward the door and extends the Holy Lance out in front of her with both hands.

"Stop it," she says. Then adds, "Right now."

Nothing happens. There's movement on the street outside. An angel winging low. Some flying demons pass the other way. The armies are inching toward real conflict.

"Stop it right now," Callie tries again. "No more fire and brimstone."

And again, no change in the horrific conditions.

Callie heaves a sigh and lowers the Holy Lance. She turns to me with a bewildered look.

"Why isn't it working?" she asks.

I have no idea. You shouldn't have put your faith in me.

"I'm not sure . . . Visualize what you want in detail and believe in your ability to stop it."

She whirls back toward the windows. I step as close as I dare with the lance active.

Callie closes her eyes in concentration. After a long moment in which nothing changes, she sighs and opens them. "It's still not working. What now?"

I'm turning out to be useless in this crisis, but I know someone who will have an answer. "Porsoth," I say. "He'll know what to do."

We walk closer to the windows, staring out into the smoke

and fire and angels and guardians and demons and hell-beasts along the road. There's still an empty sort of no-man's-land on the road directly in front of us. Sure, fire and brimstone rains down the whole way, but it's a path.

"How do we get to him?" Callie asks. "Can we call him here?"

"Best not to draw too much attention to him, not while he's babysitting Bosch. Rofocale might not realize he's here. He could be called to combat."

Callie frowns, concerned. "Bosch won't be hurt by the fire, will she?"

"With Porsoth in charge? Not likely." I gingerly take her arm, careful not to touch the Holy Lance. "We'll have to cross the street to him though."

"Take an umbrella. No, that's not going to work . . ." Mag glances around the lobby frantically for something to shield their best friend and it's one of the sweetest things I've ever seen.

"That part I can handle," I say.

I press the front door open and form a smoke canopy to cover us. After all, Mag's right. A regular umbrella would burn.

"Be right back," Callie says. "Or as soon as we can. Keep an eye on Solomon. He's tricky."

"We got it," her brother says. I'm beginning to understand what Mag sees in him. He's solid backup in a crisis. "Go."

"Jared?" Callie hesitates.

"Yeah?"

"I'm sorry. I really am oka—*good* with this." She ticks her head toward him and Mag.

"I said go," he says, playing the long-suffering brother. But I see the sheen in both his and Mag's eyes.

Hell's bells, I still feel it in my own. None of us are sure we're going to make it through this. That's the only explanation.

Callie turns to me expectantly and I say, "After you."

"Be careful!" Jared says. "I'm supposed to be in charge."

Callie and I catch eyes and almost laugh, but then the heat hits us like a smackdown.

The trip is not what I'd call fun, even protected from the worst of it.

First off, fire falling from the sky makes the place into an oven. Callie's constantly brushing sweat from her face, but there's nothing I can do about that while maintaining our covering.

Then there's the occasionally jeering demons who start to menace us, until they notice me and then they start mocking Callie. I could do without it, but we don't have time for trifles.

Sometimes priorities truly suck. World ending, et cetera. And I made a promise. A promise I'm going to see through.

At last, we stand in front of Porsoth, who grips a wide black smoke umbrella in one hand and a panting Bosch's collar in the other. He's made himself and the dog hard to notice, and we slip into the pocket of his working as if it's a niche in the wall of reality.

"You were successful!" Porsoth says. Then I watch it connect. We were successful, but things are still progressing toward apocalypse now. "What's the trouble?"

He takes in the lance with fascination, but keeps his distance. Smarter than me, but I knew that already.

"All this," Callie says. "I tried to stop the fire and brimstone, but it's not working. Why?"

Porsoth gives one of his standard owlish blinks. "Who gave the command initially?"

"Solomon Elerion, obviously." She wipes away more sweat from her forehead with the back of the hand not clutching the holy weapon. "We managed to take the lance away from him, but it doesn't seem to want to listen to me."

"He's still alive?" Porsoth asks.

"Yes." Callie swallows. I can tell she doesn't like where this is going.

"There should be two ways to stop the command," Porsoth says, going into teacher mode. "Either the person who gave it must perish . . ." When he sees Callie's horrified expression, he says, "No one could argue that the sniveling worm doesn't deserve it. We have a fine accommodation waiting for him in Hell after this . . ." He searches for a word.

"Cluster-o-pocalypse of epic proportions?" I say.

"That is not a word," he says.

"Or," Callie prompts. "What's option two?"

"Or," Porsoth says, "the Holy Lance can be destroyed. Now that it's reunified, it should be possible."

"How?" Callie asks. "And what happens if we do?"

Porsoth shrugs. "That I don't know. No one ever set forth a method in any text that I've seen or detailed the consequences."

"Great." She sounds ready to scream. "Why can't anything be easy?" She turned her phone back on en route. Now it buzzes and she checks it. I glimpse some unopened texts from her mother. A lot of them. "Mag says Solomon's awake. We have to get back. Thanks, Porsoth."

"I'm coming with you," Porsoth says.

We both stop. Fire and brimstone continue to rain down

around us. The armies of darkness and light are mixing it up a bit in the air and on the ground here and there.

"You are?" I ask.

"This is no place for a dog, is it, Bosch?" he asks Bosch.

He has a point.

Bosch doesn't look exactly zen about being out here, even under Porsoth's protection.

Callie says, "Come on." She stops for a second and peers between me and Porsoth. Then, "The lance. Luke held it, and it hurt him. Is he going to be all right?"

Porsoth studies me with concern. "And you survived?"

There's no point in lying. "Barely."

"Interesting . . . I presume so," he says to Callie. "I have no real way to know."

"Try again," she says.

I'm confused, but Porsoth takes her meaning. "It's likely he's going to be just fine."

"Better," Callie says and I want to hold her to me and keep her safe forever.

To be honest, I want to anyway.

But we don't have time. No, we have to get back to the Great Escape to prevent a not-so-great escape and to face another existential moral quandary. All this big meaning-of-life, saving-the-world business is exhausting. The lazier version of me had some things going for him.

Porsoth sweeps out a wing and effortlessly enlarges the pocket of shadow I made. Off we go, Callie's faithful hound back by her side.

The obvious answer to our current dilemma is that I take out Solomon Elerion and harvest his putrid soul. Father won't give me credit for it, but no one has ever deserved eternal damnation more.

Still, I've never had to get my hands dirty, not in that way. But the lance's reaction to me seems to confirm I'm made for the task. After all, one way or another, I'm going to see Solomon Elerion in Hell. And I'm going to disappoint everyone, like always.

This time, I fear I may also disappoint myself.

CHAPTER TWENTY-THREE

CALLIE

osch trots ahead to the edge of the shadow umbrella, and I can't help but shake my head. I'd have expected her to hide from all this. Turns out she's as good at rolling with the bizarre punches as the rest of us. She's careful not to stick her feet or nose out into the raining fire.

Shelter dogs know how to survive anything, even the apocalypse.

Luke and Porsoth's covering keeps us from inhaling the smoke clouding the air. The reek of rotten eggs is as strong here as anywhere we went in Hell. I'm sweaty and gross and have no idea what to do about Solomon Elerion.

But I have the Holy Lance and I got my dog back, so the mission wasn't a complete loss.

The front door of the Great Escape emerges in front of us through the smoke. Jared's hand-me-down car is in fact still parked in front. We could've driven over? Why didn't we think of that? Distracted by burning flame falling from the sky, I guess. Too late now.

Jared lunges forward to open the door and hustles us inside.

The spear in my hands is supposed to be all-powerful, and
yet it can't do what I want right now. It can't make this stop,
protect all these people. Protect *all* the other people.

At least, not so far.

The only comfort is even I can't blame myself for not being
prepared. This is not a test I could've studied for.

As soon as Bosch's paws hit the lobby floor, she groans and
sinks to her belly. This despite the noise of Solomon and his
followers, busy shouting and banging against the door from inside Tesla's Laboratory. But still trapped.

I'd feel relieved about that, except for Jared's and Mag's
panicked expressions.

"That bad?" I ask.

I need time to think about what the right course of action
is. I also know there isn't much to waste.

But I don't like either of Porsoth's options.

"Our doors aren't made to hold in people actively trying
to break them down," Jared says. He lowers his voice. "But we
have another problem. I forgot to pick up the keys."

"Only a matter of time until he realizes they're there," Mag
says.

Crap. The keys work on both sides of the entry door.

Luke positions himself dead in front of me, forcing me to look
him in the eyes. Problem is, I want to. When Mag called Luke
moony, it was true. But no truer than it would be about me.

I care about him. That is as scary as anything else.

"Callie," Luke says, "I could take care of him."

I've been waiting for this. As soon as Porsoth gave the option, I knew Luke would volunteer. That he'd press for this.

The idea doesn't feel right.

"Or I," Porsoth protests. "It would be but a trifle."

"It should be me," Luke says, resolved. "I botched the summoning. I should've taken their souls then and there. This is the right thing."

"No," I say. "There's got to be another way."

As expected, Luke argues. "Even if we manage to destroy the lance, Solomon will still be around. He's going to be trouble, no matter what."

"You don't kill people because they're trouble!" I shouldn't have shouted it, but I'm a little lost right now. What if he's right even though I'm sure it's wrong? What if promising to give up my soul means I'm not one to be telling the difference these days, and this powerful artifact in my hands is going to end up misused?

What if Luke takes out Solomon and we all regret it forever?

"*You* don't," Luke says, softly, coming in close. "Where I'm from, things are a little less savory. You know that."

"Where you're from is not where I'm from."

"Yes, I know," Luke says.

I need to process things the way I would normally, the way I do here, where *I'm* from. By talking to Mag.

"Can I borrow you?" I ask Mag.

"Always," Mag says without hesitation. I walk toward the hallway.

"Wait!" Luke holds up a hand. "Where are you going? We're in the middle of a conversation."

I pause. "The control room. I just want to talk to Mag in private—we'll be right back."

Jared interrupts. "It's their thing."

"Yes, talking to each other is our thing. A friend thing," I say. "It's how I decide things."

I loop my arm through Mag's, keeping the lance in my other hand, and we head toward the stairs. From up there, we can talk and I can keep an eye on Solomon via the cameras at the same time.

"Porsoth is in charge," I toss over a shoulder.

Luke and Jared exchange affronted glances. Normally, I'd laugh. But the part of me where laughter usually lives is hollow.

Mag is wise. We've figured out many things together. We can figure out this.

The door to the control room hangs open.

"I have an idea," Mag says.

See? Productive already.

They slide into the chair at the first computer workstation and click through until the screen for the room our bad guys is in comes up. They type into the box and then grin at me.

I go over and lean in to see. Mag has typed *Face it, beak-faces, you're trapped* into the monitor. The words will show on the screen in the corner of the room.

I snort and nudge them over so I can type next. "Grim wars, not grimoires . . . No, wait, got it."

I type: *Cult Leader? More like Cult Loser.*

We both laugh. I thought that was impossible. There is still one piece of light in this darkness. I relax into this little moment and it's like breathing air that counters everything nasty we traveled through to get back here.

But I know it can't last. It doesn't.

The bad guys have stopped looking at the screen and gone back to pounding at the door and searching for things to use to break out.

"It can't take much longer for them to get through," Mag says. "What did you want to talk about?"

I pull up the chair next to them. "I know. We got some answers from Porsoth, but . . ." I lay my head on the desk beside the computer, crosswise on my arms. I wish I had time to cry. Or scream. But I don't.

"Here's the problem," I say. "To stop Solomon's command we either have to kill him or destroy the lance."

Mag takes a second with it. "To get rid of it, how do you do that?"

"That's the other thing. We don't know *how* to do that. Or if it would trigger something just as bad."

Mag says nothing.

"But even if we decided to destroy it and figured out how, Solomon is still going to be a problem." I sigh. "You heard Luke offer to take care of him. What do you think I should do?"

Mag mulls it. "It's a solution, but a crappy one."

On the monitor, the cultists have broken a chair and are using it to bash through the wooden door. From the hall camera, we can see they've made a hole, and an arm comes through. Bosch barks angrily as Porsoth pulls her back.

"Any other ideas?" I try.

"Is there a way to work around the rules?" Mag asks. "Make new ones? You know, a puzzle, like when—"

"We make a new room." An interesting thought. There should be a work-around. We always make more than one pathway to the solution.

On camera, Porsoth and Luke exchange a look like they're about to go on and deal with the situation.

"I'll figure it out," I say, hoping it's true. "Down there."

And we're both up and moving. I can't help wondering if that's the last time I'm ever going to laugh with my best friend.

When we reach the bottom of the stairs, Luke and Jared are working to prevent the cult coming through. But the hole in the door is getting bigger. Porsoth is dancing around, keeping Bosch out of the way.

"Ow!" Luke gets a smashed hand for his trouble as another blow comes. I keep forgetting *he* can still be hurt by Solomon and his followers. Another point against his taking care of this.

There has to be some way . . . *Think, Callie, think . . .*

Porsoth's wings flap when he spots us. "Did you make a decision? Let me end this now."

"I told you," Luke says, his shoulder against the door. "It should be me."

I don't know if Porsoth is capable of ending a life. I suspect he is. But Luke . . .

"I don't think you can do it," I say.

He doesn't respond for a long moment, continuing to hold his position as the cultists jostle from the other side. Finally, he looks at me over his shoulder. "What choice do we have?"

What choice *do* we have?

I grip the Holy Lance.

The door bursts outward and Solomon Elerion heaves through it. "I'll be taking that back now," he says.

He's followed by his band of robe-wearing true believers.

We're outnumbered. But we have the Holy Lance and two demons.

Jared and Mag get behind me as I hold out the lance to ward him off. Luke and Porsoth flank me.

Us against them.

"You don't even know how to use it," Solomon says. "Or you'd have killed me already. Look out there, at that beautiful world ending. Let me finish it."

"Please," Luke says. "Let me finish *him*."

"Not yet." I keep searching for an alternative. There's got to be something. I consider trying to just break the lance, but if it wasn't destroyed by being separated in two that's not going to work. Destroying it might not even be the right call.

Why did Good make things so complicated?

Solomon lunges forward. As Luke moves to block him, I realize that's exactly what Solomon wanted. He backs up, holding Luke by the throat.

"Callie." Luke forces it out. "Let me."

But . . . he wants me to save him. Whether he understands it or not. If Luke really wanted to take out Solomon, he'd have done it. I've been around him long enough to know that he doesn't do or not do anything because someone tells him to.

There *must* be another way . . .

Then bless my random fact-holding brain, it gives me something to run with.

"Dante," I say.

"What about him?" Jared asks.

"Hold that thought." When we were in Hell, Porsoth said it offhand, that Dante did time as a donkey. That he was lucky they turned him back. There's that old story from Greek mythology about Circe turning Odysseus and his men into swine when they visited her island.

The princess and the frog.

Maybe *I* can take Solomon Elerion out of the equation. Assuming I can get the lance to work.

I search for the right association—what kind of animal is related to devil stuff?

I've got it.

I close my eyes and concentrate and the light of the lance floods through me and there's a flare of power so bright I hear everyone around me react with gasps.

Now to see if it worked.

I open my eyes and . . .

It did.

Luke's now standing beside a small, adorable, four-hooved, black-and-white-splotched—

"Is that a pygmy goat?" Luke asks. "You turned him into a pygmy goat?"

"Goats are Satanic symbols," I say, defensively. "So it seemed appropriate. But I wanted him to be manageable size-wise."

Luke beams at me. I can't help feeling proud.

The rest of the cult members are thrown, it's obvious. I grin at them. "Who's next?" I ask.

"No," one of them says. "No." They're flooding out the door, out into the sulfur smog, abandoning their leader just like that.

"You are a genius," Luke says. "Of some kind."

"Could've told you that," Mag says.

"It was Porsoth mentioning Dante when we were on the way to Lilith's that gave me the idea," I explain.

Porsoth basks. "Me? I inspired you? Well."

The little goat shakes and tests its feet, skidding a little at first on our slick flooring.

"He's so cute now," Mag says. "I can't deal with this."

The pygmy goat chooses that moment to prove that he's also definitely still Solomon in there, as he rushes forward and tries to headbutt Bosch. I step into his path and he falls over.

"He's a *fainting* pygmy goat," I say.

"Is that even a thing?" Mag asks.

"Don't know," I say. "Is now."

"We do still have a larger problem," Jared points out, meaning he literally points outside. Where it's still fire and brimstone city.

Right, Solomon's still Solomon in there. He still exists.

"You've made him easier to do away with," Porsoth says. "We can stop this now."

"Yeah, I know," I say. "But not the way you mean."

I grip the lance and more light floods through me. "I rename this goat Cupcake, and declare him a friend to all living creatures."

Bosch goes over and gives the fainted pygmy goat a sniff like the good girl she is. I walk over and scratch behind my dog's ears.

The goat wakes, staring up at Bosch, and then climbs to his adorable feet and nuzzles against Bosch. Who allows it.

"No more Solomon Elerion. Only Cupcake." The full scope of what I've done hits me and takes the shine off my triumph. "Wait—was this actually good or is wiping someone out of existence wrong?"

"For Solomon, it's a major upgrade," Luke reassures me as we watch Cupcake and Bosch become fast besties.

Porsoth tilts his head. "You got him out of damnation later, so on balance you did him a favor."

Mag nods in agreement. "That was some rules hack."

"Good job, sis," Jared says.

Outside, the fire and brimstone have stopped, leaving only clear air. It was a onetime thing, and no one had to kill anyone. Not really. I remind myself I promised Luke my soul anyway. So if it *was* wrong, I'll be punished.

Not that people should do right just to avoid punishment. But guilty twinge or no twinge, I'm going with my friends on this one.

I'm counting it as a victory.

Luke strides over to the door. "We *do* still have a problem," he says with regret. "Two armies are still about to collide in a final battle."

CHAPTER TWENTY-FOUR

LUKE

Callie stands silent at my shoulder, peering out the windows.

I don't know what frightened me more—the idea of having to strike Solomon down or of Callie watching me do it. The last is why I hesitated, that I'm sure of.

I could imagine her expression of disappointment. Then, in reality, that resolve I've come to recognize crossed her face as she gripped the lance, and suddenly *poof*, no more Solomon. Only Cupcake, a fainting pygmy goat.

I want to laugh.

Well, I wanted to until I took a fresh peek outside.

The fire and brimstone stopping their ceaseless torrent should be an unqualified good, and I'd bank that everyone who had it raining down on them agrees that it is.

Everyone except the armies of the divine and infernal. They see it as a sign ending. They see it as an opportunity to be seized.

They see it as an order to advance.

Each line creeps forward, posturing as they travel to the

other side. With us smack in the middle. Heaven's brass section is so loud, we can hear the trumpets like they're in here with us. Hell's legion, never one to be outdone, cries out and shrieks and howls, the only instruments their voices and clanking weapons.

"Can I stop it, with this?" Callie asks. She means the lance. "Should I be using this for world peace or something?"

I turn my head to gaze into her now-familiar green eyes, then sweep mine down to the Holy Lance. The Spear of Destiny. The thing that almost killed me. Her question is fair, and I consider it. I can only come up with one answer.

"It's a weapon," I say. "Filled with divine power, yes, but a weapon nonetheless."

Callie understands instantly. "And weapons aren't good at world peace. How would I even know what to command? How long before I start randomly turning anyone I think is bad into goats?"

"It wasn't random," I say. I don't say she has a point.

Mag steps up to the other side of her.

"I love you," Mag says, "but I don't think you should have the One Ring."

Ah, a Tolkien reference point. Just what the conversation needs. The Ring of Power created by Sauron. Father *loves* that story cycle.

"You are all a bunch of nerds," I say with mock disgust.

"Guilty," Callie says.

"No one should have the One Ring," Jared says. "Look what happened to Frodo."

Porsoth hoots softly. "I always fancied visiting the Grey Havens and journeying into the West."

"Nerds," I repeat. "Back to the task at hand. The lance is

first and foremost, in essence, a weapon. There must've been a reason it was split up all these years. What did it feel like when you used it?"

I watch Callie carefully to gauge how the question registers.

Her fingers tighten around it. Her eyes flicker shut then back open. "Like it would be happy to cleanse with fire. Does that make sense?"

My body shudders at the memory of holding it. "It does to me, as someone who has felt it attempt just that."

"I wonder," Porsoth says, lifting a wing to stroke his feathered chin, "if it was hidden not to protect it, but to protect you. Humanity. Look what's happened, in such a short time since its recovery . . ."

Callie looks over at Cupcake. "Yeah, we humans aren't too great at decisions about cleansing with fire. Historically speaking. I guess this means we destroy it. That would show everyone out there that no one's trying to end the world with it, right? Unless there's some rule we don't know." She doesn't sound entirely convinced, but she commits to exploring the idea. "But how do we do it?"

Mag clears their throat and ticks their head toward the windows. "What about asking the guardians?"

"We don't have much time," I remind them as I look out again.

Rofocale is practically on top of us, leading the vanguard on his beast, steam boiling from its nose. Opposite, a couple hundred feet away, the guardians march toward us in white and shining silver armor, armed to the hilt. Angels with hard expressions and magnificent wings fly above.

"I know they were rude," Mag says. "But could they introduce you to Michael? Could he help?"

Callie's attention returns to me. "What do you think?"

Sadly, I find I have no better ideas.

"Worth a shot," I say. "But, remember, you have the lance. Use it if you have to. They're dangerous."

"What about us?" Jared asks. "Shouldn't we all come?"

"No," Callie says. "I took this on, and Luke will be with me. You stay here. Be safe. Protect each other and Bosch. And Cupcake. Text Mom that we're okay."

Porsoth makes me meet his eyes. But when he speaks, it's directed to Callie.

"Don't let this one make any foolish heroic sacrifices," he says. "The guardians won't like him. You protect each other too. I'll watch over everyone here."

"You got it," Callie says. Then, to me, "Behave yourself."

My chest swells and I grin. "No problem. I'm naturally gifted at that."

Callie lets out a sigh.

And so into battle we go, two upstart pacifists against a universe that's been spoiling for a fight for thousands of years.

"The apocalypse is less smelly and hot than it was before," Callie says, making conversation as we venture out toward Heaven's troops. She grasps the Holy Lance with a mix of nervousness and confidence all her own. I do my best to make us semi-invisible to Father's legions.

"True," I say. "But so much louder."

I do a small working to help drown out the trumpets and the howls. Callie notices. She slides me a look. "Like having earplugs at a show without earplugs," she says.

It hits me in this moment, an extremely poor one for romantic notions, that I don't know nearly enough about her. What kind of music does she like?

"Have you been to a lot of concerts?" I ask.

I've been to Hell's, which are invariably screeching heavy metal or intentionally off-key riffs on classical pieces. We all secretly love Earth's music. There's a significant black market in bootleg streaming devices with all the good stuff, harvested off new arrivals. I've heard rumors that some souls even get targeted *for* their taste.

Callie doesn't know that much about me either, I suppose, and what she does know should have her running away. Yet, here she is. Here I am.

"Concerts?" she asks, distracted. "Not many—Mom runs a small business and I work for it, you know? They're pricy." She stops. "They spotted us."

I mean to ask her if she *wants* to go to more concerts, assuming we live through this. But she's right. Guardians have the worst timing.

Here they come with the leader, Saraya, in the, well, lead. She spins a murderous-looking multibladed ax that reflects off her gleaming armor.

"Little not-guardian," Saraya says, "the rumors are true. Here you are with the demon spawn, and I see you have the Lance of Longinus. Prepare to die as I recover it."

"Don't think about attacking her," I say. "She knows how to use it. Hear her out."

"Yes, Saraya," Callie says, subtly muscling in front of me. "Saraya the Rude is how I'd say you should be known. Hear me out."

I duck my head to hide a grin. Callie has just saddled Saraya with that nickname forever; I'd bet on it.

"Start talking," Saraya says, making an extravagant gesture with her blade. "Then you can die."

I lift my hand to shield my eyes a bit from the glow of the angels. One would wonder why they aren't leading the charge, but having met a guardian and seeing how they operate, it makes perfect sense. No way the guardians wouldn't insist on throwing themselves into glorious battle first. Angels, on the hand, they've been around for millennia. Why be so eager on the front lines?

For demons, it's more of a pride thing. Cowards at the rear, bluster and chest-beating, and all that. Probably it's where most of the smart, future Porsoths are—even though he used to be fearsome himself. I digress.

Callie's searching for words. "Saraya the Rude," she says, at last, and the other woman grimaces, "as you can see, we have reunited the two halves of the Holy Lance. Do you see me using it to fight? No, because I've only ever been trying to stop Solomon Elerion and his order—which is now done. So call all this off."

"This seems like a trick," Saraya says. "A clever one, but nonetheless."

Typical. "I didn't tell you this is what I feared they'd say, because I didn't want to say I told you so. But I could've told you so."

To her credit, Callie doesn't blink. "I propose we destroy the Holy Lance, then," she says, "to prove we have no intention of using it. To prevent anything like this from happening ever again."

Saraya roars. Other guardians come forward, weapons at the ready. "She has threatened to destroy the Holy Lance," Saraya tells them. "Seize her!"

"Saraya the Rude, it shall be done!" one of them calls.

I can't laugh because they're serious. They rush Callie and she has a frozen panicked expression on her face. Her brain must be cycling through possibilities like turning them into pygmy goats too.

"No," Callie pleads, extending the lance to ward them off. "I just want to end this."

"We know," Saraya tosses off.

They're about to overtake her and Callie looks at me. "What do I do?"

Something breaks open inside me. My body heaves, out of control, as if a new skeleton is forming under the skin, determined to make me shed it and leave it behind. The searing pain stretches on and on and I wonder if I've touched the Holy Lance again.

I haven't. But I scream.

"Luke!" Callie clearly doesn't know what's happening to me either. "Stay back!" she cautions the guardians, who pause in their progress.

The pain spikes, and then it . . . fades.

Callie stares at me. "Luke," she says again, but with a note of wonder instead of panic.

My wings unfurl from my back and I may as well be taking the first deep breath of my life.

I turn my head to check one out. Tipped with gray, the rest a killer gleaming black like my jacket.

Angels are flying toward us now too, but I beat my wings—*my wings!*—and I'm right beside Callie. An arrow barely misses me and then Callie lifts the Holy Lance and says, "Leave him alone!"

"Callie," I say, "careful with that thing. Need a ride?"

I have an idea. Never in a million years did I think my wings would arrive. That I might be in a position to help good win the day. Real good. The kind Callie is.

"Where to?"

"Heaven," I say.

She hesitates. "Don't hurt him either, you," she tells the Holy Lance, although she still arranges it in her right arm, where it won't touch me. She shakes her head and grins at me and my wings while the guardians and angels watch in shock. She loops her left arm around me. I enfold my arm to hold her to me, because I still have those obviously, and up we go. Every beat of my wings is like a breath.

Angels streak toward us, following, but it turns out that I'm magnificently good at flying, even sans practice. Blue sky and clouds stretch out and we leave the battlefield behind.

The lance should protect her from this audience.

"Michael! Hey, archangel!" I shout. "Parlay requested. Let's end this. Michael!"

Callie remains wide-eyed. "We're flying. Your wings. They're . . ."

"Black like my heart," I say.

"Don't do that," she says. "They're beautiful. They're yours. You know who you are."

I am well aware of what this means, but if I think about it right now I'll be overwhelmed. "I just didn't want to see you taken out by *deus ex* guardians."

"That's not what *deus ex machina* means—it means 'the god in the machine' because they used to lower gods onto the stage at the end of Greek and Roman plays."

"Callie," I say, amused, "call Michael."

"Right." She takes in a breath and then, "Michae—"

But she doesn't need to shout. We're flying through another bank of clouds and then up out of the Earthly plane. An elaborate set of pearly gates appears up ahead. Tall, reflecting every color within their pale gleam.

An angel who radiates light from every pore stands in front of the gates. Michael.

On sight, every part of me wants to turn around and fly back down, take our chances. He could unmake me in the bat of an eyelash.

"That's him," Callie says, because even mortal, she knows there's no question when you see an archangel.

"You're so close," I say. "End this."

She swallows. "*We're* so close."

I fly closer to Michael and set her down. Even though there's not really ground here, my suspicion proves true. She stands fine, the air supporting her.

"Approach," Michael orders.

He is nearly translucent and a little creepy because of it. It's as if instead of a heart, he has a star inside him, leaking out. His bushy white eyebrows match his milky, perfect wings.

"Possessor of the Holy Lance," he says to Callie. To me, "Lucifer spawn."

"Don't forget my mom," I say. "Lilith spawn too."

He raises his eyebrows. "Why have you come?"

Callie holds up the Holy Lance. "This thing inadvertently kicked off Armageddon. We don't know how to get rid of it, and your guardians laughed when we suggested it." She pauses. "So, we thought you could take it. Save the world by putting all that on hold."

"Why?" Michael asks. "What if it's time for it to end?"

"It's not," Callie says with a frown.

Michael spreads his hands. "How can you be so sure, human?"

"Because there are good people in it, and they deserve to live their lives."

"There are bad people too. Would not the good be rewarded in the afterlife?" he asks.

I can feel her frustration, or maybe it's my own.

"I really don't know," she says.

"Correct," he says. "You do not."

Callie sighs and her shoulders fall. But only for a moment.

"This weapon never belonged on Earth," she says. "You should've destroyed it ages ago. If you're actually on the side of good, you'll take it. You'll end what's going on below."

I worry she's gone too far with suggesting he might not be playing for Team Good. But when he responds, he sounds almost amused. "And if I don't, you'll turn me into a pygmy goat?"

"Could I?" she tosses back. She shakes her head, "No, I wouldn't."

The two of them are in a standoff.

"Hmm," Michael says. He casts another glance at me. "Is it true, that this was all a prank that got out of hand?"

Someone's been back-channeling. I can't help but wonder if it's Father.

"I wouldn't call it a prank," I say. "But yes, a giant misunderstanding. It's my fault."

"Or the fault of bad parenting," Callie says.

Can't argue there. "Look," I say, "I can confirm this world-ending business was entirely the desire of a human cult. Father had no role in it."

Michael continues to examine both of us like we're under Heaven's microscope. Then, at last, "Very well," he says.

He reaches out his hands and Callie, after only a breath, gives him the lance.

"To Earth," he says.

Callie tucks herself into my side again and we follow his flight path, off the Heavenly plane and back to Earth.

"What's going to happen?" Callie murmurs. "I don't know if I trust him."

"I heard that," Michael says without turning around.

Callie snorts, and I sense she's struggling to keep from laughing. She must be as nervous as I am.

Then the battlefield appears below us, the Great Escape dead center and just off the highway. Callie holds on tight.

Mag and Jared and Porsoth emerge and gape up at what must seem like a hallucination. Porsoth flaps with joy when he takes in that it's me—flying—using my newly grown wings.

Rofocale approaches us from the demonic side, dismounting his beast and walking the rest of the way on foot. Saraya and her guardians dash toward us from the other direction.

After they've stopped on the ground on either side of us, Michael hefts the spear high. He's allowing the humans to witness him, toning down the full glory of his form.

"This human and demon have gifted the Holy Lance to Heaven," he says. "We have no quarrel at this time, save the usual age-old grudges. Disperse."

"It's over so quickly?" Rofocale asks, crestfallen.

"She was telling the truth," Saraya says.

"Yes, Saraya the Rude," Michael pauses, hearing what he called her, and then goes on, "she was. Should she desire to be a guardian, our order would be lucky to have her."

He waits for Callie to respond.

"No thanks," she says, clinging to me as if she'll never let go. "I'm good right here."

Yes, that's definitely relief on Saraya's face.

"Disperse," Michael repeats and then he travels upward in a beam of blazing light.

Callie and I don't move, and I believe both of us are slightly in shock.

"We did it," she says.

She's right. We did it. We stopped the world from ending. And . . .

My father's clock is almost out. I held up my end of the bargain, for once in my life. The day is saved. We have to go. Why do I feel like I'm dying?

"Set us down," Callie says. "I just need to say good-bye. For now. I get to come back for a while?"

I answer awkwardly, "We can probably arrange for until your natural life span is over."

"Okay."

We float gently to the ground. My bones feel hollow.

Hell's legion is already leaving, and the angels fly away as one shiny pack. The road is clearing, and we finally get a glimpse of the TV crews that were filming in the distance. I wonder what story they'll weave to make sense of all this.

Mag and Jared rush toward us as I land. Porsoth stays back a bit, and continues to shake his head at my glorious wings.

There's someone else still present too. Rofocale. Never one to wait for the right moment, he jumps right into it.

"Time to go home," he says, polishing a scuff on his obsidian chest plate. "Have you met your father's task?"

He expects me to have failed. Who could blame him?

"He has," Callie says. Her voice is thin and serious. "I'm ready."

"What is this?" Jared asks, concerned.

"She promised him her soul," Porsoth says. "But it's Lucifer's fault."

"No way," Mag protests, and Jared is right with them.

"I made a promise," Callie says. "I have to honor it."

Jared and Mag are clearly getting ready to marshal their arguments. But there's nothing they can do. A deal is a deal. When you shake hands with a demon, that's it. No going back, not unless you want to pony up *and* get some extra pain for the trouble.

Where I'm concerned, on the other hand . . .

"We're going home," I say to Rofocale. "But Callie is not coming."

"Luke, no," she says. "You honored your promise too. I won't let you do this."

"Not your choice. Your soul's too good for me. Stay here, go inside and hug your dog, recount the *deus ex* Michael."

"Still not how that term works. Luke, he'll . . ." She searches for the right way to say it. I could help her out.

Unmake me? End me forever?

"I know." I take one step toward her, then another, until our faces are inches apart. I lace my fingers through her outreached hand. I place a gentle kiss on her lips, letting it deepen for one breath, then another. Then, I pull back. The hardest thing I've done today.

"It makes me happy to know the world has you in it," I say, which is a pretty good parting line. More, because I mean it with every fiber of my demonic being, from toes to wingtips.

"Luke," Callie whispers.

Rofocale heaves a bored sigh. "Does this mean we can leave now?"

I release her fingers and then I'm already flying away. I'm headed home to face the terrible music.

I take one last look back before I leave Earth for Hell and see Callie staring after me, surrounded by those who love her. She'll be fine. She'll be *good*.

Soon enough, I'm almost home, nearing the Gray Keep. Father stands on the upper balcony, awaiting my arrival with a grim expression.

I probably shouldn't have done that. I don't know how I ever thought I could do anything else.

CHAPTER TWENTY-FIVE

CALLIE

I stand on the Earth—something that would seem unremarkable except, before this, I was *flying* and outside *the* pearly gates—and watch as Luke's beautiful black wings get smaller and smaller and he finally vanishes into the distance. He's really leaving me here.

He refused to take my soul. We had a deal.

That noble idiot.

Okay, get a grip, I think. He's not an idiot. Or noble. He's never been noble.

Until the last five minutes.

"Why did he do that?" I ask Porsoth.

Porsoth considers. "I daresay he followed his heart."

"He should have followed his brain."

Mag comes closer, Jared at their elbow. "Callie, this is good," Mag says. "He could have taken your soul, I have that right?"

"It's not good. His father . . . Porsoth, what will happen?"

Porsoth goes quiet. Given how chatty he's been up to now, that's another bad sign. "Porsoth," I press.

"It's difficult to say."

Difficult to say how bad it will be, he means.

"Will he survive?"

Rofocale clears his throat. "What a foolish question. Lucifer will mete out justice for his failure. You've ruined his chances to achieve greatness. What does survival matter now?" He shrugs. "Ah well. I'd best get back."

I'm so angry I want to yell at him, but Rofocale disappears in a cloud of black smoke before I can. The beast he rode over here on stomps toward us and Porsoth makes a clicking noise that slows it. But then the beast disappears too.

"He almost forgot his monster-horse, didn't he?" I ask. "I despise that guy."

"Rofocale's not so bad," Porsoth says, but there's no real argument in it.

Jared checks his phone. "Mom's on her way back—they had the interstate exits closed so traffic's backed up. It'll take her a while. But . . ."

"But we should get this place cleaned up?" I ask. "Is that what you were going to say?"

"Callie," Mag asks, "what do *you* think we should do? This is over, isn't it?"

Is it? The highway is a little pock- and scorch-marked from the brimstone and fighting, and a lot more journalist-heavy than normal. But otherwise no one would imagine what almost happened here: the battle for Armageddon, narrowly averted. We stopped the end times. Cue the party music.

Luke didn't take my soul.

I couldn't have done any of this without him. He couldn't have done it without me, either. But there we are.

I owed him a debt, and he didn't collect.

The way I see it I have two options: (a) consider this my one grand adventure and a narrow soul miss and live my life as if someone else didn't sacrifice himself for it, or (b) at least try to save Luke too.

The idea of Luke not existing anymore because he refused to hurt me isn't something I can accept. I'm not planning to force my soul on him, but like with the Cupcake plan, there must be another option.

B, it is.

I even have a way to force communication with the other side. The grimoire. Like that, I have the beginnings of a plan.

"Porsoth, where's the book?" I hold my hands out for it.

The owl blinks at me. "You mean to . . . ?"

"I do."

"I won't be able to help you with the summoning, protocols forbid it. But it might work." He reaches into his scholar's robe and then pauses.

"Where is it?" I ask, waving my hands. To Mag and Jared, I say, "We're going to need to clear the floor in the Chamber of Black Magic. It already has a built-in pentagram."

"It seems I, well, I," Porsoth says, "I no longer have the book."

Time crashes to a halt. "What?"

Porsoth rocks from hoof to hoof. "It, well, ah, it seems when you and the prince went to converse with Michael, you left the Earthly plane. Your arrangement with Styx, it activated."

I can't believe this. "But I'm alive!"

"Yes, but zones of existence are rarely crossed by living

humans and so the universe must have decided to consider you, ah, briefly dead." Porsoth hangs his head. "I failed you."

This isn't good. Styx has my book, the key element of my plan. But I'm not giving up that easily.

"Take me back to Lilith's," I say. "You can zap us there, right?"

"Callie, maybe it's time to let this go," Jared says.

He's almost certainly correct. I consult Mag.

"What do you think?"

Mag stares at me for a long moment. "You'll never know if you don't give it a shot."

"I'll be back," I say. "Get the room ready. Candles. The works."

Porsoth hesitates. "Are you certain about this?"

"To Lilith's." I reach out and grasp his wing and the world goes dark and scream-filled.

When we arrive, Lilith is napping or communing with nature or something. She's reclined in her garden, World Watcher–less now, with flowering vines curling around her limbs.

Porsoth and I exchange helpless expressions. "She likes you," he says under his breath.

The short straw is mine. "Lilith," I say, "wake up. We need to talk."

Her eyes pop open. She sits up, the plants releasing her like they share one mind.

"You came back." Those same perceptive eyes narrow. "Why?"

"I need your help." I shake my head. "No, that's not right. Luke needs your help."

"You should've stuck with the first story." She climbs to her feet, reaching out for the assistance of a spiky-leafed plant.

"He's your son," Porsoth says.

"I'm aware," she says and throws her arms out in a stretch, yawning. "Did he betray you? Is that why you're here? I received a dispatch from the palace inviting me to join his disciplinary hearing. I declined."

Hell has disciplinary hearings. *Wait*, I remind myself, it also has internships. Fair enough.

"Un-decline," I say. "I have to get my grimoire back from Styx, so I need time. I need you to go there and stall for it."

Lilith comes closer, studying me. "Why do you care so much?"

"Because he doesn't deserve this. He helped me save the world, and then he didn't take my soul. He could've saved himself, but he didn't."

"Don't be fooled by one sweeping gesture."

"Trust me," I say. "I'm not. It wasn't sweeping. He didn't even give me a chance to talk him out of it."

"That's not why you want to save him," she says. She sighs. "I'll go. I can take you by Styx on my way. I make these dark chocolate pomegranate brownies she goes wild over."

Traveling with Lilith is a new experience. She conjures winds, and we leap into them. With each jump, we're carried high over the landscape miles at a time. Fiery ridges and dark forests and black-mud swamps go by in a blur. I suppose you could call it travel by witch.

The fancy cloak she put on before we left sails around her,

reminding me of Luke's wings. The thornbushes are too far below to worry about, because we never quite touch the ground.

Until the Styx's still, black waters come into view. The winds lessen, and we land on the banks.

There's no calling the goddess this time. She bursts forth from the parting waters. And she has my grimoire in one talon.

"Lilith," she says, hissing, "lesser Porsoth, dead human."

Lilith's greeting is warm, ours not so much.

"I'm not dead," I say, "so if I could just borrow my grimoire again? Please?"

Styx shows her teeth. "Ah, but you were dead enough for it to be delivered to me. The way of the world. The book is mine. A fine old book."

"I'll ask you a question, I'll give you whatever you want for it," I try.

Porsoth steps in front of me. He hesitates, and then he grows by several dozen sizes in seconds. He looms over us, nearly as large as the dragon.

When he speaks, his voice is a deep rumble that disturbs the water of the river. "Give her the book."

Styx tilts her head back and releases a gout of flame, then lowers it to Porsoth's. She slithers closer.

So *this* is how I die, in the crossfire of a giant owl-pig and a dragon. Sure. Why not?

I tremble, waiting.

"There's the merciless creature I remember," she says.

"Give it to her," Porsoth says.

Styx . . . purrs. Or at least, that's the closest word I can come up with to describe it. Porsoth is impressive—I'm proud of him—but we don't have a high-ranking prince to chime in this time. I'm afraid he's going to have to marry her.

Lilith produces a basket from her cloak. She waves it in the air.

"I'm sorry to interrupt," she says. "But I have to go, off to the palace. My boy is in some trouble. I brought your favorite. If you might entertain their request? For me?"

Styx dips her head to Lilith's and takes the basket in her teeth. She tosses the grimoire to me and I lunge to catch it.

"Let's go, before she changes her mind," I say.

Lilith is already sailing away on air currents.

Styx balances the brownies on her talon. "Not so fast," she says. "You must still pay a toll."

Always another rule.

"A question," I say.

"Try to do better with it," she says.

Porsoth shrinks back to his usual size.

"I could still eat you up," the dragon says.

"Promise?" Porsoth counters.

What is happening? Are these two flirting? They are.

"Ask," Styx says to me.

For once, I don't search for something I've read or seen a documentary about, some random piece of knowledge filed away in my brain. I choose something I lived, a truth only three beings know for certain. I'm pretty sure Styx and Michael aren't in the same social circles. And Luke's in no position to talk.

"I have one." I clutch the book to my chest and stand tall. "Who convinced Michael to call a halt to the most recent near-apocalypse?"

Styx shakes her head from side to side. "The legends spread quickly here," she says. "I know it was *youuuu.*"

Ha. "Nope," I say. "Well, yep, but not just me. It was me *and* Luke. He answered a crucial question for Michael in the crunch. So your answer was technically incomplete. Can we pass?"

Styx's neck sways like a snake about to strike and she grins with every one of those sharp teeth. "Clever girl, you shall pass."

She sets one wing flat for us. "Be careful with my book. And Porsoth? Do visit me soon."

I don't push my luck by pointing out it's *my* book. Part of me wonders how I knew I'd need it again, why I balked so hard when she first demanded it. For that matter, why was I so drawn to it in the first place? But if there's one thing I've learned in the past forty-eight hours, it's that some questions are better left unanswered. If some higher power steered me this way or that, I don't need to call them on it.

I've got another callout to make first.

As we step onto her wing, Styx uses a nail on her other claw to flip open the basket from Lilith.

I extend a hand to Porsoth. He takes it and zaps us back to Earth. I'm almost used to the screaming darkness.

We appear in the lobby of the Great Escape, met by Bosch and Cupcake racing around us in a frenzied welcome. I head straight to the Chamber of Black Magic.

Jared and Mag are waiting there amid candles on the points of the pentagram. The furniture is all out of the way, everything except the grimoire stand.

"You got it," Mag says. "What now?"

I walk over and set the book back into place, flipping to the section about calling Rofocale, the minister of Hell.

Now we see if it's possible for me to outmaneuver the devil.

CHAPTER TWENTY-SIX

LUKE

I t's not that I assumed I'd win any popularity contests in the kingdom—the opposite. Yet, somehow being confronted with a mass of demons and my father hungry for my ruin is overwhelming evidence of something past dislike. Past loathing.

Hatred.

Although, it could also be that the soulless hordes surrounding me in Father's throne room, where I sit before him, contrite, not even allowed to stand, are simply expressing the pent-up aggression they didn't get to spend on the final battle. I thwarted their bloodlust.

Now I'm its object.

Rofocale is a stern presence beside Father's throne, judgment on his face. Father's is hard, pitiless. The worst part is, I think he's enjoying this.

He has his wings stretched out at their most impressive on either side of his throne. I ruffle mine, which I still can't believe exist.

"Put those away," he orders.

I start to say I don't know how, but when I think about it they fold back in automatically. I feel smaller.

I'm sure that was his desire.

"You had forty-eight hours, which has now elapsed," Father says. "What were your orders from me?"

This entire hearing is a sham. I wish he'd skip to the punishment.

"Answer," he says.

The chair beneath me means I have to, another of his toys, like the World Watcher.

"You told me to secure Callie's soul." *And I agreed to take it, like a monster.*

"And did you?"

"I chose to release her from promising it to me," I say. "So I suppose you could say yes, then no."

"You admit that you *chose* to disobey a direct order from both your king and your father?" he asks. "For a human?"

The company around us erupts into disgusted cries. Someone shouts, "Boil him!"

"You may as well go ahead." If they're going to tell this story until the end of time, I won't be a coward in it. "Unmake me. I'm guilty. I've still not managed to obtain a single soul. What's more, I don't want to."

Father stands. His shadow falls over me.

I may be pretending I'm not afraid, but it's only pretend. I'd rather live. The consequences are beyond my control this time, though. I don't get to decide.

He does.

"Hold on a second," my mother's voice says.

Father double-takes. He was so focused on me, he must not

have sensed her arrival. "The messenger said you declined to come," he says.

"I changed my mind," Mother says, and slinks into the room in a long velvet cloak. What is she doing here? "Bring me a chair. I'd like to hear the full charges."

"Very well," Father says, and sinks back to his throne.

I catch the change that flits across Rofocale's face. It might be me alone who does. The faraway look that started this whole mess to begin with is on it.

I've been wrong before, but I'd bet my probably-not-much-longer-but-valuable-to-me life on this.

He's being summoned.

Then, he confirms it.

Rofocale holds up a hand. "Excuse me, sire, I'm afraid I need to—"

"Summoning—lot of those lately." Father waves his hand. "Go. We'll finish this."

Mother winks at me and crosses her fingers.

Something like hope arrives as Rofocale departs.

Until my father speaks again. He gazes at my mother then at me. "Maybe we don't need to humor dear Lilith. After all, the prince has admitted guilt and his lack of a spine befitting his station. We could move straight to sentencing."

The throne room erupts into cheers.

Whatever Callie has planned, it better be as speedy as this trial was.

CHAPTER TWENTY-SEVEN

CALLIE AND LUKE

The clock's ticking down in all sorts of ways. Mom is making her way home through a traffic jam. The front door has been locked to slow her down a fraction if she makes it here before we finish summoning a demon.

I might be the proud owner of a grimoire, but I never imagined actually using it.

Standing here, in the dim light of the Chamber of Black Magic, small candles burning at the points of the pentagram, with Mag and Jared forming my call-and-response circle, my hair lifts at the back of my neck as I say the words in the *Grand Grimoire*. Porsoth is in the corner, observing.

If there was any other way, I'd stop talking, blow out the candles, and leave.

But I have to try. For Luke. Because of what Luke did.

Because I'm no longer the kind of person who can walk away.

I speak the last words, no doubt mangling the French pronunciation. Do you have to get it right for the spell to work? I hope not.

The room is absolutely still, and then a wind rushes around us, fluttering the candle flames.

So it did work.

Maybe.

"I don't like this," Mag says.

Porsoth says, "It'll all be over soon."

Which might be comforting. I guess.

I'm banking that the pentagram will serve as a trap, the same way it did for Luke when he responded to the Order of Elerion's summoning. That the demon being caught up in it means there's no way for any of us to get hurt.

I hope I'm right about that.

Rofocale is suddenly in the center of the pentagram and he's angry.

"I should've known it was you," he says. His eyes glow from fires within. "What do you want?"

I swallow. Mag's and Jared's faces reflect the same terror I feel. Luke was a hot guy in a leather jacket. Sure, they saw Rofocale and other demons outside earlier, but there's a difference between breathing the same air and breathing the same air in an enclosed space.

Rofocale is monstrous, and not in the cute sort of way that Porsoth is.

"What do you want?" he repeats, enunciating slowly.

I can't let Rofocale see that I'm afraid too. My palms are sweaty and my heart thumps in my chest like I'm running a race (and I hate running). No, Rofocale can't see that weakness. Neither can who I really want to talk to . . .

"The boon I seek is an audience with Lucifer. Call him here, now."

Rofocale rolls his pinpoint red eyes. "Not likely. Name another."

"Can *you* save Luke?" I ask.

"No one can."

I cross my arms. "Except Lucifer."

Rofocale waves a hand. "Not likely. What else can I give you? Riches? Power?"

I stand tall. "You are trapped here, until I release you, correct? We'll charge admission to see you, here, near the site of the mass hallucination that some people claim was real. A live demon, captured." I shrug. That's the official story, according to Mag and Jared: mass hallucination. Lots of people dispute it. The fire and brimstone seem to have disappeared without causing much actual damage—Solomon must not have been specific enough in his command, mostly for show—like historical reports of storms of falling frogs and all the other things I always assumed were fake but might have been real. It turns out most people are all too glad to have a lie that's easier to believe than the truth. "Given the nature of our business, no one will think you're truly real. So unless you want to be a sideshow attraction, I suggest you try to get Lucifer here."

Rofocale stares at me. Smoke rises around him. He shifts and he finally sees Porsoth over in the corner.

"Get me out of here," he says.

"I can't interfere," Porsoth says in his demon voice, staying put. Mag and Jared flinch at hearing it for the first time, but they hold position.

"You'll regret this." Rofocale spits it. "All of you."

I shrug again. "Not your problem."

"Fine." He tosses the word like a knife and closes his eyes. After a long moment, he opens them.

"Well?" I prompt.

Jared whispers, "*Is* this going well?"

"Depends on what you mean," Rofocale says.

The room begins to heat and there's a glow below us. Rofocale steps to one side, still trapped, to make way.

Lucifer ascends through the floor until he's in the center of the pentagram.

He has Luke with him, holding him by the arm. Seeing him is good, even in these circumstances. We weren't too late. He's still breathing.

Luke asks me, "What are you doing?"

"Why, son," Lucifer says, unfurling his wings, "obviously she didn't want to miss the show."

"I, um, wanted to talk to you," I say. "About Luke."

Lucifer gives me a lazy smile. "Too late for that. And after this stunt from you, I don't see how I can do anything less than unmake him. You can watch."

I never thought Callie and I would be in the same place again, able to look each other in the eye. I want to say so many things to her.

But that's not to be.

Father will consider the interruption of his grandstanding as the ultimate insult. Whatever leniency I might have gotten due to Mother's presence, that is gone now. Porsoth may think he's hidden in the corner, but he'll be lucky not to be unmade himself.

I've seen unmakings before. A being exists one minute, then is unraveled piece by piece, cell by cell, atom by atom, until nothing whatsoever remains. I hate the idea that Callie might have my dissolution in her head, an ugly memory.

I don't want that to be the way she thinks of me.

"Wait," I say.

"What's this?" Father asks. "You feel like answering questions without being forced? All I ever asked of you was that you fulfill your duties, learn your trade. Giving Rofocale a deadline to report on you started as a way to motivate you to do your best. And instead, here we are. I'm about to lose my son and it's all your fault."

"Mother's about to too. She won't be happy."

Father says nothing. Then he says, "Last words? Do you have them?"

I consider the tactics available to me. What story could I weave to make him forgive me? I could promise to do better, to become so good at soul-gathering that I'll be ready to inherit in no time. I could volunteer myself to be publicly tortured for humiliating him.

I face Callie. "I'm not sorry I did it," I say. "I'd do it again a thousand times. Good-bye."

I close my eyes and wait. And wait.

I open them.

Father is gathering his power, which means he's planning a spectacular show of my demise. Callie interrupts him.

"Lucifer, now that I've got you here, you can't leave without my, um, leave . . . correct?" she asks.

His seething is answer enough. Her shoulders relax a fraction—she wasn't sure. My brave Callie.

"You're trapped in that pentagram," she continues. "So stop whatever you're doing. Don't do a thing to Luke. If you want out of there, you have to hear me out."

My heart in my chest has never felt so much like it belongs to someone else.

Luke's looking at me like I'm a star in the sky, something to wish on. He's the only one.

Lucifer growls. "That both of you put me in this position will not be overlooked," he says, training his gaze on first Rofocale and then Porsoth. Porsoth raises a wing.

"You wished an audience? You want me to hear you out. Talk, human."

Behind him, Mag and Jared grip hands like their lives depend on it. I can't afford for this to turn worse than it already almost did. I have to do this. Make my case.

"Explain to him, Callie," Porsoth says, and I don't know if that means he's given up on getting out of this alive himself or that he's filled with courage and not willing to let Luke go either.

"Explain to me," Lucifer says, heavy with irony.

"I also want to hear this," Luke says. No snark, completely sincere.

I'm making my case to Lucifer, I know that, but once I decide to talk *to* Luke it gets easier. "You wanted Luke to prove that he could get a soul—first it was nonspecific, but then you changed the game for it to be mine. I agreed," I say. "I told him if he helped me stop the world from ending—which he did—then I'd let him have my soul. Just as you said."

"I know this." Lucifer motions for me to speed it up.

"I made that promise believing that he'd follow through. That he'd take my soul. I was willing to give it up for something bigger than me."

"What a hero you are," Lucifer says.

Rofocale snorts, and Lucifer quiets him with a glance.

Luke simply watches and listens, riveted.

"Imagine how surprised I was when he decided to back out of our deal."

"Another strike against him to be sure." Lucifer sighs. "How long is this going to take? We left a throne room full of demons."

"As long as it has to," I say. "Now, here's where things get interesting. You wanted Luke to learn how to get souls, right?"

"Yes, it's a bit essential for a demon," Lucifer says. "Keeping the universe in balance."

"But you're always hoping for humans to surprise you, too, right? Luke told me that."

"They rarely do," he says. "You're an exception there, and I forget *why* I ever want it at the moment."

"I think you want more than humans to surprise you. Why else would you leave Heaven?" I take a breath. "For a while I wondered if maybe it was Lilith, something to do with Luke's human half, and then I remembered Porsoth saying she's immortal now. And I don't think it mattered anyway. I realized that Luke being more than what you want him to be has nothing to do with either of his parents. Maybe in spite of you," I say, pushing it.

Lucifer's eyes narrow.

"I always hate in books when a big deal is made out of someone being half demon or half this or that. That's not how being a person works. Luke isn't just a part-demon, part-human, or all-demon. Just like you're not only an angel or a demon or whatever. He's a *person.*"

"Does this have a point or is it intended to bore me out of my anger?" Lucifer truly does look about to go to sleep.

Luke has a concerned expression, but he's still listening.

"Luke's a good person," I say. "You know how I know?"

Luke's mouth drops open. "I'm not *that* good . . ."

I shut him up with a look. "Good isn't something you are. It's something you do. And I submit Luke's behavior over the past forty-eight hours—most of it, anyway—as proof that he's good."

Lucifer gives me a look like I've lost my mind. He turns to Rofocale and Porsoth. "Are you hearing this? I don't think she understands that being good isn't on the menu."

"Ah," I say, "so you *don't* like being surprised, then?"

"I didn't say that," Lucifer counters.

"And wouldn't you say it's surprising that Luke did get a soul this weekend?"

"Whose?" Lucifer demands.

"His own."

After dropping this stunning revelation, Callie steps inside the pentagram, and she must know that will break its hold on us. She's risking everything.

She walks to me, and she places her hand over my heart. It responds by beating a symphony, serenading her from within my chest. I lift my hand and put it over hers.

"Luke has a soul. And he let it guide him. He did the right thing, even knowing this might happen. That you might *unmake him for it.*" Callie angles her head toward Lucifer. "He's exceptional at being Luke. You should reward him for it. You can't claim he didn't surprise you."

Father's lips gather. I can practically see the wheels and gears—think torture rack—turning in his head.

"You're saying," he says, finally, "that my son is exceptional. That I should pardon him because he did obtain a soul. His own."

Callie takes a moment, maybe making sure that's the size of it. "Yes," she says.

Father's attention wanders to each and every witness in the room. Mag and Jared, who wisely look down to avoid meeting his gaze. Porsoth, who stares back encouragingly. Rofocale, who might have indigestion, it's hard to say with him.

Then he settles back on me. One elegant shoulder lifts. "All right, you convinced me."

In a puff of smoke, he's gone.

"You didn't deserve that reprieve," Rofocale says and adjusts his suit jacket. "I'll see you at the office tomorrow . . . once I figure out what you'll be doing from now on." Then he disappears too.

"I'd better get back and begin recording these events," Porsoth says. "I'm proud of you, Prince. Until next time," he says to Callie, and he leaves.

Callie and I stare at each other. I rest my forehead on hers. Our hands are still gathered at my chest. My heart beats *for her.*

"You didn't have to do that," I say.

"I did."

"No," I protest. "Having to do things is very rare. I'll give you an example," I say, my lips tilting in a smile that she matches. "*This* is something I have to do."

Luke presses his lips against mine and my body lights up like a fuse, but it's my heart that goes off like fireworks, bursting with happiness.

I can't believe it worked. I can't believe he's still here. I gather the fabric of his shirt in my hands and keep on kissing him for as long as I can. Until Jared's voice interrupts from right next to me. "Callie, um, bad news . . ."

"Hello, everyone," Mom says.

We pull back. Luke blinks as if dazed, and I stiffen because we are so busted.

Mom bustles into the room, stopping to pick up a votive and blow it out, set it back down. She repeats the task.

"You must be Luke," she says over her shoulder.

"Er, I am." Luke looks at me, then at her with panic. "You're Callie's mom. Should I be going?"

"Probably in a bit," Mom says.

"Mom," I say, ears burning, "how did you know Luke's name?"

"Oh, right," she says. "Did I forget to tell you guys our security system means I can get all the video feeds on an app on my phone? No need to fill me in. I know just about everything."

She knows just about everything.

"I'm proud of you, Callie."

She's proud of me. I didn't mess up. I saved the damned day.

Luke tightens his hand on my side like he senses how much that means to hear.

"It's a good thing our insurance covers acts of god." Mom sighs. "I am going to miss our painting of Tesla's pigeon. Congratulations to you two, by the way." She points between Mag and Jared. Jared beams, Mag smiles shyly.

Luke steps away from me, not far, but I feel it. Sure, it *feels* too far after not knowing if I'd be able to save him, but I don't freak out. We made it through this. We made it to heart fireworks. No way am I letting go of that anytime soon. I don't think he is either.

"Let me take care of that," Luke says.

And he produces an exact copy of the painting of the pigeon with gray-tipped wings, missing only the hole where Mag planted it on Solomon Elerion's head. He presents it to my mom with a bow and flourish. Charming her already.

"That's handy. Thank you." To me, she says, "And yes, before you ask, we're keeping Cupcake. It would break Bosch's heart if we didn't."

We all look at each other. Mag and Jared break first, then Luke and I.

We're laughing together, and, somehow, that feels like the best possible way this weekend from Hell could end.

CHAPTER TWENTY-EIGHT

PORSOTH

SOMETIME LATER

finish brewing the tea for Rofocale ten minutes before he arrives. He's still angry at me for siding with the humans, even after I explained it was for Luke's sake.

This is the first time he's agreed to get together since all the excitement.

Luke caused a sensation on his first date with Callie. They went to Lexington's Comic Con and he won a costume prize just by leaving his wings out. He's changing, but not that much. I'm proud of him. I can lure him into the library much more easily, now that Callie has dispensation to come and go. She only has to present the young master's handkerchief for her toll these days.

Lucifer's growing to like her. Or Lilith is making him play nice because she was upset he didn't bring her along to the Great Escape to see Callie's performance. She's since seen a rendition of it—heavily edited to make Lucifer look like the hero—in one of our own demonic repertoire theaters.

"Is that tea cold?" Rofocale asks when he enters.

"Rather," I say. "It was warm when you were meant to be here."

Rofocale picks up the cup and heat radiates from his hand as he warms it back up.

"It's still more polite to be on time," I tell him.

"Sorry," he says. "Luke's fault. He and Callie have hatched this plan to offer souls here on lesser infractions second chances on Earth. I told him Lucifer will never entertain it, but . . ." He shrugs.

"I think it's sweet," I say. "You never know. Have they figured out yet?"

"About Callie?" Rofocale grins. "Not yet."

Callie isn't entirely human herself anymore. All that traveling back and forth combined with the extended contact with the Holy Lance.

But we've agreed not to spoil the surprise. We'll leave that secret for the two of them to discover.

THE END (. . . OF THE BEGINNING)

ACKNOWLEDGMENTS

To the author pals who went along with my serendipitous plan to do an escape room next door to our hotel in Murfreesboro at the Southeastern Young Adult Book Festival (SEYA) in 2017: Court Stevens, Megan Shepherd, Sheba Karim, Lauren Gibaldi, E. Katherine Kottaras, I. W. Gregorio, and Andrew Maraniss. Did we escape? YOU BET WE DID. And I had the first spark of this idea on my drive home from the festival.

To my writing group, the Moonscribers, for general support and for reading and assisting with parts of this book. To Kami Garcia, for being the world's best accountability buddy, and to Sam Humphries for always sending a "you got this" text at the right moment. To the Lexington Writer's Room, a wondrous place filled with wondrous people. To Jennie Goloboy for supporting Romancing the Runoff with a generous bid for an advance copy of this book. To all the romance authors whose work has brought me joy and helped me survive the quarantimes.

To my fabulous editors on this book, Tiffany Shelton and Jennie Conway, and the entire team at St. Martin's, who are rock stars of the first order. Speaking of, thanks to Mary Moates, DJ DeSmyter, Marissa Sangiacomo, and Kejana Ayala for their publicity and marketing work, and to Kerri Resnick for her cover design and Louisa Cannell for the character art. To my agent, Jennifer Laughran, for letting me do what I want and supporting me even when it's a little out of left field.

To the menagerie: Izzy, Sally, and Puck, good dogs every one (Bosch might bear a certain resemblance to Ms. Isabelle), and Stella and Phoebe, co-queen cats. To Christopher Rowe, my husband, for meals and moral support and generally being the best romantic lead I can imagine.

And, as always, to all the readers who've supported me along my author journey and to the new ones. I love you all. Thank you, thank you, *thank you* for reading.

ABOUT THE AUTHOR

GWENDA BOND is the *New York Times* bestselling author of many novels, including the Lois Lane and Cirque American trilogies. She wrote the first official Stranger Things novel, *Suspicious Minds*. She also created *Dead Air*, a serialized mystery and scripted podcast written with Carrie Ryan and Rachel Caine. *Not Your Average Hot Guy* is her first romantic comedy for adults.

Her nonfiction writing has appeared in *Publishers Weekly, Locus Magazine, Salon*, the *Los Angeles Times,* and many other publications. She has an MFA in writing from the Vermont College of Fine Arts. She lives in a hundred-year-old house in Lexington, Kentucky, with her husband and their unruly pets. She believes she may have escaped from a 1940s screwball comedy. She writes a monthly-ish letter you can sign up for at her website (gwendabond.com), and you can also follow her on Twitter (@Gwenda).